DEAD FESTIVE

R Young

Sulk Media

Copyright © 2021 Ross Young

Copyright © 2021 Ross Young All rights reserved
The characters and events portrayed in this book are fictitious. Any similarity to real persons, living or dead, is coincidental and not intended by the author.
No part of this book may be reproduced, stored in a retrieval system, or transmitted in any form or by any means, electronic, mechanical, photocopying, recording, or otherwise, without the express written permission of the publisher.

To everyone who reads this… both of you.

CONTENTS

Title Page
Copyright
Dedication
Little Things	1
The Start of the Trail	47
Shopping	105
Business talk	150
To the Guillotine	198
Gnome Sweet Gnome	241
Not a Hope in Hell	284
B Team	331
The Morning After	371
Afterword	391
Acknowledgements	393
About The Author	395
Books By This Author	397

LITTLE THINGS

He pushed back the heavy cowl and tapped a skeletal finger against his skull. "I'm sure I put them up here," he mused.

With a grunt, he picked up a cardboard box but slipped as he tried to move it to one side. The box tumbled from his hands. A cloud of dust exploded into the air as it hit the floor, and the worn cardboard split open. Books tumbled out. Paperbacks mingled with ancient tomes as they landed with a clatter and a thud, billowing up yet more dust.

"Oh, I'd forgotten about these."

He leaned forward and, with one hand on his back, stacked the books. As he did, he slipped one or two that took his fancy inside his robes before turning once more to the range of boxes spread out around him.

In amongst the rectangular tombs to things forgotten were old standing lamps, a large ancient electric fan, and a mannequin. Try as he might, he could not recall where the mannequin had come from, but he considered taking it back down the several flights of stairs and giving a bit of thought to robe design.

"This is just ridiculous," he muttered, or at least, he attempted to mutter. The Grim Reaper can't say things 'under his breath' by virtue of having no breath to get under, but he tries. "I put them right here last year."

He kicked a box in frustration, then looked around to make sure nobody had seen his fit of pique. Which is when he noticed the tiny hoofprints in the dust. His first thought was of Beelzebub, Lord of Hell, nemesis of the Grim Reaper... well, nemesis of everyone, really. That was sort of Beezy's whole raison d'être. Not the most helpful of chaps.

Hooves, or cloven feet, were definitely a Beelzebub thing, and recent events had led Grim to believe Beelzebub might bear him some specific ill-feeling. The prints were, however, tiny. Not that it would be un-Beelzebub-like to shrink himself just to prove a point. It just seemed unnecessary in this situation.

Death, the Big Sleep, the Grim Reaper, got down on his hands and knees and crawled across the creaking floorboards of the attic of the Office of the Dead. He followed the hoofprints until they came to a large rectangle on the floor that was almost clear of dust but for a very thin layer.

"Hm," he said, because there was nothing more to be said. He took a seat and patted at his knees to clear them of dust. He flicked the cowl back over his skull and put an elbow on one knee, propping up his chin in the palm of his hand. "Oh, Grim, what have you done this time?"

A breeze through the cracks in the roof tiles caused his robes to billow for a moment, and he saw something out of place fluttering in the wind.

"Oh, what's pink and fluffy?"

Beside the pink fluff were three words written in the dust.

"Oh dear."

Unbelievable

There are many ways to die: exsanguination, heart attack, illness, stroke, injury, accident, murder, drowning, hanging, decapitation, patricide, fratricide, matricide, the other -cides, poison, radiation sickness, being crushed beneath the weight of a large mammal, choking, electrocution… it's a long list.

Let's stick with there are many ways to die… for the average mortal.

But what about the others? A hope, a dream, an idea, something that exists only in the mind of a child held there by the innocent, naïve belief of something other, something else, someone else.

The child was excited; the mother was tearful and fearful. The apartment was cold, and the single glazing did nothing to hold out the icy fingers of Jack Frost. On this special day, though, she turned on the electric heater. Perhaps just for this morning.

A meagre offering would rest upon the three-legged table later today when they huddled together before the television, watching happier people in other places.

"Sarah said he brought her a train set," the child said, beaming as they took a seat under the tree.

"Oh, well, I don't think we've room for a train set. Perhaps he brought us something we need instead of something we want."

"What do we need?" the boy asked.

The answer was long and complicated. It was sad and cruel: money, help, friendship, for the system not to be geared to fail them, to be treated like people.

She offered a weak smile instead. "I need nothing except you," she said, squeezing the child close.

"Can I open it?"

"Of course you can, but try to remember there are things we need."

The wrapping paper was more expensive than what lay inside, and the child seemed to realise. He carefully peeled back the tape and unfolded it rather than tear it apart with excitement.

"A coat," the child shouted, bouncing up and down on her lap. Lifting it up and inspecting it. "It's got pockets and a hood."

"Do you like it?"

"I love it, Mummy, but I love you more. Thank you, I won't be cold now when we walk to school."

She couldn't hold back the sob. "I'm sorry there are no toys."

"It's not your fault, Mummy. I know he's not real. I love my coat. Thank you for getting it. All I need is you."

If he ever was real, she thought, I hope he burns in hell. What kind of monster tells their children that some mythical man brings them all the riches in the world but treats others as if they're a failure, unworthy of his love? He'd better be watching, he'd better be listening, and how she hoped he'd never be sleeping.

The child stopped believing.

That is how you kill the others.

Ne'er-do-well

"Disgusting!" the woman shouted as she swung an umbrella at a stuffed snail toy.

The toy, inhabited by a bewildered demon, ducked its stalked eyes, and the umbrella passed through the air above its head.

"Oi!" Detective Augustan Blunt shouted. He was standing behind the woman and caught the umbrella in one hand on its upswing while she prepared for another attempt.

"Gerroff," she screeched as she whirled around, tugging at the umbrella. When she came face to face with the detective, she froze. "Don't I know you?"

"I think I'd remember meeting a nasty piece of work who assaults people for no good reason."

"It's not 'people', it's a demon. They torture people."

"Do they? I don't remember being tortured by any cuddly toys recently," Blunt said, letting go of the umbrella.

They were standing on the corner of a street beneath a flickering neon streetlight while the early morning rain, which was lighter than mid-morning or late morning rain, mingled with the heavy mist of Gloomwood daybreak. A cloud of exhaust fumes battled with thick fog in their ever-present war on visibility.

She lowered her makeshift weapon. "Not here.

In Hell."

"Oh, so you've been to Hell? I'm not sure they should've let you out."

"That's not what I meant. Those horrible creatures are Satan's spawn."

"Technically, he doesn't spawn them. He's not a frog. You might take things a bit too literally. Also, I think he prefers to be called Beelzebub, not sure why —"

"How is that relevant?"

"Aha," Blunt said, lifting his hand and flicking the underside of the homburg he wore. Water that had pooled in the brim splashed on the angry woman.

"Ew, you dirty bast—"

"The point I am making, madam,"—he said, with a heavy emphasis on the word 'madam'—"is that you don't have a clue what you're talking about. This furry snail did nothing except walk, crawl, whatever it does, across your path while you weren't looking where you were going. So, why don't you leave the cuddly snail toy alone and go about your business?"

The woman scowled beneath her blue rinse perm, which was almost hidden beneath a floral-print scarf. "I recognise you now. You're that idiot detective who keeps causing problems."

"That's me," he said with a smile.

"You're as bad as the demons," she shouted, swinging the umbrella at the detective.

"Bloody hell, leg it, snail!" Blunt shouted as he

put one hand on his hat and ducked out of the way. "I mean, slug it… I don't know. Shove off before she Ableforths the pair of us. Merry Bleakest Eve."

Suit up

"This stinks," the Kallikantzaroi said as it peeled the suit off. The furry pink costume fell to the floor, falling into a heap around its cloven feet while it tugged the head off.

"It's you that stinks," one of its brethren said as it removed its own headpiece, the hollow head of a teddy bear in green fur. "Only been in the suit a few hours and it already stinks? It must be you."

"Yours stinks just as bad. You stink worse."

The bickering between the gaggle of them, seven of the strange little creatures, went on and on like this. They were mostly blind but had acute hearing and senses of smell. Their skin was a dark green colour, though the short downy fur that covered them from head to foot was lighter, making it look like they were glowing.

"Did you get the decorations?" a voice rumbled from the darkness.

"Yeah, yeah, yeah," one of the Kallikantzaroi said, waving a hessian sack from one of its black-clawed hands. "Simple enough," it lisped. They all lisped. Something to do with their tongues being too large for their mouths.

"Then hand them over," the thing in the shadows rumbled.

"We had a deal," the Kallikantzaroi said in unison. They stood shoulder to shoulder in a line, each in the same pose. Arms crossed, bellies pushed forward, head tilted to one side.

"Yes, yes, one step at a time, you idiot mole people."

"That was rude," one said, followed by a chorus from the others.

"Rude, rude, rude!"

"Ho, ho, ho. I can't tell you how little I care about your feelings. There's probably some tiny form of empathy inside, but buried beneath so many layers of disgust and disdain, I fear it has reached pressures and temperatures that it cannot handle in its normal form. Instead, it is like a diamond. Its properties have changed, so to unleash it now would probably result in me squeezing your tiny little heads until they popped. Shall we test our theory?" The shadow shifted around the edges of the room as it spoke.

The row of creatures formed a circle facing outwards. "Don't understand, trying to be clever, too many words, what's the next job?" they said, sniffing at the air as they spoke.

A single lightbulb lit the warehouse. Around them, half-finished soft toys covered every surface. Beneath them, machines for stitching and moulding lay rusting and dormant. The glow of the light refracted on motes of dust that floated through the air.

The creatures didn't care; they craved the darkness and the nooks and crannies of spaces too small for most to inhabit. The urge to slip in where they were not wanted drove them to crawling and stealing into homes in the night. They longed for darkness and warmth.

"Where to go next?"

From the shadows came a sigh. "Hardly a surprise that people stopped believing in you strange little house gnomes."

"Cut down the tree now?"

"No. I will tell you when you can cut down the tree."

"Now?"

"Not even a minute has passed. You have more jobs to do. A narrative to build."

Mantrakoukos, their leader, if there was such a thing, let out a growl. "Don't enjoy building, like cutting down trees and making trouble, that's what we do."

"Then you shall make trouble."

They released a chattering sound that was something akin to laughter.

"In the suits."

The chattering changed to a disappointed murmur.

A Grim Case

The door to his office opened while Blunt was staring out of the window at the brick wall of the building opposite. Looking down, there was a narrow alleyway just wide enough to be filled with rubbish and never emptied. In the time he had been in the office, the rubbish had risen by several feet, and not because he kept throwing things out of the window.

At least, not only because of that.

He spent hours standing there, mainly so he could have a cigar and convince himself that the howling gale outside sucked all evidence of the fumes out into the city below. It also made for a much more dramatic scene when people entered the office.

"There's someone here to see you," Ursula Panderpenny, former assistant to the Grim Reaper and Blunt's business partner, said. "Also, I'm not your receptionist, and your cigars are stinking the place out."

"Thank you, Miss Panderpenny. Please send them in," Blunt said as he turned around.

The office had the welcoming feel of a jail after turfing out the drunk and disorderly from the night before. Unlike the empty jail cell, the office still housed its inmate. He was guilty of all charges.

Ursula gritted her teeth and entered the room, closing the door behind her before she turned to glare at Blunt. "Stop calling me Miss Panderpenny."

"It's your name," Blunt said.

"I know that. You keep saying it like I'm your assistant, or receptionist, or something. I'm not."

"How would you like me to say it?"

"Ursula. Just call me Ursula, and stop this embarrassing routine. As for 'Please send them in', how about shifting your arse and greeting them yourself? Send them in," she muttered as she opened the door again. Before leaving, she turned around. "Do us both a favour and get a present for Sarah while you're out today. I won't hear the end of it from your little bunch of friends if you forget."

"I've already got one."

"If it's that ridiculous game on your desk, then no, you haven't," she said before disappearing out of sight.

Blunt let out a sigh and glanced around the office. It was the kind of place for which people used the phrase 'It's seen better days', except in this case, it actually hadn't. It had never been used before Blunt had moved in, and though it was chaos, it was his chaos.

Sitting on his desk was the present he had bought for Sarah. He wasn't sure if they were in a relationship. If they were, it wasn't in any sense that Blunt understood. Apparently, everyone else around them thought differently. He wasn't even sure if Sarah thought they were in a relationship, but there were definitely expectations he didn't understand. Blunt hadn't been in something he would call a relationship since he'd died. When he thought about it, which he avoided, death hadn't really changed matters.

The gift was badly wrapped in brown paper. Wrapping that a toddler would manage with applause from the recipient because it showed quite impressive hand-eye coordination. For a toddler.

Something about making a flat piece of paper wrap around any object, even a perfectly symmetrical box, eluded him. Added to that was the ingrained belief that nobody in the history of present wrapping had ever thought to cut up little pieces of tape before beginning the wrapping process.

Now, he thought to himself, wasn't the time to worry about that. He needed to look presentable, or at least more presentable than the thing on his desk.

Blunt tossed his cigar butt out of the window to the street below. His office, at 4B Pale Avenue, was on the second floor of a building that looked like it had been built by a child with the dullest set of lego bricks ever invented.

This room was in better shape than the one down the hall he lived in. The furniture was in need of repair, or of burning. There were three chairs, a working lamp, and a desk that only needed one leg propped up on a pile of books. It even had his name on the door.

He grabbed his hat off the hat stand, the homburg he was determined to make into his calling card, and placed it on his head before stepping out of the office door.

In the hallway, against one wall, was a sofa. It was the most luxurious piece of furniture in the building if you didn't include Ursula Panderpenny's office. The reason it was so nice was because Ursula had bought it and put it outside her office for her clients.

To prevent any arguments about who sat on it, Blunt had been diplomatic, a skill he was learning. Rather than buying a second sofa or tidying his previous office, he had simply moved his office to the room next door to Ursula's. Now it would be churlish for Ursula to complain about Blunt's clients sitting there too.

Sitting on the sofa today, dressed in a black and purple robe that literally had bells on it, was a skeleton.

"Hello, detective." Death, the Grim Reaper, that which awaits us all, gave an awkward one-handed wave.

"Um, your Lordship," Blunt said while running through a mental list of expletives both vast and inventive, which, if he survived, he would be sure to deliver to Ursula in full.

"No need for formalities. I'm here for your help."

"My help?"

Grim, as he was known to his friends, of which he had very few, stood up. There was a distinction between being imposing and being intimidating, and Grim was both.

Blunt took a step backwards. It was involuntary, and he cursed himself for doing it before mentally excusing himself. It was only reasonable that he took a step back. Death was very tall, and taking a step back made it easier to look him in the eye... or rather, eye socket.

"Yes," Grim said, looking up and down the corridor. "It's about my baubles."

"Your baubles?" Blunt asked.

"Hm," Grim said. His voice didn't come from within, it came from without, meaning he didn't need to move his jaw to talk. Despite this, he leaned towards Blunt until he was inches from the detective's ear, a distance one might call intimate. "I would rather not discuss my baubles here. It's quite a delicate matter."

Moments later, they were inside Blunt's office. The detective was having a hard time trying to look professional while the Grim Reaper was sitting in the chair opposite him. The chair was too small for someone the size of the embodiment of the big sleep. It was too small for most people. It was only now that Blunt noticed how small it was.

Now that he was faced with having a client in the room, he noticed other minor details. The filing cabinet was lower than most. The rectangles of slightly less discoloured yellow paint, where pictures and certificates might once have adorned the walls, were lower than most people would hang their pictures. The walls themselves were a colour that was probably found in a Dulux colour chart under the moniker of nicotine stain.

"Sorry about the chair," Blunt said. "Do you want to swap? Mine's normal size."

"Normal?" Grim said. "An interesting way to put it. What's normal about the size of that chair compared to this one?"

"I just meant… a more conventional size, then."

"Ah, yes. Convention is the mother of invention, you know."

"Is it?" Blunt said, nodding in that fashion that people do when they have no notion of what is being spoken about.

"No. I don't think that's right at all. Maybe it's convenience."

"Is it not necessity?"

"Convention a necessity? Well, I haven't thought of it that way, but—"

Blunt picked up a sheaf of papers lying on his desk and shuffled them to get the conversation back on track.

"So, your"—he tried very hard not to look in any way inappropriate—"baubles?"

"Ah, interesting you should bring them up, detective. I actually have something of an issue with my Bleakest Day decorations."

"Those are the baubles you were referring to?"

"That's right. What did you think I was referring to?"

Blunt, who was fortunate to be gifted with a face that made concrete seem friendly, smiled.

"That's what I thought."
"Oh, good. They've been stolen."
"Right."
"And it may have been demons."
"Bollocks."
"Baubles, detective. I've been quite clear."

Bureaucracy

"I don't understand why we're debating this," Sarah Von Faber said. "The Grim Reaper said they could stay. He's in charge, end of story."

Across from her, on the other side of an olive green table that did not hide its age or cheap manufacture, a woman with a mouth the size of a pea and eyes like saucers shook her head.

"It's not whether they're allowed to stay. It's whether they're citizens. Can they work? Do they get the same benefits as everyone else?"

"Why wouldn't they?" Sarah asked. Her tone was neutral, balanced, in the way that only someone attempting to remain calm can manage. Her face flickered in and out of existence for a moment, temporarily leaving the other woman staring at the inside of Sarah's skull.

The woman's mouth fell open, which, as it was the size of a pea, wasn't actually particularly noticeable.

Sarah's face popped back into existence, and she smiled. "Sorry, that happens sometimes. Now, as I was saying, they should get what everyone else gets."

"Well, it's not how it works, is it? It's not like this is their afterlife," the woman said. Her tiny mouth had no relationship to the volume of her voice as she grew louder.

"They're not asking for special treatment.

They just want to carry on like everyone else."

"Yes, I can see that, but is that really fair?"

"What?"

"They had their afterlife—"

"They were in Hell."

"I understand it wasn't ideal, but it's not the city of Gloomwood's job to look after everyone. If we just let everyone in… well, everyone would come here."

"And?"

"Well, we can't support everyone that comes along who says, 'We like what you've got, can we have some?'"

Sarah Von Faber, one of the most brilliant minds this afterlife had ever seen, now on a temporary sabbatical by choice, definitely by choice, let out a sigh. She put her hands on the table and nodded.

"I hear what you're saying, I just disagree. But I respect your opinion."

"It's not an opinion—"

Sarah held up a hand, which flickered, interrupting the tiny-mouthed woman. "Actually, it is. It's your opinion. You feel, because these people didn't walk through the mortal veil, that they don't have a right to the things everyone else does. Fortunately, in this situation, your opinion is irrelevant because the decision has been made. They are citizens of Gloomwood because the Grim Reaper said so. Just out of curiosity, did he ever say that you were a citizen of Gloomwood?"

The woman let out a noise that sounded like the tiniest puncture in an old bicycle tyre while someone far too large for it rode over rough terrain. It was a titter.

"Of course not, but I came here when I died—"

"So you're not a citizen then?"

"Of course I am."

"Because?"

"Because a reaper brought me here, like every normal person."

Sarah leaned back in the chair, a brave move considering the condition of the seat, and gave a thin smile. The smile she reserved for those moments where she had proven a hypothesis, where her investigation had led to the desired conclusion.

"A reaper? Just an ordinary, run-of-the-mill reaper?"

"What's your point?"

"Well, you're a citizen because of an everyday, run-of-the-mill reaper. The demons are citizens because of the Grim Reaper. Technically, that means they belong here more than you."

"No it doesn't."

"I'm afraid so. Maybe you aren't a citizen."

"You're being stupid. I deserve to be here just as much as them."

"So we're all equal?"

"Of course we are!" the bureaucrat said, her enormous eyes narrowing as she scowled at Sarah. "Fine, I'll sign the papers."

"Thank you, Dina. I knew you were the person

to see. You're always so kind," Sarah said without a trace of sarcasm.

"Well, we could all do with being a little kinder," she said, unaware of Sarah's arduous efforts to scrape the sarcasm from her words.

Death's Attic

Clouds of condensation formed in front of his face as he puffed, red-faced, for breath. He didn't need to breathe, but then, technically, humans don't need to scratch an itch, but they still do. Blunt's walk up several flights of stairs had led him to a doorway at the top of a small staircase.

From the moment they had left Blunt's office, the Grim Reaper had not uttered a single word. Blunt had followed while the de facto ruler of this afterlife walked down the flight of stairs and out onto Pale Avenue.

People in the street had stopped to stare as Death walked towards a nondescript, though clearly expensive, black saloon and slipped into the back seat. A driver, a nervous man by the name of Wheatley, had opened the passenger door, and Blunt spent the journey in silence.

When they had arrived at the Office of the Dead, he had followed the Grim Reaper. He attempted to walk beside the imposing figure of Death but, despite his efforts, always seemed to end up following in his wake. They had ridden the elevator up to the floor where the Grim Reaper had his office, and then, much to the surprise of Grim's receptionist, who didn't seem to realise it was there, exited through a door to a staircase.

After what felt like hours of climbing, Blunt stood before the door, waiting to be told what to do next. The door was wooden, round and set into the wall with a sign hanging from it that said, 'Grim's stuff, keep out,' written on a wooden board in a childish scrawl.

"Is this your bedroom?" Blunt asked the black-robed figure next to him.

"No," Grim said, breaking the eerie silence that had lasted so long.

"Did you write the sign?"

"Maybe. Come on. I believe you would call this a crime scene." Grim reached forward and opened the door with a twist of a metal ring before ducking through the entrance.

Inside, there was dust. A vast accumulation that spoke of centuries of neglect. It moved beneath Blunt's footsteps, billowing up and leaving his footprints behind.

"Here, detective, evidence of a demon."

"Footprints?"

"Yes. Little odd-shaped footprints."

"That's why you think it's a demon?"

"I think nothing."

"Wish I'd recorded you saying that."

"I'm referring to this specific scene. However, there is a reason to believe it was a demon. The feet are shaped like little hooves."

"Maybe it was your friend Beelzebub."

Grim turned. He was crouched beneath the low beams of the ceiling, and it brought his skull face, once more, uncomfortably close to Blunt's. "His hooves are rather larger than these."

Blunt couldn't stop himself from taking a step back. Something instinctive took control, and he grimaced for a moment. "Right. Isn't there anyone else in the city who might have hooves?"

"Yes, many people. Minotaurs, centaurs, horse people, Mister Ed… but all their feet are larger. I suppose there are some with smaller hooves, but there's also this." Grim reached out with one long hand and pointed to some fibres caught on a splintered beam.

"What's pink and fluffy?"

Grim's face betrayed no emotion, because it wasn't a face at all, but it seemed even less friendly than usual when the empty eye sockets looked at Blunt.

"It was a joke. What's pink and fluffy? Pink fluff."

"Mhm. Then there's these." Grim pointed towards several more footprints. They were all small, but there were various shapes and sizes. Paw prints, claw prints, and several round prints with no toes. "Now, about my decorations."

"This seems like a huge deal," Blunt said. "This looks suspiciously like an average attic in a family house where stuff has been dumped for a very long time. Are you sure you didn't just misplace your decorations? What do they look like?"

"They are in a cardboard box, sealed with brown tape, which clearly says, 'Bleakest Day decorations, do not touch, extremely powerful.'"

"Right."

"It seems someone did not read the label."

"Yes, if only they'd read the label," Blunt said. "Shall we look around?"

"No. I've already done that. They're not here."

Blunt's smile, which had faltered many times over the course of the journey to the attic, struggled to maintain some integrity. "Right, but how about just one more check?"

"I am not an idiot," Grim said, and his voice caused the rafters to rattle, showering the pair of them with dust.

"No," Blunt said, wincing. "I wasn't suggesting you were. When I investigate missing items, I've often found that an extra look saves people a lot of money. I mean, the number of times when I was alive that my wife looked for something… Well, let's just say that pride seems to come before finding something where you've already looked."

"You're referring to something known as the spousal vanishing hypothesis."

"You what?"

"When one person cannot find something and insists they have looked for it in all the places mentioned, then when it is looked for in the same places, it appears. It's a known phenomenon. Here, the role of the spouse has been played by several members of the Artificer's team, who have searched this very room multiple times."

"Oh, the spousal vanishing hypothesis."

"The box isn't here, and there are these cute little prints and the fibres… pink fluff. It seems quite demonic. There's also only one way to get in here if you don't come through the door. That's through that ventilation shaft, and, as I'm sure you know, they're too narrow for a person to crawl through despite what television suggests. And then there's this." Grim stepped over a box and pointed to a message written in dust. It read, 'Demons done it.'

"Right, well, that seems definitive. It couldn't possibly have been someone trying to incriminate demons. I'll start looking for pink demons with hooves."

"I doubt it will be that simple, detective."

"No? Well, that would be a shocking twist."

"You're being sarcastic again. It's quite tiresome. I must stress that this is a very delicate matter."

"Yeah, a delicate matter about your—"

"These decorations are important. They come from beyond here."

Blunt nodded, though he wasn't sure why. People could 'bring' things with them when they died, if they were supposed to. If someone was buried with a watch, a bag of money, or some prized heirloom, then the Office of the Dead would arrange for the item to be remade in Gloomwood. It was a tradition, one which infuriated everyone who died with nothing.

"Who gets buried with Chr... with festive decorations?"

"Nobody. Well, I can't say that for sure, but it would be quite unusual. No, I brought them here,"

Grim said before he let out a sigh.

There is something 'wrong' about Death sighing. As if eternity has been turned on its side and what seemed like forever is only a thin slice cutting through what we know as reality. A sigh shouldn't make people nauseous, yet Blunt swallowed as his mouth watered in that oh-so-unpleasant way.

"So, can you sense where they are?"

"I'm quite certain we've had this conversation before, detective. It might make people more content to believe that I am some omniscient being, or even semi-omnipotent, but I am neither. I am just one person, and one person alone—"

"You *are* Death, though. You have command over, well, death."

"It really sounds a lot more special than it really is. I mean, you're in command of death too, or you were when you were alive."

"No. I could've killed someone, but that's not the same as being responsible for lifting the mortal veil and—"

"I'm essentially an animated signpost."

"What?"

"My job is to turn up when people die and point them in the right direction. Hm. That might be a bit of an oversimplification. An escort, then. I am a professional escort who will turn up for a brief tête-à-tête, a passing casual encounter. Possibly some money exchanges hands as I have to pay the ferrywoman. We have a rendezvous, and then we never speak again."

Blunt rubbed his chin. "I think you've just described yourself as a prostitute."

"Oh. Well, they say it's the oldest profession of them all… though I would beg to differ."

"So these artefacts," Blunt said, trying to turn the conversation away from prostitution. "Are they dangerous?"

"No," Grim said. "I wouldn't have dangerous things lying around."

"Oh, that's a relief."

"Unless somebody were to use them in some nefarious way, they're perfectly safe. That's why I keep them up here, away from nefarious people."

Blunt took his hat off and rubbed his face to control the ticking time bomb of frustration that was moving ever closer to exploding.

"So they are dangerous if somebody tries to do something with them."

"Yes, extremely, but nobody would… ah, but somebody has taken them, and that is nefarious."

"Isn't it just? So what can they do?"

Grim tapped his teeth with one bony finger. "That's a good question."

"So you want me to find the decorations?"

Grim didn't answer.

After several uncomfortable minutes passed, he tried again. "Are you hiring me to find the decorations?"

"I don't think demons did this," Grim finally said.

"I am both flabbered and ghasted by this hypothesis."

"You know, you are quite an unpleasant man."

"I've been told that before, but you didn't come to see me for my sparkling personality. What would you like me to do?"

"I think you should go see the demons. Whatever is happening has something to do with them."

"You think I'll find your decorations there?"

"No, but it is where our villain will expect you to go."

"Great, will your driver take me?"

Season's Greetings

Gloomwood is cold, wet, and misty and has winds that howl through every alleyway and avenue as if it's a living thing aiming to make its presence known. The streets themselves seem designed to create a moaning and wailing that pairs perfectly with the rattling of thousands of ill-fitting doors and window frames. Nobody had ever visited Gloomwood for the weather, but then the number of people who had 'visited' Gloomwood could be counted on one hand.

Festive lights had been strewn across storefronts, and the street vendors had made a poor effort at including tinsel on their carts. Baubles and furry accessories were the order of the day. As if the fire hazard the carts already presented wasn't great enough, they could only be more hazardous if they were doused in petrol.

There are religious celebrations in the city, the major religion being the Church of Meep, though they have come under considerable fire in recent times because of some misplaced enthusiasm on the part of its members. The small matter of a failed resurrection and the distinct lack of the end of days had done a little to damage their reputation, but they had weathered that storm because of having no direct involvement. They'd just watched on, waiting to jump in and claim the rewards.

Religions sparked into and out of life much

quicker in Gloomwood than in the mortal realm. For any religious institution, having parishioners who are dead can make building a flock quite tricky. Which is why religious celebrations aren't what citizens really look forward to.

Instead, there are four big celebrations in a calendar year. There's the Changing of the Keys ceremony, which has all the pomp and flair of a wet autumn picnic with the side of the family that nobody wants to speak to. Then there's Cup Final Day, where tribalism is lifted to its highest level as the same two teams that have reached the final for the last seventeen years once more play out a defensive game of football. It frequently ends in violence among both players and fans.

The third is Apologies Day, a relatively recent public holiday introduced by the Grim Reaper, where everyone says sorry to other people. The Grim Reaper is very keen on apologies. It's like Thanksgiving, but a little more honest. Then there's the one that everyone really looks forward to.

Bleakest day,
Darkest night,
Shadows sleep,
No sky tonight,
Rest in peace,
Give up the fight
Just once a year,
all will be right,

*On one and all,
Death shines a light.*

Bleakest Day is a celebration of gratitude that the residents of Gloomwood haven't been abandoned in the abyss for all eternity. Lights are lit throughout the city to mark Death's stand against the darkness and solitude of the everlasting abyss. It is not, and the Grim Reaper is adamant about this, anything to do with Death himself.

Bleakest Day is about everyone being together in Gloomwood. Standing together regardless of what they once were and celebrating the fact that, despite dying, everyone still has free will, which, according to what they knew about other afterlives, was not the case for most who died.

It is also a day for remembering.

For Sarah Von Faber, it is a day when she tries to restore what little faith she had in dead society.

"I don't understand," Morgarth, democratically elected representative of the demonic refugees from Hell, said.

Sarah sighed and rubbed her closed eyes with her thumb and forefinger. "I know you don't, Morgarth. It's because you're different."

The blue furry dinosaur was standing on top of a cardboard box. Her tail moved back and forth as it hung over the edge while she faced Sarah, who was sitting on the other side of a desk.

"Isn't the idea that we're all different?"

"Yes," Sarah nodded. "But not too different."

"So we should all be the same."

"Exactly."

"I'm very confused right now."

"It's important that everyone is different but that we're also the same. You're more different than they're used to, so they'll need to... adjust."

"So we're allowed to be here, but we're not allowed to be here?" Morgarth said.

"That sounds about right. Before you can get jobs, you need to be in the system."

Morgarth nodded. "We had something like this in Hell. Nobody was supposed to be punished until they had been assessed and placed in the right circle of Hell."

"Okay," Sarah said. "That sounds similar, let's say it's like that."

"So we will be pre-tortured and undergo the pain we have inflicted upon others for a thousand years?"

Sarah stared at Morgarth, then shook her head. "Not exactly. We just need to fill in lots of paperwork and try to change the law."

"Paperwork... that is quite terrifying. A clever form of torture. A thousand years of paperwork with pens that do not work? Do we write in our own blood, or must we write with the blood of those we have made suffer while listening to the anguish that we caused?

"Ah, you mean to provide us with paperwork in a language we never understand that bursts into flames every day and a new language the next day, leading to an eternity of tormented frustration as we rush to complete it but fail over and over again?"

"No," Sarah said. "It's just normal paperwork and a lot of waiting. It really isn't that bad when you consider your perspective."

"Waiting?" the demon in the dinosaur outfit asked. "As in... boredom?"

"It can be tedious."

"This is horrible. Waiting, unable to do anything, a cruel, vindictive torture."

Sarah pursed her lips and brushed her hair behind her ears. Understanding the logic of demons was difficult. She, like most things in Gloomwood, had died. Even those who hadn't been living individuals—the hopes, dreams, and promises—had all at least died.

But the demons had never experienced a change. They existed in Hell; they existed in Gloomwood. It was more like they'd taken a holiday and stayed... except the holiday was from Hell.

"How are the others holding up?" Sarah asked.

"They go out every day looking for work, for something to do that will give people a reason not to hate us, but there is nothing. Sometimes they don't all come back. I tell the others that they must have found jobs, but they doubt me. I am a demon, after all."

Sarah stood up and put her hands on the desk. Her white coat was open at the waist, showing her sensible black trousers and white shirt. Everyone else in this line of work had moved on to cardigans and comfortable trousers within minutes, but Sarah still looked every bit the scientist she still believed she was.

"Don't do that. Don't demonise yourselves."

"It's in the word. We are demons. Have you tried asking for a job and explaining that yes, you're a toy, but you're also a demon? Do you hear our voices? We spawned from the depths of Hell. People don't really care that we might actually be quite nice. It will take time. I know that. The others know that. We'll be patient. There's no need to get upset on our behalf," Morgarth said.

The dinosaur hopped down from the box and walked towards the door. She had to jump and hang on the door handle to turn it, then placed one foot against the interior wall to swing it open before dropping to the floor.

"I'll keep trying. You're as much Gloomwood citizens as anyone else."

Morgarth raised a tiny arm. "Thank you for your help. We appreciate it."

"Just doing my job," Sarah said, but the dinosaur was gone.

She sighed. Her job seemed to comprise arguing with people about demons and apologising to Morgarth, even though she expected nothing to change.

She was supposed to be helping a lot more people than the demons, but Gloomwood had never dealt with a sudden influx of people before, and there was nothing in place for them.

They escorted most people to the afterlife when they died. That was how it worked for norms. They lived, which was considered quite an ordeal, then they died, and a reaper popped up to bring them here.

The Hopes and Dreams she'd interviewed said that there was no living part. Instead, there was a sudden, terrifying awakening and some vague, amorphous recollection of a prior existence.

Gods would tell you their lot was the hardest of all, believing themselves immortal and fully aware of the afterlife and everything in it, only to discover they were no longer believed in. Finding themselves needing a place to go lest they drift away into nothingness.

Everyone was angry about dying. Demons hadn't died, so everyone was angry with them instead. Anger needs a focal point.

A small part of Sarah, one that she didn't care to acknowledge, was grateful to the demons. They had provided an opportunity for those insecure members of society who so desperately needed someone else to blame for their deaths not being all they wanted. It also meant they were interesting. Which was why she had volunteered to help them. Scientifically, it was fascinating. From a thaumaturgical standpoint, there was nothing quite like them.

It was going to be her break back into academia. A research paper like no other. Of course, the title was the most important thing. 'Walking with Demons'? 'Demons Among Us'? It was a work in progress. Nobody could deny the demons were taking pressure off the parts of society that had suffered outsider status for so long.

The graffiti that had littered the walls of this neighbourhood, sadly lacking in vibrant colour or artistic flair, was changing. The newest layer of hate-fuelled vandalism was covering up the previous one. Where once the walls had shouted hatred at Hopes and Dreams, now it attacked demons.

She pulled at the lanyard around her neck and straightened the pens in her lab coat pocket. It was a uniform of sorts. She couldn't let people forget she was a scientist. Something was missing from the research, something crucial and important, but she couldn't quite put her finger on it. Figuratively speaking. Though with her vanishing body parts, it could equally be taken literally.

The Artificer

Lavender Holt remembered dying. It wasn't unusual to remember dying, but when most people said it, they meant remembering how they died. Peacefully going to sleep, staring down at an eighteen-wheeler heavy goods vehicle, struggling for breath... They were statements of fact. People remembered what happened, but most didn't remember the actual process.

Lavender remembered the sensation of dying. She could recall the feeling of her mortal coil slipping free. If she was asked, but often also when she wasn't, she would explain that it felt like pulling off a sock. One long sock that covered the whole body. 'Like a sleeping bag?' people would ask. At that point, she would fix them with a glare over her half-rim semi-circular glasses. If she had meant a sleeping bag, she would have said it was like a sleeping bag.

Her death, like that of many in Gloomwood, had been the making of her.

They had exsanguinated her following the conditions of a directive for the correct treatment of cephalopods in captivity. Thanks to a wide-sweeping rule, all cephalopods had been categorised under one central welfare rule. So, when Lavender, whose actual name cannot be heard by mortal ears, never mind pronounced, was captured by a secret underwater military operation, they killed her according to the rules.

Slow, terrifying underwater exsanguination. Her lifeblood escaped her while she desperately battled an underwater vessel and its metallic arms. The people inside it had been terrified, in their warm pressurised box, of the creature who had just been on her morning commute. Worse still, she'd ended up in the afterlife with a lot more of the creepy, dried-up humans.

"Miss Holt, we were wondering if the green tinsel would do?" asked a man wearing blue overalls and a festive hat, complete with large pompom, interrupting her daydream.

"It will not."

"But—"

"The green tinsel is for the seventh, twelfth, and fourteenth tiers only. If you add tinsel in willy-nilly, we'll end up with more tinsel than tree. It will be tacky. Do you want it to look tacky?"

"No, Miss Holt," the man said, scurrying away with a cardboard box under one arm.

She was the Artificer. The creator of 'mood', of theme, of emotion. Most of her work was for commercial bodies, building an undercurrent of feeling, sprinkling the seeds of the zeitgeist, that grew to a crescendo on release day. Lavender's deft touch and understanding of the populace's mood allowed her to manipulate public perception.

Queues of the dead standing outside shop fronts in the middle of the night were what companies wanted. News reporters waving microphones in the faces of fans desperate to pay full price to be the first to hold coveted products were all part of the spectacle. That was the job of Lavender 'Tentacular' Holt, and she was the best at it.

Corporate sharks came no more bloodthirsty than Lavender, even if she was more squid than shark. Her reputation preceded her, the master of smoke and mirrors, or rather, of ink clouds. She was ruthless. Except, of course, for one day a year. Bleakest Day, the one day of the year when she turned her powers to good… sort of.

"Miss Holt," a nervous-looking child asked.

"Don't try the snivelling orphan routine on me, Doris. Some people say you've been dead longer than the Grim Reaper."

"Fine. Lavender, we wanted to check if you really wanted us all to hold toys."

"Why not? It looks like you've received a gift. That's what it's all about."

"Yes," said Doris, who looked like a six-year-old girl, complete with hair in pigtails and missing front teeth. "But soft toys are a bit… sensitive right now."

"Of course, the demons." Lavender nodded and folded her tentacles. She had four where two arms appeared on most people. It was impossible to be sure if she had a further four beneath her large skirts, but it was safe to assume as much. "Fine, no soft toys. Replace them with wooden toys. Things that look festive. Like those hand rattles you get at football matches."

"People don't really use those anymore."

"Do I look like I give a shit, Doris?" Lavender said, arching an eyebrow. "Somebody tell me where the hell the decorations are for the main event."

"Can't find them," the man in overalls said from beneath a tall dead tree. "His Lordship said he was busy when I asked for them, so I checked. Been up in the attic and everything."

"The attic?"

"Aye, above the clock is the attic. Where the decorations are."

"Are you telling me the Grim Reaper's... things are missing?"

"You can call them baubles; he does. And yeah. Even moved the old suitcases up there."

"Why are there suitcases in the attic of the Office of the Dead? What is going on?"

"I don't know. It's an attic, that's where suitcases live. You might've asked why anyone would even need suitcases anyway. Isn't like anybody's going on holiday soon."

Lavender turned to look up at the huge dead tree that loomed over the centre of Dead Square. It had been up for weeks, but it needed further embellishment for the Bleakest Eve address.

The towering building of the Office of the Dead gave the momentous, and very repetitive, annual event a suitable backdrop. The building was a shining beacon of brass and concrete, curves and archways that demanded attention, a geometric masterpiece that had fallen into decline—because this was Gloomwood.

For one day a year, it was transformed into a festive extravaganza, where dead children sung songs that spoke of the season and people wrapped up warm, holding tight to hot drinks and bathing in the glow of faux-festive nostalgia for a time that had never existed in the afterlife.

It meant something to people. It meant something because Lavender Holt, the Office of the Dead, and the Grim Reaper had colluded to ensure it meant something. In Death's own words, 'It is important that people believe there is something to believe, and that they believe that some among them believe, even if they themselves do not believe.' Which Lavender had always found confusing and yet perfectly proper. If you're going to manipulate people, it should always be proper. If it isn't, well, that way lies politics.

In the mortal realm, most festivals, special days, and causes for celebration of a similar ilk had long ago been co-opted by commercial enterprises who used them as an excuse to milk the public of their hard-earned cash. This allowed them to pay the little people again so the cycle could repeat.

And each time, the rich people would continue to reduce the amount given back to the poor people in the hope of one day discovering how big a gap could be formed between the haves and have-nots before something breaks...

The answer, in case you're wondering, is

exactly as big as it gets just before a revolution resets the experiment.

Grim had noticed this cycle, and, to ensure people felt at home in Gloomwood, he wanted to ensure this tradition continued. So he created Bleakest Day—on the surface to offer thanks, to remember what has gone, and to sentimentalise (which was last year's fresh addition to the Wordaliser, which in the mortal world is more often called a dictionary). The true meaning of Bleakest Day, however, was to ensure everyone spent a lot of money, because that was traditional.

"Everybody stop," Lavender screeched, a high-pitched sound that, if there had been any in the city, would have made dogs whimper. "Where are the decorations from the attic?"

"I've just picked these up from the office," a woman said, waving a gingerbread man that looked like it had required reconstructive surgery.

"Not that crap, His Lordship's decorations."

All eyes were on Lavender as confused minions paused in the middle of their assigned functions.

"Should we get some more?" asked a man with antlers, though these were his own rather than a festive affectation.

"Yes, get some more. Did you think we'd just leave a gap in the tree? Idiots."

"Could check the bargain bins at the off-licence. They've always got a few things knocking about—"

Just then, there was a crash and the sound of breaking glass. Lavender and her team whirled around to see three small soft toys opening boxes filled with treat-sized bottles of cold mulled wine and spilling them over the road, stopping traffic.

"Stop them!" Lavender called with a roar. She lifted herself up and, with great slaps of her tentacles, closed down on the toys.

"Merry Bleakest Eve," a teddy bear with static features said before the toys scuttled away through the crowd of technical staff, presenters, and the huge crew it required to arrange the event.

"Demons! Spiteful, hate-fuelled beasts," Lavender said as she stormed away from the tree and towards the three doors that led into the Office of the Dead. Behind her, desperate lackeys worked to complete the decorating of the tree.

As they worked, all of them studiously ignored Ralph Mortimer as he hopped from one foot to the other in front of a large wooden room purposely built to the left of the stage. It had been named the dressing room, and, despite being less than one hundred metres from the entrance to the Office of the Dead, it was where the Grim Reaper would prepare himself for the evening ahead.

THE START OF THE TRAIL

The Grim Reaper's laugh is an unpleasant sound. Like gurgling water coming from every direction, but dry at the same time. It wasn't something Blunt was in any rush to hear again. Though, he realised in hindsight, asking for a lift on Bleakest Eve with everything else going on was probably daft. Fortunately, he had a travel card.

Starting a case the right way wasn't something he had done for a long time. Since dying, Blunt had either lost himself somewhere in a bottle or become entangled in something he didn't want to be involved in. The chance that had been handed to him was probably the last one he was going to get. True, he wasn't over the moon about being one half of a partnership with Ursula Panderpenny, but beggars can't be choosers, and Blunt had been pretty close to begging.

He stopped by a stall as he walked towards the canal docks, picking up a copy of a newspaper emblazoned with the headline 'The Devil's Work'. It was a snappy title for an article about demons finding jobs. Of course, in the eyes of many, they were 'illegal' demons trying to find work. What made them legal or illegal seemed to be up for debate.

From behind the stall, a woman glared at him. "Does this look like a library to you?" she asked.

"Libraries contain things people might actually want to read," Blunt said.

"Oh, so hurtful. As if I'm the one who writes the bloody things. Anyway, you've clearly never been to our fine city's library. It's full of heads. Now, are you going to buy the bloody paper or just stand in the way of anyone who might actually be a customer?"

He sighed and put the paper back on top of the stack. "Nah, it's the same crap every day."

"I'm sorry,"—the woman said, looking around—"you might have confused me with someone who cares about your opinion. Get out of the way of my customers."

"What customers?" Blunt said looking around.

"Sod off."

"I'm going, bloody hell. Happy Bleakest Eve," he said as he walked away.

"It would be a lot happier if people actually bought something!" she shouted after him.

It was around noon, and he'd gained many questions but very few answers. The time of day meant office types were busy marching backwards and forwards or standing in queues to buy sandwiches where they got to choose every filling. The idea of pointing at each section of a sandwich had never tempted him, and watching a stranger in plastic gloves that they kept on all day assemble said sandwich seemed beyond tedious. He could make his own sandwiches, and he could choose what to put in them himself. Not that he ever did. Still, queuing for the opportunity to micro-manage the construction of a mediocre lunch seemed a waste of a lunch hour, but everyone had time to spare.

He weaved in and out of the pedestrian stream, every potential collision calculated with the 'Will they move, or should I' algorithm. Most people understood how it worked until they were drunk or so blindly arrogant they believed everyone else should move for them.

His sense of smell told him he was approaching the canal before he saw it. The pungent sulphurous aroma of the strange purple-black fluid people embarrassingly referred to as water grew stronger with each step until it subsumed all other scents and mysteriously became bearable. Like a friend who has been around for so long that you think they're normal when, in reality, they're obviously not.

The plastic pass he flashed at the gate guard was a new purchase. It was a canal boat season ticket to ride on Gloomwood's public transport system. The canal was in a permanent state of near-completion and ongoing repairs. The Office of the Dead had posted signs on every available surface that read 'Travel at your own risk' or 'We accept no liability for loss of possessions, limbs, or sanity'. It was an unpleasant experience, and he'd discovered that it only got worse as Bleakest Day approached.

The overburdened system was collapsing under the weight of the desperate clamouring of the Gloomwood populace. People were eager to spend anything they might have saved throughout the year on things that would ensure a moment of joy. Most gifts went to a place under the stairs to gather dust forever more.

He couldn't help but think about the comfort of having his own car. Selling the automobile had been the price of his half of the partnership in the business. Even then, Ursula had been generous. It would take an eternity to dig his way out of the debt he owed her, but then he had eternity, and she seemed happy enough to have her own detective on hand.

Boarding was the usual nuanced affair, and he found himself in the personal space of several other people. One of them had an extra pair of arms. When trapped in a floating tin can with barely enough room to breathe, additional elbows are not something anyone would ever wish for. And yet, Blunt scowled, here they were.

Somebody, presumably in collusion with an evil mastermind, had strewn yuletide lights and decorations across the ceiling of the barge. They were at the perfect height for the gentle irritating brush of tinsel to combine with tiny wreathes, which repeatedly hit anyone standing in the face as the boat rocked.

Decorations, Blunt thought. *Why does the Grim Reaper have magical sodding baubles?*

There were four stops until he reached Formaldehyde station in the northwest of the city. Development in the area was a mishmash of former warehouses and factories that had fallen into disrepair. In recent years, developers had purchased many of the buildings and, rumour had it, change was coming.

In the meantime, it was an excellent area for destitution, poverty, and desperation to hold their weekly meetings. And somewhere in this neighbourhood was a warehouse full of soft toys with glowing red irises who spoke in voices straight from the depths of Hell.

With every stop, it seemed fewer people disembarked and more flooded on. The boat groaned in protest, and the dark, murky waters below rose a little closer to the windows.

The boat lurched to one side, and those lucky enough to have seats watched the people standing for entertainment. The haves and have-nots had been decided in the boarding scuffle. Now the standing few were little more than a cheap comedy act as the boat rocked. Teeth were gritted as people steeled themselves against the force of gravity, its effect indifferent to the fact that this was the afterlife. Knuckles turned white as people held the few available handles, many of which were sticky for reasons nobody could explain.

Blunt tried to sway against the boat's movement. His method was working until Jonny Ten Elbows slipped, delivering a sharp blow to Blunt's nether regions. He winced and lost his footing. His balance went with it, and he became the first domino.

He tumbled into a woman with eyes on either side of her head like a deer. She let out a squawk as she toppled over the lap of a man who was sitting reading a newspaper. The front page was largely filled by an angry looking demon unicorn beneath a title about 'impending demonomics catastrophe'. The paper was a broadsheet of the type designed for inconvenience on public transport, but the increased spread feigned the quality of class. The deer woman ripped it in half as she fell, and the man, rather than helping her to her feet, scowled at the affront.

"Merry Bleakest Eve," Blunt muttered as the boat slowed to a halt to stop at Formaldehyde station. He straightened out his coat, repositioned his hat, and barrelled off the boat onto the platform.

Blunt took his time stepping out the doors, damned if he was going to make it easy for anyone else to get on. It wasn't like anyone had made it easy for him, and he had no compulsion to be the first on the fruitless journey towards respecting his fellow dead.

Thanks to Blunt's few friends, he knew the demons were camping out in a large warehouse in this rundown part of town. To call it accommodation would be disingenuous. It was a place for them to lay their heads and nothing more. There was no running water or electricity, and even the most ardent of virtue signallers had shied away from stepping forward to support the demons.

Blunt didn't hold an opinion either for or against integrating demons into Gloomwood society. It wasn't careful fence-walking that dictated his position but a mix of apathy and ignorance. As far as he was concerned, the demons were as welcome as anyone else in his personal sphere of death, meaning that they weren't.

Nobody else had stepped off the boat. The few who had rushed on to it looked like they might have spent half an hour standing on a platform they'd arrived at in error. As if the only people to visit this place did it to win a bet, to prove a point, or by mistake.

A sign painted onto a square sheet of metal hung from one chain and clattered against the brick wall of the platform gate guard's office. It read, 'Tickets, please?' The added question mark turned it into a pleading request rather than the demand it would have been elsewhere.

"Christ on a bicycle, looks like there's somewhere in the city you can get away from the crowds after all," Blunt muttered. He stepped through the guard's station, not seeing the need to flash his new commuter pass, and headed out on the road.

It was quiet, but he knew that some of these buildings were still active businesses. A lorry with a faded image of a rag doll and the slogan 'The child in you is dead too' rolled by.

"That's disturbing," Blunt said as it trundled around a corner and out of view.

He might not have had an address, but in their conversations, Sarah had made it simple enough to find the building. Step out of the station, then go straight across the road. Keep walking until you see the graffiti of a big red demon with a speech bubble saying, 'Don't worry, I'll bring Hell to you', then turn right. His destination was the second warehouse on the left side of the street which had an office with a blue door.

When Blunt arrived, Sarah was standing outside reading something on a clipboard.

"Sarah," the detective said.

"Blunt," she replied, lowering the clipboard to one side. "You found us then."

"Clearly," Blunt said with a shrug. "Any chance you've got a cup of coffee in there?" He nodded towards the door.

"Only instant." Sarah turned and walked into the office out of the howling wind. At least it wasn't raining.

Inside, the office was tiny. A desk, small though it was, took up most of the room, and on a spinning display was a collection of leaflets for government services with a perky sign at the top saying, 'What are you entitled to?' Sarah poured hot water over a brand of instant coffee that bore no relation to what it claimed to be.

"Isn't the answer nothing?" Blunt asked with a wave towards the display.

She turned and nodded. "For a demon? You're probably right, but when they are entitled to things, it might get useful."

"It's a good thing you're doing. I mean, I don't think it's altruistic. You're far too single-minded for that. But still, it's a good thing."

"Why can't it be a good thing for them and for me? What's being done to them is pretty terrible, and working out the science of what they are, how it all works, is going to help them as well. All I'm doing is pulling back the curtain and showing the monsters we're all afraid of are just like the rest of us."

"You're in danger of becoming political, you know."

Sarah gave a smile and winked at Blunt. "Don't worry, you won't need to hate me for a while yet. So, you've got a demon-focused client. This sounds intriguing. Let me grab a pen."

"Sorry I cancelled the other night. Turns out investigating stuff is pretty time-consuming when you've got a partner on your case."

"That's good news, isn't it?"

Blunt nodded. "Ursula is no slouch in business. She's got more letters after her name than she's got in it, which is saying something with a name like Panderpenny. My offer is still open, you know. Actual cases are arriving rather than gross, 'catch my husband banging the secretary' divorce cases. You could make a difference there, too. Of course, the lab won't be as fancy and expensive as the last place you worked."

"Oh. Well, fancy expensive equipment is the only reason I do this work." Sarah placed two mugs on the table. Both were chipped; one had a teddy bear holding a heart on it.

"I didn't mean it like that. I know it makes a difference to have the respect of your peers and everything, good standing in the scientific community. You probably deserve that. Not sure why it matters what a bunch of lab coat-wearing arrogant sods think, but still."

"Oh my, I'm not sure I can cope with such a compliment."

Blunt's eyebrow twitched as Sarah pushed the bear mug towards him.

"Really?" he asked, turning the mug to examine the picture.

She took a seat behind the desk, ignoring Blunt's question. "I'm never going to work for Ursula 'business before people' Panderpenny. You're just trying to push my buttons."

Blunt tilted his head in a 'perhaps I am' motion.

"So, you're calling in a favour?" Sarah asked.

"Well, it's not really a favour…"

"No? I'm pretty sure this is work-related and you're asking for help, so… that's a favour."

"What are you getting at?"

"Just wondering how you're going to make this up to me," she said as her entire torso vanished, leaving Blunt standing opposite a pair of sensible trousers. Sarah's right foot began tapping while they waited.

When she reappeared, she continued talking as if nothing had happened.

"You can tell me when we see the horde. You *are* here to see them?"

"The horde? You're really going with that?"

"It's got a certain quality, don't you think? The demonic horde and me? My demonic life? Demonic misconception? Oh, I like that. Doesn't that sound just lovely and strangely naughty?"

"Yeah… lovely."

Exorcists

"Hello, my name's Dan, and I'm pleased to be here standing up for dead people," said the man at the front of the upstairs area of the Rusty Guillotine.

The Rusty Guillotine was a pub on the west side of Gloomwood city centre that hosted themed discos at weekends. It also had one of the worst pub quizzes on offer in the entire city. It was a popular norm pub of the kind that welcomed any joke that came at the expense of someone who wasn't welcome. At the last time of checking, that included anyone who wasn't one of the norms' kind.

Dan—or Dangerous Dan the Man, to those who stood on either side of him while he attempted to belittle anyone foolish enough to stand opposite him—was an 'important' man. He was important because he knew what was wrong with society in Gloomwood, and it was simple. The problem with society was that it was unfair.

Exactly why it was unfair had changed several times over the twenty years Dan had been holding forth in the Rusty Guillotine. Fortunately for him, the same regulars had been there just as long. They understood it was easier just to agree with Dan and his friends.

When questioned about their continued apathy towards Dan and his strident points of view, anyone who frequented the pub just said it was easier. 'We've always gone to the Rusty Guillotine, haven't we? Seems silly to stop now just because Dan's an offensive twat sometimes. He'd had a few beers. He'll calm down by the morning. Anyway, he's entitled to his opinion.' Which was not, technically, overwhelming support for Dan's tirades.

In fact, convincing themselves that what Dan said, or did, had nothing to do with their presence as an audience was something that many locals in the Rusty Guillotine had become so adept at that they had discovered they could actively take part, and agree, with him. Provided they never attempted to have any kind of conversation with anyone who disagreed or tried to form any opinion of their own before hearing Dan's perspective. It was easier just to listen to what Dan said. Then, if he cornered you in the pub, as he was wont to do, you just said what he wanted to hear. Of course, that meant you had to believe it too, but anything for a peaceful life.

"Hello, Dan," a few people in the audience said. There were only sixteen of them, and two of them were working behind the bar.

"I'm here because I am a representative of a political movement some of you may have heard of: the exorcists," he said from behind the podium, which was actually four crates of bottled beer covered with a sheet that had once been white but now had suspicious yellow stains on it.

"Now, we have had some bad press recently where people have been saying we're some kind of hate group, but that's not true. We don't hate anyone. In fact, it's the opposite. We love

Gloomwood and the people of Gloomwood, which is why we exist. We're here to protect our fine city from those who might wish it harm."

While Dan expounded further on why the exorcists were, in fact, a friendly, supportive, understanding group, a figure in a long green hooded coat watched from the darkness at the back of the room. They remained in shadow, sipping on a pint of Gravestone's best bitter. Each time they raised their gloved hand to take a drink, there came a tinkling sound. They'd brought their own tankard from home. Nobody questions someone who brings their own tankard.

The general hubbub in the room was one of consensus as Dan drew closer to his conclusion.

"And that's why all good citizens of our fine city should be concerned about the demons who have turned up, uninvited, demanding our jobs. Did they die?" he asked. "No, exactly. Did they exist as part of the living world? No. Now you're seeing my point. This is the afterlife, not the neverlife, not the 'I don't like where I have to die so I'm going to move to your place' afterlife. Now, it's got nothing to do with them being demons, or demonic, and I wouldn't want to go to Hell either, but why should I have to support them?"

A hand went up in the crowd. It belonged to Erica. She only had the two, but they were both right hands, so she could write with both.

"Yes, Erica?" Dan said.

"Well, it's just, aren't we all here because the

Grim Reaper created this place and said we could be here?"

A murmur went through the crowd.

"That"—Dan said, raising a finger—"is an excellent point. The Grim Reaper created this place for us, not for them—"

"Yeah, but didn't he say they could stay here?"

"Yes, Erica, he did, but it's not their afterlife. He didn't make it for them. I think we all know what I'm saying," Dan said, nodding his head. Nobody knew what he was saying. "They are demons, with demonic ways. They came from Hell. *The* Hell. It's an actual place. Which means… well, it means that they've probably corrupted the Grim Reaper."

A collective gasp went around the room, and with that, Dan had them in the palm of his hand.

Unfortunately for Dan, he did not know what to do beyond this point, because Dan was not a leader. He had the qualities of a supervisor who only had the position because he'd worked for the same company for thirty years.

But it didn't matter that he had no more to add. That would come from further up the chain. He was a grassroots campaigner, and he was doing his job.

The figure in the shadows drained their tankard and stood up with a slight wobble.

The Horde

Morgarth's tail swept from side to side. It was too slow to call it wagging, though, she admitted, it happened sometimes.

"Detective Blunt, it's been a while. We could've used your help."

"Could you?" Blunt asked, gritting his teeth.

Morgarth's voice could reduce him to a mewling puddle of flesh. It grated and clawed at the inside of his skull as if something in there wanted to escape, but he resisted its power. The worst part was Morgarth was attempting to tone her voice down.

"I think you might need to learn a bit about how this city ticks. The last thing you need is to be associated with the man voted 'Gloomwood's Worst Person'. The same charity Sarah now pretends she works for planned to sue me for... what was it called?"

A small smile flitted across Sarah's face as she said, "Defamation and hate speech against minorities."

Blunt was about to continue but caught himself and looked at Sarah. "Really? That's so much worse than I thought it was."

"It's fine," Sarah said with a wave of her hand. "It was for publicity. You were an easy target."

"The way you say that makes it sound like you knew they were going to sue me."

Sarah nodded and, with nothing approaching

remorse, said, "It was my idea. How many people do you think work for this charity? It's me, Aunt Agnes, and a handful of volunteers, most of whom are doing it for community service or as part of the seventeen-step program."

"Seventeen steps?"

"I think they called it the twelve-step program when you were alive."

"Right. You…" Blunt paused. He found he needed to put his usual plethora of insults needed to one side around Sarah. "You're mean," he finished, twisting his face in disgust.

"I'm helping people, Blunt, remember? It's a good thing. Now, I'm going to leave you with Morgarth because this bit is boring, but I'll be expecting details later."

The demon and Blunt watched as Sarah walked out the main doors of the warehouse, popped open a small umbrella she seemed to pull from nowhere, and disappeared from view.

"Woman's an enigma," Blunt said with a shake of his head.

"Mhm, and if I still had a working female form, I'd do some things to her," Morgarth said. Her tongue, also fluffy, flicked out, and she licked her oversized lips.

"Hmm. Well, that's both disturbing and inappropriate. Also, as a demon or T-Rex, I'm not sure you're her type."

"I'm everyone's type if I want to be. Anyway, detective, what is it that the horde can do for you?"

the little blue dinosaur asked.

"You realise Sarah's my... well, she's... we're sort of..."

Morgarth raised a furry purple eyebrow.

"Oh, you know. You're just winding me up."

Blunt looked around the inside of the warehouse. He had expected far worse, but it still wasn't a pretty sight. The demons had laid out blankets on the floor. Each one was neatly aligned with the one next to it, forming a vast rectangle. Cuddly toys lay sleeping on some of them as if a child had placed them there.

"So, how's Gloomwood treating you?"

Morgarth rolled her oversized eyes. "If you're just going to keep dragging it out, then I can ask one of the other demons to help. We're quite adept at getting to the root of the matter."

"I thought you were all trying to make more of an effort to integrate? This is a normal conversation," Blunt said as he followed Morgarth around the edge of the sleeping area. "Most people have a little small talk, a lead up to whatever it is they're going to say."

"Why?"

"Because... I don't know. It's polite?"

"Ah, politeness is something we're working on. It's a bit of a strange concept for us. Please and thank you are easy enough, but asking people how they are when both parties do not want to talk about it seems like a deliberate waste of time. It also seems quite unlike you, Detective Blunt. I think the phrase

I've heard you use is 'stop beating about the bush'?"

Blunt opened his mouth, then stopped himself from correcting Morgarth by offering a more imaginative phrase.

"Look, it's confidential. I can't discuss it out here."

They reached a door, and Morgarth leapt up onto the handle to open it. The door swung open to reveal a room that could only have been a storage cupboard in a previous life.

"This is my office. What? I'm supposed to have an office," Morgarth said, catching the look of bewilderment on Blunt's face. "I know. I write nothing down, and this is where they kept cleaning products, but I come in here for conversations with a different meaning. And it gives the others something to talk about. Come in."

Blunt didn't speak until he pulled the door shut and found himself in a room smaller than his own arm span.

"Small offices seem to be a bit of a theme today... Right, well, this is for the best, anyway. What can you tell me about baubles?"

Morgarth nodded. "I wondered when people would question us about things like this. Baubles are not the most effective form of torture—"

"Stop. Never ever mention that again. I'm talking about decorative baubles, the festive type that are all over the city for Bleakest Day."

Morgarth's furry eyebrows furrowed. "What would I know about decorations? Interior decoration was quite low on the list of desirable skills in Beelzebub's elite guard. I can spray the walls of most rooms in blood so quickly and efficiently that the victim would wonder if the walls were painted red before they passed out. That's sort of to do with decoration. Psychological punishments might include lining interior walls with the stretched-out skin of loved ones."

"Right," Blunt said, swallowing the rising bile. "So nothing about actual baubles?"

"Ah, yes, a lot can be done with someone's—"

"Still talking about decorations."

Blunt watched the tyrannosaurus in front of him. Its cartoon-like appearance made it easy to read, but Blunt wasn't about to accept the reaction from a recently reformed, millennia-old evil being at face, or snout, value.

"That means nothing to me. Should it?"

"Someone thinks demons stole their baubles."

"Ah, I see."

"You do?"

"No."

"I can't actually think of a reason you would want to steal decorations," Blunt admitted. "To be honest, the whole thing sounds ridiculous."

He rubbed a hand across his chin. Despite having shaved only hours before, he could feel stubble. It didn't seem to matter that he shaved at all. Even when he didn't bother, there was only ever a shadow of stubble.

"It is confusing. Really confusing. You mind

if I look around in case any of your, um… is horde the right word? Anyway, just in case one of them has decorated their space on the floor with stolen decorations?"

Morgarth's head bobbed up and down. "That seems unlikely, but please feel free."

"Demons wouldn't do that?"

"Oh no. We could definitely do that. We have the skills to steal them, and some of us literally existed only to cause misery. Stealing festive decorations sounds quite appropriate. Flaunting the fact we stole them by putting them up in plain sight… yes, that too is something we would do."

"Misery-making as a way of life?"

"Essentially. We all have our niche. I don't believe we have a specific person with this fixation. There was Flixiver of the broken fairy lights, very seasonal work, but around Chri—"

"We can't say the C-word. It gets people all jumpy. So this Flixiver might be the sort to steal a load of decorations?"

"No. He would ensure that the lights didn't work, that there was a bulb missing from a series circuit or a chewed wire, or just tangle them to induce murder-causing rage, if nothing else would do. But Flixiver isn't part of this horde."

"Ah, still in Hell?"

"I do not know. It really depends on where he's most effectively deployed or if he's obsolete. Things change."

"Obsolete?"

"Technology changes. Demons who are too specialised can become obsolete if they can't retrain. There was a demon who used to cause problems with sticking typewriters, but there's not much call for that now."

"So they became obsolete?"

"Well, no, that's a poor example. They started a whole new section responsible for paper jams, ink problems, and even failed wireless connections on printers. They're a big deal now."

"Wait, so a demon handles... Bastard. Absolute bastard."

"She even came up with the whole idea of printers being cheap but ink being expensive. Genius, really."

"Is this demon here?" Blunt asked, his hands balling into fists.

"No. Why would she want to leave Hell? She's a huge deal."

Blunt nodded and took a breath. "You know, Hopes and Dreams don't tell people what they were when they were on the living side. I suggest demons do the same thing."

"If you say so. I'm not sure it's that big a deal."

"It really is. It really, really is. Morgarth, I don't mean to be rude, but you lot were demons, but you're not anymore. How are you going to defend yourself as a bunch of toys?"

Morgarth's dinosaur mouth broke into an open grin. "Violence is about will, not strength, detective."

Blunt had a moment of recollection. Months ago, Ursula Panderpenny had been decapitated. How was never really made clear, but it had been Morgarth, all two feet of blue fur and foam of her, who had separated head from body.

Morgarth was the reason that Blunt's business partner now had such an affection for scarves.

Bunny

She didn't know when it happened, but it was quick. The seeping in of emotions, an awareness of what others think on more than an academic level.

Demons, despite what people might say, can be very insightful. Selling temptation, fuelling jealousy and spite, it all takes an understanding of underlying psychology. Before they had come here, it had all been theoretical, knowledge to be applied, but within minutes of arriving, empathy had set in like the onset of some insidious disease to take hold of their emotional systems.

Tremoria, like the others who had stayed, didn't want to turn her back on what she had gained. It was like someone had opened a window in a room that had never been exposed to the outside world. As if a door they had never known was closed had now opened, and they were free.

There were downsides to the revelations of empathy and free will. Tremoria missed her eight-foot-tall body. The ability to tear the spine out of a mortal with one clawed hand had been useful. She would have applied her skills differently now, of course, perhaps in surgery. That body was in Hell, presumably still lying on her bunk in the demontory, which is like a dormitory, but more... demony.

She was now housed in a rabbit. To be more specific, it was a fluffy grey bunny, which bore almost no resemblance to an actual rabbit. Trem, as she was usually called, shook her head, and her ears whipped around, slapping her in the face. It was not what she was housed in, she reminded herself.

It's not a vessel, it's who I am. A former demon.

Morgarth had told them they needed to integrate into Gloomwood society. They were just the same as everyone else. If Gloomwood could accept former gods and individuals who were once only ideas in the mortal consciousness, then they could accept former demons.

She carried several sheets of paper in one hand. Copies of something Miss Von Faber, from the charity, had called a curriculum vitae. Trem spoke Latin. All demons did, but apparently that wasn't a very useful skill anymore. Neither, it seemed, were many other things on her list, but then she had probably put too much emphasis on the torture and dismemberment and not enough on her soft skills.

'Fear inducement' had not been one of the soft skills Miss Von Faber had been referring to.

She turned into a clothes shop that had a 'Help wanted' sign in the window. As she made her way between the racks towards the counter, a woman nearly stood on her.

"Excuse me," Trem said.

"Ew, get away from me! Oh, my bag! Thief!" the woman shouted, snatching at her bag, which was hanging over her shoulder, nowhere near Trem's reach.

"What are you talking about? You nearly just

kicked me," the demon said. Her voice, despite Trem making it as gentle as she could, still sounded like a V8 engine trying to drive through a meter-deep sewage flood.

"Can I help you?" a woman with the name 'Delilah' on a tag attached to her blouse asked.

"This woman—" Trem began before it became apparent she wasn't the individual being addressed.

"Yes, this thing was trying to steal my purse," the woman with a serious spatial awareness problem and needlessly pointy shoes screeched like a tortured parrot.

"I'm sorry, ma'am," the Delilah said as she looked down at Trem, "I'm going to have to ask you to leave, or I'll be calling the police."

"What?" Trem asked. "I was literally walking to the counter to ask about the help you wanted."

"We don't want any help," Delilah said. She cast an embarrassed look towards the woman, who was clutching her bag.

Trem held out the pages in her hand. "But the sign—"

"It turned out we were just being lazy and we can do the job as we have been. I meant to take it down but forgot. So there's no job. You can leave."

Trem's ears perked up and straightened out, rising on the top of her head. "Okay, well, I'll just look around."

"We don't do clothes for... toys. This woman says you were trying to steal from her. That's a serious accusation, and we don't want any trouble," the shop assistant said.

"I do!" the parrot woman screeched. "We should lock them up. She's a demon, you know. From actual Hell. We're lucky she's only one of the thieving ones. There are much worse ones, you know!"

Trem turned and walked out. The CVs in her hand crumpled and creased as she gripped them too tightly. As she stepped out into the street, a figure in the shadow of a nearby doorway called out, "I've got a job for you."

"What is it?" Trem asked.

"Look," the voice said, and a small demon stumbled out of the shadows.

"Moki?" Trem asked. "Is that you? What are you wearing?"

"Tell your friend," the voice said.

"It makes us sound different," Moki said. Through the mask, her demonic growl vanished, as if filtered to be bearable by mortal ears.

"That's amazing," Trem said. "How?"

"Come with me, and you'll see, a world of vocal transformation," the figure in the shadows said before bursting into warm laughter. "Ho, ho, ho."

Floor Demons

"These are your decorations?" Blunt asked.

Morgarth was standing in front of a twig in a red bucket. There was nothing in the bucket to make it stand up straight and no decorations to be seen.

"Is it inadequate?"

Blunt shrugged. "I'm not sure. I mean, I've got no decorations at all, I haven't bothered, but somehow, this stick in a bucket is worse. It's… just really sad, Morgarth."

"Sad? It's called Bleakest Eve. That sounds like it should be sad. We can make it bleaker… perhaps some limbs of our enemies? A weeping mortal placed atop the stick?"

"I'm no expert on this—"

"That's never prevented you from giving advice before."

"—but I think the idea is that in the bleakest of times, there's always a light, shining."

"The same is true in Hell. There's always a fire burning."

"Right, yup, but the light we're talking about here is more metaphorical and not as terrifying as the fires of Hell."

"Stupid mortals, it makes little sense. Also, isn't it quite inefficient?"

"What?"

"Keeping a light on throughout the night. Don't mortals sleep? Even demons sleep."

"It's a metaphorical light," Blunt said. "There really is nothing here," he continued as he turned around, taking in the warehouse. A large hole in a part of the ceiling let the rain pour through, and a few working strip lights flickered. The ceiling tiles had fallen loose in most places, letting foam insulation spill through. "Do you even have possessions?"

"We're trying to cut down on the possessions. People don't seem to like them."

"Possessions… Ah, I don't mean demonic possessions. Taking people over and controlling them and all that. I mean stuff."

"If it's something that belongs to us, then isn't it technically a demonic possession?"

"I… right. So no stolen decorations?"

"We are without baubles."

"You're doing this on purpose, aren't you?"

Morgarth nodded without a smile, as if the need to force bauble-related comments into the conversation was a task she took extremely seriously.

"Decorations mean nothing to demons. Demon accommodations in Hell are simple. I had my personal space."

"Like a demonic palace?"

"A cabin."

"Oh, a place somewhere away from everyone?"

"No. Like a cabin on a boat. A room with a bed. I had some decorations." Morgarth was referring to posters she'd had of her favourite demonic musicians. "Most people have cellmates."

"So they're cells, like prison cells?"

"Yes."

"Hang on, cellmates don't count as decorations."

"Not even if they're hanging from the walls?"

Blunt let out a sigh and straightened his hat. "Okay, I don't think you're hiding anything here. How many demons have pink fluff?"

"I do not know. Is that something they might collect? Seems like a strange thing to—"

"How many of you are pink and fluffy?"

"Oh. Be more specific with your questions, please. Quite a lot of us are pink. It seems to be a very popular colour for cuddly toys."

"Great. I'm going to need a list. How many of you have hooves?"

"Oh, less. I'm not sure any of us do. Even those of us who might have hooves seem to have rounded soft feet, stumps, instead. I can check. Are your phenomenal powers of deduction going to cross-reference the two, creating a Venn diagram of likely suspects?"

Blunt looked like he was chewing a wasp.

"I'll find your list, even if I think it's a waste of time," Morgarth said. "If, in return, you check up on a few demons."

"Do I look like your sodding assistant?"

"No. He's a green frog wearing a tartan dress. Why is that relevant?"

"Fine, I'll check up on your fuzzball friends."

Morgarth looked at Blunt and eventually rolled her eyes. "If something is happening to the demons, doesn't it seem likely it would be the same people who are trying to frame us for this decoration heist?"

"Maybe... You ever think about being a private investigator?"

"Yes—"

"Well, don't. All you get are people being know-it-alls."

The Machine

"Where are we?" Trem asked as she walked behind the tall figure.

"This is where you'll be working." Its voice was deep. "You'll have a roof and food."

"That's good—"

"As long as you do your job."

"Why wouldn't I do my job?"

"You might not like it."

"I used to torture people," Trem said. "My speciality was playing horrible music over and over again really loud. Did you know it's possible to make someone's ears bleed like that? It's not just a thing people say. You have to find the right song though. And insert the speakers inside their head so they claw at it, trying to open their own skull."

The figure walked on. "In here," it said as it pushed open a door. Trem followed it inside into a room dominated by a dentist's chair on a raised platform. A single light bulb over the chair gave little illumination to a drab-looking room, on one side of which was a bench.

From Trem's position, it was difficult to see what was on the bench, but wires hung down over one side of the table.

"This looks familiar," Trem said. "And not in a nice way."

"In the chair."

"I didn't do those things by choice, you know.

Demons don't have free will. Or at least, we didn't. We do now…"

"Good," the figure said. "Now, hop up into the chair. I don't want to pick you up. It's very demeaning."

"I don't—"

"I really must insist."

Aunt Agnes

Of the 506 demons who had arrived in Gloomwood and requested to stay, ten had not returned to the warehouse for several nights. Three of them had known whereabouts. One of them, a pink elephant by the name of Phil, sounded a likely suspect in the case of the missing baubles.

Blunt had to find the demon if he wanted to get any further. When dealing with missing persons, it was sensible to start with people who knew them. It was also not unusual for the person simply not to want to be found.

It was mortal realm logic, and Blunt had learned his lesson when it came to trying to apply policing methods he had learned on the mortal side of the veil, but he had to start somewhere.

His first stop was Aunt Agnes' house. It was probably the most famous home in the city. No mean feat when considering the desperate cries for attention that come from people trying to maintain their celebrity status for decades at a time.

That was one problem with being dead; people didn't pass the flame on to a new generation. Instead, they tightened their grips and fought tooth and nail to keep it. Aunt Agnes was famous in her own way, but for very different reasons.

There were no paparazzi outside the run-down terrace house. Technically, Aunt Agnes lived at number seven, but someone had purchased numbers five and nine on either side of her home and donated them to her charitable work.

If the Office of the Dead was the cold, calculating, reptilian brain that stamped its authority on Gloomwood's citizens, then Agnes was the heart. Her home was a haven for the city's waifs and strays. For those who had hit rock bottom and needed help to bounce back. She offered them food, accommodation, and a sympathetic ear, and it was the latter that was in shortest supply among the dead. Sympathy was, at least. Ears were available in abundance at most supermarkets and corner shops.

At this time of year, the entire street, populated by former residents of Aunt Agnes' home, was bedecked in seasonal decorations. As Blunt stepped out of a Gloomwood black cab, he couldn't stop himself from turning on the spot to take in the spectacle.

"Come on, who are they trying to kid? This is blatantly just Chri—"

"Detective Blunt," a voice interrupted him, and he turned back towards Aunt Agnes' house. She was standing in the doorway, holding a pie in her hands. She offered him a theatrical wink. "Never say what you were about to say, even if you think nobody is listening."

He gave her a grin. It was difficult to do anything else when faced with just about the only friendly little old woman in the city. She was everyone's grandmother and nobody's at the same time.

"That pie looks interesting," Blunt said.

"Well, it is Bleakest Day, so I'll be charitable and not say anything about whether you really need a piece of pie," she said, turning into the house.

Blunt broke into an awkward three-step jog to the doorway. "We both know you just called me fat, don't we?"

"I didn't say that," Agnes said over her shoulder. "If that's what you heard, then perhaps you should wonder why."

"No, you're not playing that game with me. You called me fat. Now, about that pie."

Aunt Agnes' kitchen was a constant hive of activity. That was hardly surprising, considering that her pies, cakes, and cookies were constantly being offered, for free, to anyone who asked.

But there were rules to asking for food from Aunt Agnes. First, she might say no, and you never argue if she does. Second, you can only ask if you're having a chat or if you're genuinely desperate, and she would know if you weren't. Third, taking the piss would destroy you. For simplicity's sake, the rules were something that Aunt Agnes herself was completely unaware of, and it was her neighbours and friends who saw to their enforcement.

Without asking, Blunt took a seat at the table that sat at the centre of the busy kitchen. Every surface had piles of baked goods on top of it, but he kept his hands to himself.

"So," Agnes said. "I'm guessing you didn't come here just to say hello."

"No small talk?" Blunt asked, casting an eye over the mouth-watering sight in front of him. "Are those mince pies?"

"Yes, and we can do small talk if you like. You look well. A lot better than the last time I saw you. I assume death is treating you a little better now?"

Blunt reached for a mince pie, short-crust with powdered sugar on top of it, and received a sharp slap to the back of his hand for the effort.

"Ouch! Yes, much better, thanks."

"Miss Panderpenny is a tough taskmaster."

"You as well? Everyone keeps telling me she's amazing. I don't need to be reminded that she's got more qualifications than you can shake a stick at. She made the offer, I accepted. It's business."

"Ah." Agnes smiled. "There's the characteristic resentment. For a second there, I was worried that the chip on the shoulder may have become a little lighter, but it seems to be where it's always been."

Blunt scowled. "Well, it's lovely to see you as well."

"Don't be so grumpy, Augustan. That inherent bitterness you carry around is only part of you, but it's an important part. Nobody suggested you change."

"Actually, loads of people have suggested that I change."

"Well, I'm just saying there are worse attributes to have and there's a balance to these things. Nobody's perfect."

"Try telling that to the Office of the Dead."

"Oh, I do. Regularly. And they often listen. Now, what exciting case brings you to my door?" She handed him a saucer with a teacup on it. Blunt didn't recall seeing her make a pot of tea or get a teacup and saucer from anywhere, but there it was.

"Thanks," he mumbled. "It's a little… uh—"

"Would you like a mince pie?"

"That's what it needs."

"Mhm," Agnes said, nodding at the table. "Be my guest."

"You're not going to hit me?"

"I didn't hit you last time. I merely reminded you of your manners with a mild physical memory aid."

"You slapped me."

"Detective, don't be rude. Speaking of which, you have bought a present for Sarah, haven't you?"

"Of course I bloody have. Why's everyone asking me that?"

"Everyone?"

"You and Ursula."

"Ah, so people who might be concerned about your welfare?"

He frowned but grabbed a mince pie before she rescinded the offer. "Right. So, I'm here about missing demons," he said between bites.

"They have been causing a *hell* of a stir."

"Everyone's got a demonic pun today."

"It's the holiday season. Everyone loves puns but especially during the holidays."

"Mmhf," Blunt said with a mouthful of mince

pie. The sickly sweet inside was dribbling into his hands as he looked around for a napkin.

"Those poor creatures. Demon is just a name. It would have been sensible not to have used it at all and simply called them people who had been wrongly placed in Hell."

"They're not, though, are they? I mean, they're from Hell. Made in Hell might as well be stamped on their feet. Actually, they're toys now, so they probably do have some kind of Made in Gloomwood mark on them. Not that it's relevant. Morgarth—she's their leader, I guess—said at least one of them came to see you, a demon called Phil?"

Agnes nodded. "Yes, Phil was here for a few nights, then we found him a job and a place to stay. He's doing well."

"He is? That's disappointing."

"It isn't for Phil. He seemed quite happy. Thrilled, in fact. He gave the distinct impression that things were better than in Hell."

"Well, obviously it's good that he's integrating into society, but I'm looking for demons who've vanished."

Aung Agnes frowned. On her wrinkled face, a frown and a scowl were very similar. "So would you have preferred my response to be, 'Sorry, Phil vanished'?"

Blunt stuffed the last of the mince pie into his mouth and took a sip of the tea, wincing as it burnt his tongue. "Hot."

"Yes, that's how you make tea."

"Well, maybe Phil has some idea about where the other demons have gone. Any idea where can I find him?"

"At this time? He'll be on his way to work."

"Oh? Night shift, is it? I guess it's because they can see in the dark."

Aunt Agnes shook her head. "I don't think they can."

"No? Then what's with the glowing red eyes?"

"You're a tough man to like sometimes, detective. Here." She handed him a piece of paper.

"You had that ready?"

"Sarah called me before you arrived."

"Oh, so you just—"

"Just wanted to see how you were, dear."

Phil and Bill

As Blunt entered the shop, the bell above the door jingled. Music from speakers discreetly hung in corners around the room played in the background. A noise with too many jingling sounds, nostalgically plucking at something he remembered from life. Festive.

"Happy Bleakest Eve," said a creature with the body of a man and the head of a goose from behind the counter. "Last minute shopping trip? We've got you covered. Anything I can help you with, sir?"

Blunt desperately tried not to catch the earworm of the tune playing while he stepped up to the counter. It was an establishment that made its money selling cigarettes, booze, and those last few things you'd forgotten to pick up during that week's big shop. It offered a mishmash of items, tins of food standing alongside chocolate-filled calendars, which were now reduced to a fraction of their cost from twenty days ago. After tomorrow, they'd be practically free.

"Actually, Mister Goose," Blunt said as he placed his fingertips on the edge of the counter. "I'm looking for Phil."

"My name isn't Mister Goose. Are you Mister Human?" the newsagent said. "Anyway, why do you want Phil?"

"I'm here on behalf of Panderpenny's, investigating a case."

"Panderpenny's?"

"Private investigations."

"Okay." The man nodded. He wore an apron with 'Season's Greetings' printed on it, and as he spoke, he picked up a small green felt pointed hat from the counter and pulled it over his feathered head. "What's that got to do with Phil?"

"It's about demons."

"Look, Phil's a good lad. He works hard, and he wouldn't harm a fly."

Blunt shook his head. "No, no, he hasn't done anything wrong. I'm not here to give him a hard time. The opposite, so there's no need to worry about that. It'll only take a couple of minutes and"—Blunt looked around—"I guess I'll buy a few presents for people, if it helps?"

The shopkeeper didn't look happy about it, but he craned his long neck to look over Blunt's shoulder at a bargain bin of 'last minute get out of jail' gifts and back at Blunt.

"A few?"

Blunt shrugged. "Completely forgot Bleakest Day was around the corner. I'm pretty fresh. My first one."

"Oh? Well, you're in for a treat. Nobody likes to admit it, but Bleakest Day is basically just the same as Chr—"

The bell above the shop door rang, and a figure, wrapped in a coat and scarf with a large woollen hat on, stepped through the door. It was a little over three feet tall.

"Evening, Phil," the shopkeeper said.

"Hello, Bill," the bundle of clothes said in a voice that made Blunt's skin crawl.

"Really?" Blunt said. "Phil and Bill, the corner shop men? Also, Bill Goose, I mean—"

Bill shot a scowl at Blunt. "My name isn't Bill Goose, it's Bill Morris. You're unpleasant." The gooseman looked back at the mound of clothes. "This fella is asking after you. Seems okay, if rude. Have a word. Then there's stuff in the back that needs putting away, and it's a stock count tonight."

"Stock count? Outstanding!" Phil said as he began unravelling the scarf.

With the outer layer off, Phil turned out to be a pink stuffed elephant with a fully mobile trunk and, despite his voice, a very cheery demeanour.

Bill pointed through a door at the back of the shop, and Blunt followed Phil through it. They sat down in the back room, where Phil always worked during opening hours to avoid any confrontations with customers who might not look kindly on a demon.

"I'm here because there are demons missing from the horde."

"Missing?" Phil asked.

Blunt nodded. "I've spoken to Morgarth and Aunt Agnes. Now I'm going around trying to locate the missing demons and find out if they actually *are* missing or if they've just found a place for themselves."

Phil's trunk lifted, and he scratched the top of

his head. "Can't imagine anyone running off telling nobody where they were going. I mean, we're not very well-liked. I understand it. If you hadn't been in the grey, then we might have been torturing you for all eternity. We were this close"—he held up a tiny paw, a thumb and mitten hand—"to being the worst thing to happen to you. Now we're standing here asking for help."

"Huh. Hadn't really thought of it like that."

"Well, that's one perspective. The other is that we were enslaved against our will and put through eons of forced labour torturing people, which is also torture. But unlike mortals, we couldn't decide our fate. Mortals got a choice, but we didn't."

"Uh, yeah, that too. Maybe let's stick with this minor problem I came here about. Any idea where these other guys might be? I'm specifically looking for anyone pink and fluffy," he said, looking Phil up and down.

"Hey, I'm pink and fluffy. Could you be looking for me?"

"Given your reaction, that's... quite unlikely. Do you have hooves?"

The elephant eagerly jumped to the floor and pointed his feet up towards Blunt. "Sort of, only not really. They're just circles."

"Right."

A cough came from behind Blunt, and he turned to see Bill, the shopkeeper, peering into the back room. "You, um... Whatever it is you're doing, do it somewhere else, right?"

"I was just looking at his feet," Blunt said.

"Oh, because that makes this better?"

"It's nothing weird. I'm trying to make sure he wasn't at a crime scene by seeing if he has hooves. I didn't ask him to do"—Blunt waved at the elephant—"that."

"Yeah, well, whatever it is, finish up and sling your hook."

Blunt shook his head and turned back to the elephant, who was still on the floor with his feet in the air.

"Will you get up? You're making me look like some kind of… I don't even know what. Now, any ideas about the rest of your missing friends?"

"No, sorry. I'm pretty low down on the demon totem pole. Not that there's really any of that anymore. If Morgarth doesn't know, then I'm worried about them."

Blunt sighed. "Shame. I'm not having much luck in tracking them down. Other than you, there are only a couple of names. Do you know of anyone else who might have given them a job? Maybe someone else sympathetic like your boss, Bill?"

"Bill found Aunt Agnes. He just called her up and said I've got a job, has she got anyone worth giving a chance to, and she sent me. Bill was pretty surprised. But he said if Aunt Agnes said I was okay, then I was okay. Bill's a nice guy."

"Yeah. Well, thanks for talking to me, Phil—"

"There was another guy who offered me a job though."

"Who?"

"I don't know. I didn't go with him because it seemed a little weird. He just saw me on the street and said, 'Hey you, I've got a job if you want it,' and I said, 'What is it?' and he said, 'I'll show you, come on,' so I said, 'No, this whole thing is weird,' and walked away. He just laughed."

"Can you describe him?"

"He was mostly in the shadows. He was a norm, I think. I can't always tell with you people. Some of you look really weird."

"Some of us? Right, anyway, anything else?"

"Think he had a beard."

"Brilliant, because that's really unusual."

"Is it?"

Vague Incompetence

"Now what do we do?"

"We put up a cordon, guv?"

"Yes, excellent answer, Corporal Falstaff. You put up a cordon. Now, who can remember why we do that?"

Captain Sowercat, head of the Gloomwood police, looked around the room. In one corner, sitting on a police issue folding chair, was a frightened-looking man in spectacles and a cardigan that was at least one size too small.

"To stop the public from interfering with our investigations," Corporal Falstaff answered. She was tall and moved with the grace of a battleship as she stuck yellow tape across the door frame in a large X. "Done, Captain."

"Good work, Falstaff. Now, come and survey the scene with me and Constable Darwin."

"Um, sir—"

"What is it, Falstaff?" Sowercat said, turning to look back at the door. Falstaff stood on the other side of the police barrier she had just created. "Oh for... Right, take it down, come in here, and put some more up."

"That was my last roll, sir."

"Constable Darwin, please assist soon-to-be demoted Corporal Falstaff in crossing the barrier she made and create a new cordon."

Darwin spoke little. He was a dour man with

a shaved head and huge eyebrows that, on closer inspection, were definitely hairy caterpillars that were tethered to his face.

Darwin was part of the Gloomwood police's greater representation program—an effort to better reflect the citizens of Gloomwood. Following the public revelations of the harassment received by Gloomwood's first Hope police officer, John Jacob Jeremiah Johnson, the Office of the Dead had taken a much more involved role in the police department. Sowercat and his officers had come to terms with it. Darwin wasn't so bad. He did the job and barely spoke, exactly what Sowercat wanted in a corporal.

Without a word, Darwin tore down the tape, stepped aside, and allowed Falstaff to step back into the room. The caterpillar-browed police officer then taped up the doorway once more.

Sowercat clapped his hands and turned back to the scene. "Right, let's try again. What do we see?"

"Looks like someone pulled the stuffing out of a bunch of stuffed toys," Falstaff said.

"Yeah, it does. The question we've got is a little trickier. Are they someone's toy, or are they demons?"

"Toys either way," Darwin said, his voice staccato and quiet.

Sowercat raised a finger. "Yeah, good point. A demon body is a stuffed toy." The chief of police turned to the frightened, bespectacled man in the room's corner. As Sowercat turned, his nose flapped. It was cheap and made of thin rubber that inflated when he forgot he couldn't breathe through it. Usually, this happened when he was angry. "Well then, Mister Hollis, what makes you think these are demons?"

The man opened and closed his mouth several times before finding the gumption to produce words. "I didn't know what they were. I just found them and couldn't help but wonder."

"You just thought that knackered toys might be demons?" Falstaff asked.

"Shut it, Falstaff. That is not how we address a member of the public," Sowercat snapped.

"It was last week. Last Monday, you called a woman a Babylonian whore who should keep her mouth shut."

"Falstaff! For your information, Mistress Ventria is a prostitute who was Babylonian before she died, and she was giving us information on her boss, who walked into the room as we were talking about him. I was being reasonable. Right, Mister Hollis, is there any reason you have for thinking these toys were, before something happened to them, demons?"

"It... it smells like sulphur here?" Hollis said.

"Sulphur?" Sowercat turned to his subordinates. "Does it smell like sulphur?"

Falstaff and Darwin made a show of sniffing the air while stepping around the table in the middle of the room. Upon the table was a splayed-out toy puppy. Spilling out of its stomach was white foam, and a googly eye dangled from a thread on its face.

Someone had hammered nails through each of its paws, holding it in position. If it had been a demon, it had been tortured. Hanging from the ceiling, like the skins of flayed puppets, were more soft toy carcasses.

"Eggs?" Falstaff asked.

"Yeah," Darwin said. "Sulphurous eggy smell."

Sowercat let out a sigh when a cough came from the taped-up doorway. Everyone turned towards it to see Sarah Von Faber, the former head of forensics for the city, standing there beside the two-foot-tall demon, Morgarth, who was hopping from one foot to the other.

"This is nice tape," Sarah said. "It's new."

"Things have changed a little since the police came under more scrutiny thanks to your bloody detective friend and his insufferable pet reporter," Sowercat snapped.

Sarah forced a smile, tilted her head, and fluttered her eyelashes at the chief of police. The nose hanging from the police chief's face like a broken water balloon grew larger.

Morgarth stepped under the tape, her head passing well underneath where it crossed the door, and walked across the room. She paid no attention to the police officers or the terrified Hollis, who was watching the little furry dinosaur with his feet up on the chair and his arms wrapped around his knees.

She leapt onto the table and stared down at the body. "It's not one of us."

"How can you tell?" Sowercat asked.

"I know all the demons in Gloomwood, and none of them were in this body."

"So what is it?"

Sarah ripped down the tape.

"You can't do that," Corporal Falstaff said.

Sarah's smile didn't falter. "Oops, sorry… Corporal," she said with a look at the bars on her shoulder. "Officers. That's also new."

"We're a modern police force now," Falstaff said.

"Sure you are." Sarah shook her head, the smile finally dropping, and stepped up to the table. "This is horrible."

"What do you think it means?" Sowercat asked.

"It looks like a threat," Morgarth said. "We demons understand threats."

"But you would never have seen it if it hadn't been reported," Sarah said.

"Not much of a threat then, is it?" Sowercat said, looking at Morgarth.

The demon inspected the split-open toy, then nodded. "Not a threat. Strange though. Maybe it's a Bleakest Day thing?"

"Skinning toys? What's celebratory about skinning toys?"

Morgarth shrugged her tiny T-Rex shoulders.

"Exorcists?" Sarah asked. "Maybe they were practising?"

"Well, that's a bloody dark thought," Sowercat said.

The Demon Sous-chef

Blunt waited until the door was about to close before stopping it with his foot and waiting for a beat to make sure nobody was on the other side. The alleyway he was standing in contained four large skips that were already full to the brim. Festive music floated out of the door he held ajar, and he let out a snort of frustration.

"Just give me one place without the music, just one."

He pushed the door open and ducked into a dark corridor before shutting it behind him, being careful to be quiet.

Pallbearers was an exclusive high-end nightclub that catered for the people who didn't understand that most of the population worked from paycheck to paycheck. Customers who said things like 'Just buy a new one' whenever anything broke, regardless of its value.

It wasn't that they would have refused their staff being questioned for an investigation. The problem was that the manager of Pallbearers, Vinnie the Fish, hated Blunt.

A few months ago, Vinnie the Fish had invested a lot of money in a prime-time television show featuring an acerbic talking bear. Blunt may have had some small involvement in revealing the bear to be a corrupt netherworld villain on a veil-hopping heist to steal time from the reapers themselves. It had not ended well for the bear.

Some people, Vinnie in particular, hadn't missed the fact that the bear had enjoyed attacking Blunt on his popular show. Had it been a coincidence that Blunt was embroiled in the case? Yes. But would Vinnie ever believe it?

Which is why Blunt had decided to sneak in through the back entrance to get to the kitchen, hoping to catch sight of Jargle the Exsanguinator. The demon, commonly known as Jarg, was a fluffy blue octopus with a purple top hat permanently attached to his head. According to Morgarth, his skill with knives, not to mention his multiple arms, had landed him a job in the kitchen at Pallbearers, where they only served raw food. The reasoning for that was to sidestep licensing as a restaurant.

It was far too early for the club to open, but preparations for their Bleakest Eve party were well underway. As Blunt kept a watchful eye out for any management who might recognise him, he made his way to the kitchens in the depths of the building's basement.

He held his breath. Not that breathing was something he needed to do, being dead. Giving up on living habits still didn't come naturally after months of deceased existence. He passed by a door with a frosted glass panel. The frosting was a festive addition and had snowflakes etched in it. Across the ceiling of the corridor hung tinsel, and, despite the 'nothing cooked' rule, there was the distinctive smell of roasting meat with an undercurrent of mulling spices. Nostalgia raised its head and chuckled at Blunt's attempt to ignore it.

"Bastards should leave some things for the living," he said in a whisper.

A pair of aluminium double doors beckoned, and the smell of food grew stronger and the sound of clattering metal and voices grew louder as he pushed them open to reveal the kitchen.

The kitchen staff at Pallbearers were a veritable who's who of the ne'er-mortal world. People who had skills but scared off society's more conservatively minded norms.

Blunt shook his head as he looked around, though it wasn't their appearances that bothered him. There was a hooded figure, who seemed to be nothing but mist with a pair of floating blue orbs for eyes, and a woman whose eyes and mouth had swapped places. No, the cause of his consternation was the fact they were singing a merry festive tune.

*Oh! The littlest wraith woke up
on a cold wintry morning,
He sat with a scowl and let loose with a
howl to give all the mortals a warning.
For the loneliest place, for the littlest
wraith, was on the wrong side of the veil.
But along came the man with a cunning
plan and skull face ever so pale!
Oh, have no fear, for the reaper lives here,
and he'll bring you Bleakest Day!
Oh, gear up, my dear, and be of good*

cheer, as it's time for Bleakest Day!

Blunt knew there was more to the song, but the voices quieted as the kitchen team noticed his arrival until the only person left singing was a small furry octopus who was wielding several knives as he cut something that looked like beef into slices thin enough to see through.

"...for Bleakest Day!" it sang in a voice like an industrial grate being lifted.

"Can we help you?" asked the woman whose face looked upside-down with something approaching a growl.

"Hello. Yes, please. I was hoping to speak to Jarg quickly," Blunt said, trying his best imitation of good cheer. "Merry Bleakest Eve, that was lovely. Please don't stop on my account."

"Jarg," the woman said. "Do you know this"—she hesitated as she looked Blunt up and down slowly—"clown?"

Blunt took off his hat and scratched his head. "Have you actually seen a clown?"

"I was being pejorative."

The detective's mouth moved, but words eluded him.

"Nope," Jarg answered.

Blunt ignored the chef's slight as his wit, like his vocabulary, abandoned him. Turning to Jarg, he said, "I'm here because demons might be in trouble."

Jarg's top hat waggled as he nodded. He hadn't

stopped slicing the beef. All but one of his tentacle tips were covered with some kind of rubber mitten, and he held knives in three of them.

"I imagine so. People don't like us."

"Five minutes," Blunt said. "Maybe less. Your fellow demons might need your help."

The octopus stopped cutting and looked towards the woman.

She scowled, a unique arrangement with her particular features, then sighed. "Go on then. It is Bleakest Eve, after all."

"Thanks, Chef," Jarg said before rising on his tentacles and scuttling across the countertop. He discarded his rubber mittens with blinding speed.

"Don't get seen," the woman said. "I recognise you, Blunt. Vinnie wouldn't take kindly to you being in here."

Blunt nodded. "Appreciate it."

"Well, us oddballs have to look out for each other."

"Us?" Blunt raised an eyebrow.

The chef let out a chuckle. "I don't think the norms count you as one of theirs."

Jarg took them into a refrigerated room where meat of no discernible shape or type hung from the walls.

"Cold in here," Blunt muttered.

"Makes a pleasant change for me," Jarg said with a smile on his cartoonish face. "Though it's a shame they don't bother with bones. Something quite satisfying about cutting through bone."

"Why are there no bones?" Blunt asked while looking at a hanging ball of flesh.

"Because there're no cows, or pigs, or anything else."

"But where does it come from?"

"Same place as your meat sack. Different factory, but it's all the same stuff, apparently. I'm pretty new to this. If you just wanted to ask questions about food though, speak to Chef."

"No, no, sorry. Morgarth told me you were here. There are a few demons who have landed themselves jobs, and I'm trying to catch up with you all."

The octopus nodded. "Okay. Hello."

"Right. There's a bit more to it than that. It looks like some demons who haven't returned to the, ah, horde might not have landed on their feet, or tentacles, as well as you. I was wondering if you'd heard from any of the others?"

Jarg's enormous eyes seemed to grow larger for a moment. Blunt couldn't be sure if they actually did. Soft toy physiology was hard to read.

"Some of us are missing?"

"Possibly. I'm just trying to clarify."

"I haven't heard from any of the others. Oh, except Moki. We were an item."

"Right, of course." Blunt tried not to think about how that might work as he nodded. "And where can I find Moki now?"

"I thought she'd gone back to the horde. We had an argument. She said she'd heard of a job and wanted me to quit and join her. Said it would be worth it, but I like it here and I'm good at it."

"What was the job?"

"I don't know. She said some man approached her, read her CV, and asked if she had any friends. She might have gone and met him."

"But you've no idea who he is?"

"No. I thought people here were all good?"

"I don't mean to sound harsh, Jarg, but this isn't Heaven."

Jarg fixed him with a look. "You don't know what this is like compared to Hell."

SHOPPING

The music had gone from irritating to soothing. He didn't bother with the playlists like the bigger stores. The radio had to do. They had warned him that even that required a license if he wanted to play it in the shop. He hadn't paid the license, but he was beyond caring if they hit him for it.

Last Bleakest Eve, they'd cleared the shelves. He'd had people begging him to look in the back room to see if there was some kind of cuddly creature to give as a gift. Anything that might assuage the last-minute panic that the festive season brings to all those people who have better things to do and get caught out by the 'Let's not do presents this year' story that never holds true.

When the chime above the shop door rang, Geoff started choking on his mulled wine. It was Bleakest Eve, and he had forgotten to close up because things had been so quiet. He knew it would probably be the last Bleakest Eve he spent in business.

"Hello, good sir. I love your decorations. This place has a very festive feel."

The man who had entered was wearing a

priest's collar and a woollen bobble hat over the horns that topped his goat's head. The hat was Gloomwood purple, the colour that was plastered everywhere at this time of year.

"Well, I ain't feeling so festive. Shop's closed. Nobody wants this stuff anymore." He gestured around the shop with his half-full mug.

"Oh, well, that's disappointing. I'm actually here to purchase quite a few things. Though I'm not sure if you'll have them."

Geoff squinted at the goat-faced man. "You a priest?"

"Vicar. Could I persuade you to be open for a little longer? I would rather not interrupt your celebrations, but—"

"Ain't celebrating nothing. Going out of business, ain't I? Stupid bloody demons. Who wants a toy in their house now that the demons are here? Everything I've got now looks like a demon. It's completely ballsed everything up."

"Ah." The vicar held up a human hand. "Well, I might just be coming to your rescue."

"How's that?"

"The Lord moves in mysterious ways. I need toy accessories."

"Accessories?"

"That's right. Helmets or hats, specifically. And do you remember those masks from a few Bleakest Days ago where you sounded like Tuck the Duck if you wore them?"

"Talk like Tuck? Yeah, I remember them. Don't

think they'll fit you though." Geoff's slur was fading. "I might have some lying around in the back room."

By which he meant he had nearly three hundred, which he had bought before Tuck the Duck starred in the predictably named adult film. He had offloaded some of them to adult stores, but on the whole, nobody wanted to talk to Tuck after what he'd been up to.

"Wonderful. This is a fortunate turn of events. I imagine the demon thing is quite a boon for some businesses."

"How's that then?"

"Well, suddenly there's a market for these accessories and clothes. Nobody wants the toys, but the demons still need clothing and everything else."

Geoff dropped his mug, and it shattered into pieces. "Well, call yourself Santa and jump down a chimney, that's it!"

"If you're considering changing businesses, might I suggest giving Toywood a call? One of my flock, Mister Sweet, is looking to expand his business."

Muffle Mouth

"Just do your job, Blunt," Ursula Panderpenny snarled down the phone before hanging up.

Blunt was left holding the receiver, listening to a dial tone. He was standing in a phone booth beneath a streetlight while the rain hammered down outside. Car headlights blurred through the rivulets of rain running across the glass.

Around the booth, neon street signs were flickering into light, contrasting starkly with the gas lights that lined the road. Behind the mist rolling through Gloomwood's streets were Victorian-era buildings with gothic architecture.

The neon lighting created further spectral monstrosities to play optical illusions on citizens. A moment after the street signs turned on, festive lights burst into life as if someone had flicked a switch. Purple, green and red lights hung from lamppost to lamppost so that they stretched across the street where traffic rumbled by.

"Accident waiting to happen," Blunt muttered to himself as he looked at the low-hanging lights.

He placed the receiver back in its cradle, removed his hat, and wiped his brow. The brass phone was a throwback to a time before he'd even been born. Progress in Gloomwood was slow. Payphones and desperate searches for a few more coins were a constant challenge when Blunt was on a case.

Ursula Panderpenny had solved that problem within a few days. On the inside of his hat was a pouch, where he now kept coins exclusively for when he needed to use a payphone. Ursula was full of good ideas. He fiddled with the pouch until he pulled out a half nail coin.

Phone numbers were another thing he was having to get used to again. Memorising them wasn't an option. There were people in Gloomwood who could remember a phone number after hearing it only once, but Blunt had died when technology had already usurped any need for that kind of skill.

He reached into his coat pocket and withdrew the little black notebook in which he kept his phone numbers. In his other pocket, he had a different pad of paper on which he wrote case notes, his shopping list, and anything else he worried he'd forget.

Blunt flicked through the little black book until he found one particular page with a phone number at the top. Beneath it was a list of names: The Voice, Informant Number One, Shadowman, The Cloak… Each one had a line through it.

He dialled the number. It was a rotary dial, another anachronism of a time gone by. It only took a few moments longer to use, but it felt like an age.

"Hello?"

"It's me," Blunt said.

"Blunt? What do you want?"

"Anything breaking about demons?"

"Demons?" The voice was distorted, muffled, as if it was coming from a distant room before it reached the phone. "Interesting you should say that. The police have just been to a scene where a stuffed toy made to look like a demon had been tortured. Apparently, it was disturbing."

"Hm," Blunt grunted as he balanced the phone on his shoulder while pulling the other notepad out of his pocket. "What was it like?"

"I just said it was disturbing. The head demon, Morgarth, identified the toy as not being a demon. I guess the police will have to take her word for it."

"You think they shouldn't?"

"I give information, not opinions."

"But you just gave your opinion, it was inferred—"

"There's another thing as well. Someone reported an abduction to the police, but it was a toy."

"Are the police investigating?"

"Took a statement."

"Who was the witness?"

"You didn't hear this from me."

"I don't even know who you are."

"No, have you thought of a name yet?"

"I was thinking something like Cloak and Dagger."

"That would be two people, Blunt. That doesn't make any sense."

"Fine... How about The Informant?"

"Come up with something better, for crying out loud. It's not that difficult."

"You do it then."

"I'm the mysterious one, you're supposed to

come up with the name."

"Just give me the name and address."

Blunt scribbled down the details on his trusted notepad with the phone receiver balanced between his neck and shoulder.

"Right. It's something, at least. What about where the toys were found, anyone there?"

"Just a bloke who was trying to pick up a present. It was a tailor's shop, but nobody had been there for days. You're welcome."

"Yeah, yeah, thanks… Muffle Mouth?"

"No."

Fuzz bucket

Glenn was a sunflower. A furry sunflower, complete with a furry bucket and two large fronds for arms. When he'd been in Hell, he had been a mid-level demon responsible for finding new and interesting ways to contribute to what they referred to in Hell as the other straw. A name that came from the phrase 'The straw that broke the camel's back'.

It stood to reason, to demons, that if there is an event that makes a person snap, then there must have been sufficient irritations elsewhere for them to have reached that point. Glenn had been a manager in the Straws Division. The Straws Division was not held in very high regard, but they were a vital part of the complete picture. They provided the fibre in the balanced diet of damnation: the seven sins.

He had been envious of those demons who handled the big events, the real breakers, but that kind of work was beyond the imagination of the likes of Glenn. His only real claim to fame was realising that making tiny sachets, like those for ketchup in restaurants, really hard to open would cause lots of people a lot of minor irritation. By Straw Division standards, it was a big earner, which is why he'd made it into management.

Glenn had tried to explain to several prospective employees that he had a wealth of mid-level management experience. He had even written 'problem-solving' as one of his key skills, right next to 'people management', on his CV. But people couldn't see beyond the fact that he had honed those skills in Hell.

As he trudged through puddles that reflected the hanging coloured lights above, he fiddled with the necktie he wore. Miss Von Faber had given it to him to wish him luck on the job hunt. It wasn't helping. To Glenn, it seemed like he had been asked to wear a noose.

Perhaps it was a symbol of his willingness to be subservient, but, as a demon, he would have thought that was quite obvious. Demons weren't wilfully anything. Most of them were struggling to come to terms with not being given direct instructions to do something. Free will was a lot harder for people to cope with than people realised.

Glenn was management though—well, middle management—so he had treated himself as his own subordinate. He had given himself an order, 'Go find a job,' and there would be trouble if he didn't find one. Glenn tried not to think about that. He knew he was pretty severe with punishment, and he didn't want to think of what he might think of.

"Excuse me," a voice said from down a dark alleyway. Though given that there isn't an overabundance of well-lit streets in Gloomwood, it would be fairer to say it came from down a darker alleyway.

"Are you talking to me?" Glenn asked. His voice was sibilant and filled with something that could be mistaken for longing.

"Yes," the figure grew closer until it was a tall outline just out of reach of the glow of a streetlight. "Are you a demon?"

"I don't want any trouble," Glenn said. When you have the voice of a menacing demon who comes in the night to make sure your toilet roll somehow gets damp and all the sheets stick together, it's hard to sell your friendly passive side.

"No trouble here, friend," the figure said. Its voice was loud, friendly. "I think I may have a job you'd be interested in. Is that your CV?"

"This?" Glenn waved his papers in one hand. "Yes, it is. I have a lot of experience in people management, and I'm very good at problem-solving."

"That's good, very good. Why don't you come with me, and we'll have a chat about an opportunity I think you'll be interested in?"

The Witness

As he climbed the three steps to the front door, Blunt could see the decorations through the window. A dead tree covered in bright lights and baubles. Candles and lights that gave the house an orange glow. He shivered as a gale whipped through the street and nearly took his hat away.

There wasn't a doorbell. Instead, a big brass door knocker surrounded by a wreath beckoned. He took hold of it and knocked three times. He could hear voices on the other side of the door, and when it opened, it revealed three people dressed in jumpers that screamed 'festive' in a way that only hand-knitted jumpers can.

"Merry Bleakest Eve!" a woman said. "Oh, we thought you were bleak singers. Are you okay?"

He gave a small smile—the kind reserved for acknowledging awkward situations—and persevered.

"Happy Bleakest Eve. I'm afraid I'm not really one for singing. I'm looking for Abigail Scott."

"Oh, that's me. How can I help?" the woman who had answered the door said. Standing on either side of her, in a narrow hallway, were a man and a woman. The woman had a long straight beak, like a toucan.

"I'm actually here because I'm investigating a case. My name is—"

"You're Augustan Blunt," the man said with a

big smile. "Everyone hates you."

Blunt gave the same smile he had used a moment before. "I... Yes, I am, and I believe they do. Most people, anyway—"

"Because you always say horrific things and make everyone feel bad," the man continued. "I can't imagine you're looking forward to Bleakest Day."

Blunt frowned. "I hadn't really thought about it."

"You're being rude, Arnold," the beaked woman standing to Abigail's left said. "Come on, he wants to talk to Abby. It must be important. Who would bother people on Bleakest Eve if it wasn't?"

"He would. He doesn't care about other people. Did you hear about—"

"Arnold," Blunt said. "I really need to have a word with Miss Scott on her own."

"Oh, right... Well, you're a tosser! There, I said what everyone's been thinking. Who's done that before, eh?" Arnold said. He was waving a wine glass around, and his grin was suggesting to Blunt that it needed removing.

"Actually, many people have. Usually smartarses who think it makes them a big man to call someone a tosser, especially when they're hiding behind someone else. Never anyone who actually knows me, though, because they realise I'm usually just doing my job. Like when I spend my Bleakest Eve running around the city watching everyone enjoy themselves because I'm trying to make sure nobody is being hurt, or attacked, so that they can stay at home and drink their wine while calling me a tosser all wrapped up and secure. Now, why don't you piss off so I can do my job?"

"Oh, there it is. See, that's why nobody likes you—"

The beaked woman grabbed Arnold's arm with a claw-like hand and pulled him back down the corridor while he continued to ramble about how much of an unpleasant person Blunt was.

"I'm not as bad as people say," Blunt said to the woman standing before him. "I'm told it's mainly a reaction to the difficult situations I put myself in."

Abigail looked at him, her eyes wide, and nodded. "How can I help?"

"I understand you witnessed something strange yesterday and reported it to the police."

"Oh, yes, that's true. They told me it wasn't of interest."

"I imagine those are exactly the words they used."

"Well, no, but I don't use that kind of language, especially not today. It's not proper."

Blunt grabbed his hat as another gust of wind tried to take it from his head. "Terrible weather tonight."

"It's normal. Bleakest Eve and Day are the worst days of the year."

"Looks nice and warm inside."

"Yes, thank you, it is."

Blunt waited, but the invitation he was hoping for wasn't forthcoming.

"Right, well, can you tell me about what you saw? All I know is there was a demon, and it looked like it was being coerced into a van."

"Yes."

"Can you tell me anything else about it?"

"Oh, it was small and furry. I think it was some kind of cat, or possibly a squirrel? It was very cartoonish."

Blunt pulled out his notepad and flicked to a blank page. "Right, squirrelly cat-like demon, furry. What colour was it?"

"Pink, mostly pink. Dazzling pink."

"And what happened?"

"Well, the van was parked up on the end of Existential Avenue, you know, in the Philosophers Quarter. When this little pink demon, it was quite cute—"

"You like the demons?"

"We're academics, Detective Blunt," Abigail said, as if that was some kind of answer. "I believe you're an associate of Dr Von Faber? Actually, we're looking forward to her research on the creatures from Hell. I'm sure it'll be a disaster."

Blunt bit his tongue. It was the only way he could stop himself from saying anything. Externally, he offered a thin smile. Internally, he imagined stabbing the pencil in his hand through the woman's eye and pulling it out to show to her.

"Anyway," Abigail continued, "it was just walking along the street when the side of the van opened and a figure in green jumped out. It tried to grab the demon, but it was quick. You don't realise that when you look at them, I suppose, but thousands of years in Hell must make your reactions very good."

"Hundreds of thousands, at least."

"I'm sorry?"

"Hundreds of thousands of years. They usually say eons, or millennia untold, or something like that. It's a really long time. So, this person who tried to grab the squirrel-cat demon, what did they look like?"

"Well, it was quick, and I wasn't really paying very close attention. I think it was a man."

"Uh-huh," Blunt said, making a show of scribbling on the notepad. "Male, any idea how tall?"

"Taller than the demon."

"Yup, I can believe that. Taller than you?"

"Oh yes, I think so."

"What about me, taller than me?"

"Possibly. I mean, probably. How tall are you? You look much bigger on television."

"I'm tall enough, thanks. And you don't think the demon knew this person?"

"Oh no, or if it did, it didn't like them. It shouted at the man—yes, I'm sure it was a man—in its demon voice, and the man froze. They do have scary voices."

"Yes, they do. They can make someone freeze up if they're not used to the sound of them."

"I think he was quite taken aback. Then the demon ran away. Well, it ran like a little bunny rabbit, the cutest thing."

"The demon ran like a bunny?"

"Yes. I hardly think the terrified man in the van was about to hop around."

"What time was this?"

"Yesterday afternoon, at about three, I had just finished lunch with Arnold and Imelda. At Carlini's. It's a delightful little bistro. Probably trying a bit hard with the cinnamon and pumpkin spiced lattes, but isn't everyone at this time of year? We had the—"

"Sounds delightful, ma'am," Blunt interrupted, "but I'm a little more concerned with someone potentially snatching Gloomwood citizens off the street in broad daylight. I'm surprised nobody intervened. It isn't like the people of Gloomwood are known for standing by and watching events unfold."

"Oh yes, an excellent point. Nobody seemed very interested. It's probably the whole demon thing. They're not very well-liked, you know."

"I had heard. What about the van? Can you tell me anything about that?"

"The van! Yes, of course, it had the most ridiculous advertising on it. A rag doll. I suppose it could have been a demon. It said, 'The child in you is dead too'. I mean, really, how awful!"

"Yes, good point," Blunt said, recognising the description. "Well. Thank you for your time, and have a lovely Bleakest Eve."

"Oh, yes, Merry Bleakest Eve to you. I hope you

catch your demons."

"I'm not trying to—"

She didn't wait for him to finish before closing the door. Blunt could hear her let out a sigh before shouting, showing a distinct lack of awareness of the true soundproofing ability of a single door, "Arnold, you're probably right! Complete arse, but he wasn't horrible to me at least. Probably frightened of our intelligence."

Blunt stared at the front door for a moment longer as he savoured the rage and the range of expletive-laden insults that flew through his mind. A feast ranging from the obscene to the brutally accurate, cruel, vile, and nuanced.

"Knobs," he finally said.

Vellmar

Vellmar strode down the street, ignoring the looks of passersby. A small gaggle of people stood on the steps to a building that appeared to Vellmar to have religious significance. They were singing. It wasn't an unpleasant sound, but she hurried onwards, not wanting to be caught out as night swept over the city and the temperatures plummeted.

She had developed fear. Other emotions were tumbling into place like the missing pieces in a jigsaw puzzle that created the demon's psyche. The move to Gloomwood had not been one she had taken lightly, and the trappings of free will and individuality were still catching her by surprise.

Fear was something she had delivered, fostered in others, but it wasn't something she was used to feeling. Of course, demons technically feared retribution for mistakes or when their lord was in a bad mood, but it wasn't the same. It was okay if they were wiped from existence by Beelzebub in a fit of rage. He was divine, and that was what was meant to happen.

But fear of the unknown was new.

The people singing had smiles on their faces. Something about grouping together and repeating known words to a tune seemed to infuse them with a glow. It made little sense to Vellmar. Grouping people together to recite words in unison usually ended up with a lot of blood and some kind of possession. It was fun for demons, but less so for the people.

She turned a corner and witnessed more of the same. People, neighbours perhaps, were going from door to door and delivering items from baskets.

"Happy Bleakest Eve," a man wearing a striped scarf and a large coat said to her.

"Uh, thanks," Vellmar said. The moment she spoke, his smile faltered. "Sorry, it's my voice, I can't —"

"No, no, it's Bleakest Eve. Nobody should feel bad about the way Death made them, especially not tonight. Would you like a chocolate?" He opened a box in his hands and leant down to offer them to her. "Oh, do you… I mean, can you eat chocolate?"

"Yes," Vellmar said. "Thank you." She reached out with one soft paw and plucked a barrel-shaped one from the centre of the tray. "Merry Bleakest Eve."

The man smiled and nodded as he closed the box and began walking away.

She popped the chocolate into her mouth, and it exploded with flavour. Caramel and chocolate sent her taste buds into panic as they recoiled, then bounced back again at the intense sweet sugar hit. Chocolate, Vellmar realised, made being dead quite worthwhile.

As she crossed a road, a large van pulled to a stop. On the side of it was a rag doll. The side of the van opened, and three short figures wearing black jumped out.

"Get it!" a voice bellowed from the front window of the van.

Vellmar hesitated for a moment before she realised they were talking about her.

"No," she said, and the small gaggle in front of her froze. "Get back in the van." They didn't move, seemingly confused.

"What are you doing? Grab the sodding toy and let's get out of here!" the voice shouted.

"I can't," one of the compact figures in a balaclava said. "It's terrifying."

"It's a furry little hippo. Ugh, I'll get it."

"You won't," Vellmar said. Her voice rumbled and rolled towards the driver as if it was a physical object, and his eyes grew wide in terror.

"Uh… get in the van. That one's not like the others," the man stuttered.

A moment later, the van was gone.

They were right, of course. Vellmar was not like the other demons. There were only five others like Vellmar. She was one of the Elite Guard who had turned their back on Beelzebub. She allowed herself a small swagger.

"Yeah, I've still got it," she said to herself as she continued on her way back to the horde. "Fear? I'll show you fear."

Then she stepped into a deep puddle and panicked while trying to wade out.

A Nose for the Truth

Good detective work is about following evidence, asking questions, paying attention to detail, and having a network to rely upon. Blunt's network was growing, but it still wasn't where it needed to be. When questions that needed an intimate knowledge of the inner workings of Gloomwood raised their head, he would call upon his friend at the Office of the Dead.

Nine times out of ten, that would be the end of it, but he had learned that getting straight answers to simple questions was never as easy as it ought to be. Asking for details about who owned a particular van or company would never work. He needed someone with a little more of a nose for the truth.

Leighton Hughes was a well-known mild irritant to the city's establishment, and no amount of soothing balm could stop the itching. Criminal enterprises, corrupt politicians, unscrupulous landlords and restaurants with low hygiene standards had all come to find Leighton Hughes vaguely annoying. Like a mosquito that buzzes around when the lights are off but is impossible to locate when you turn them on again.

After being hired as a roving reporter for Channel Two News, she had little time for the long investigations that had once been her bread and butter. She still knew how to find a story and chase a lead.

Blunt knocked on the door of the haberdashery that had closed at a reasonable hour, just like every other shop in the city, especially on Bleakest Eve. Sales signs blighted almost every space in the window display, and he had to try and find a gap to see inside.

Leighton rented the apartment upstairs, but Blunt knew the buzzer was broken. He knocked again, louder, and peered through the window in the top half of the door. Darkness lay like a shroud over the interior. It made the shop stand out in the terraced neighbourhood, where purple and yellow lights seemed to have infested every available interior, whether they were shops or homes.

Above his head, a window slid open. "Who is it?"

"It's me, Blunt," he said, looking up to see Leighton hanging her head out of the window. She was wearing a coat.

"What do you want?"

"Uh, help with a case?"

"Oh well, Merry Bleakest Eve to you too. I thought you were here desperately trying to find a present for Sarah."

"I've got her a present. Why does everyone keep assuming I haven't got her a present?"

"What do you need help with? I'm about to go back out to cover the Bleakest Eve speech."

"Speech?"

"The Grim Reaper gives a speech every year, and then the thing happens. Wait there."

The window slammed shut, and Blunt hopped from one foot to the other while rubbing his hands together to warm himself. The chill of night was seeping through the layers he wore. Warmth on the streets of Gloomwood was as scarce as compassion.

He could hear Leighton banging around upstairs before her footsteps went down a flight of stairs and she threw the door open. "You better make this quick. I've only got about ten minutes before the van gets here."

"Okay, in a weird coincidence, I need to find out about a van," Blunt said as Leighton ushered him into the shop.

"Ugh, you're here for Argyle, aren't you?"

"No, I'm here for you. If you're going to use Argyle, that's nothing to do with me. I've no idea how that stuff works."

"Nice. I see you trying to sell it as a skill."

"Skull magic is—"

"It isn't skull magic. It's just a network of information."

"A network made of the skulls of people who have faded into next to nothingness? Sounds pretty magical to me."

"Last time,"—she said as she pulled aside the curtain to the changing room—"you said, 'isn't it just the intercage?'"

"Internet. It's called the internet."

"Yeah, well, same difference."

Blunt peered in as Leighton took a seat in front of a black typewriter with a skull attached to it. She hit the carriage return key, and the eyes of the skull lit up red. As the rest of the shop was in darkness, it seemed even more ominous than usual.

"Is that tinsel?"

Leighton looked at Blunt, then back to the typewriter. She had stuck tinsel to the skull's head with sticky tape. "Argyle is a person. Somewhere in there. The least I can do is help him celebrate Bleakest Day."

"Assuming that he would be fine with having his head attached to a typewriter and you sticking tinsel to his head, and that he likes the whole Bleakest Day thing, and that it wouldn't be kinder just to smash his skull to pieces and release him into total oblivion."

Leighton turned and glowered in Blunt's direction. "I didn't invent this thing. If you want to be all high and mighty about it, maybe don't come around asking me to use it for you. Hypocrite."

Blunt nodded. "Yup, that's all fair. So, I need to find a van with a rag doll on the side."

"What? How am I supposed to find that? A rag doll, well, that's going to be unusual, isn't it?"

"It's got something about your inner child being dead on it as well."

"You think telling Argyle that will give you a lead, do you?"

"I don't know, do I? I'm just a lowly detective, not the self-proclaimed investigative reporter extraordinaire."

"I'm a roving reporter now."

"Yeah? Is that a step up or down?"

Quackers

They led her through a doorway into a room with bunks lining either side. On three of the bottom bunks were demons playing cards.

"Trem?" one of them asked as it looked away from the cards in its paws. "Is that you?"

"Yeah, it's me. What are you all doing here? I thought I was on my own."

"We took the job offer," a donkey said. Trem knew her as Bacter. "You did too, right?"

"Nobody else was offering," Trem shrugged as she walked into the room.

"Same here," said a pink cat toy with a patch over one eye, "so we're all in the same boat now."

"Moki? I haven't seen you for days."

"I've been here. We all have."

"The chair, and the—"

"We know," Bacter said. "We know."

"Well, we have to escape. With our voices together, we can—"

"Ah, brave little bunny," a booming voice interrupted. "I'm afraid your special voices have no power here. Or anywhere else soon."

"Release us," Trem shouted. Usually, her voice could strip paint from walls, but this time it came out with a quack.

"Don't, Trem," Moki said. She laid an oversized paw on Trem's arm. "Our voices don't affect him. We've tried everything. It's best just to go along with things. The others must be looking for us by now, right?"

"Um, yeah… we were all wondering where you were," Trem said.

"Were you?" Bacter asked.

Argyle

"You can't be serious? He found something? Wow, Argyle actually found something from that crappy description. The van belongs to a company that went bankrupt," Leighton said as a black piece of paper with white writing spooled out of the typewriter.

The skull settled back into position with a judder, and Leighton snatched up the paper and held it away from Blunt as she stood up.

"I'm going to need details, Blunt."

"Haven't you got a report to do on a big tree?"

"It's a speech, and yes, but first, details."

The sound of a horn from the street outside pierced the quiet of the darkened shop.

"You're not going to like this," Blunt said.

"Oh, now you've said that I definitely don't want to know any more. Thanks for the warning. Phew, dodged a bullet there."

"All right, sarcasmo the clown, fine, but only because you've got something I need."

She shook her head. "Oh great, so you'll ask for a favour from a friend, but you won't tell them what's going on unless they give you something in return. Real Bleakest Day spirit there."

"It's only Bleakest Eve. Ask me tomorrow."

"Spit it out."

Blunt let out a sigh. He knew this wouldn't end well.

"This is confidential information, not for reporting on. Even telling you this could get me in more trouble than it's worth."

"Right, 'You can't include this in any news, Leighton,' as usual. Come on then, Mister Confidential Informant."

"I'm being absolutely serious. This would be my job if it got out. I think Panderpenny would probably sue me as well."

"I get it. My lips are sealed."

He let out a sigh, then nodded. "I'm working for the Grim Reaper because someone's stolen his decorations."

Leighton's mouth twisted as she held back a furious onslaught of abuse before she took a breath. "Okay. Well, that's not what I expected. The Grim Reaper's decorations… like his tinsel and knick-knacks for the tree? Are you… are you trying to be funny?"

"No. I wish I was. This is ridiculous."

"I hope you don't mean the weird glowing orbs that go on the Bleakest Day tree, because that's serious. What's this got to do with a van?"

"That's a fantastic question," Blunt said. "The van has been implicated in the abduction of demons."

"It was a toy factory that went bankrupt. They closed up only recently. 'Tis the season, I guess."

"Careful, I'm supposed to be the miserable bastard around here."

Leighton flashed a grin. "Oh, don't worry, I'm

all for the festive spirit."

"Give me the stuff on the van," Blunt said, reaching out for the black paper in Leighton's hand.

The horn came again from the road. Leighton cast a look in the door's direction. "You're investigating the demon kidnappings?"

He finally wrenched the paper from her hand. "No, don't trick me into giving you some kind of quote. You've stung me like that before. This is all off the record, understood?"

"You're supposed to say that before you tell me things," she said while nodding. "But I'm prepared to guarantee you anonymity."

"Just keep your bloody mouth shut, Leighton. This is my job, my livelihood... wait, is that one of those words that doesn't apply anymore?"

"Not the time, Blunt. Spill."

"I'm trying to find a pink fluffy hoofed demon, and Morgarth will give me names if I find the missing demons. I mean, there's a chance it's one of the missing demons."

"So you're trusting a demon when all the evidence points to a demon."

"You make it sound daft."

The horn came again.

Blunt turned to the door and shouted, "I swear to God, Dennis, if you hit that horn one more time, I'll come out there with a rolled-up newspaper."

Leighton shook her head. "I've got to go. Keep me in the loop?"

"I'll do what I can. Have fun at the tree thing."

Leighton's eyebrow twitched. "Do you practise being miserable?"

Grim

To the right of the largest dead tree in Gloomwood, which had been painstakingly designed and constructed by faux-life artists over the course of the last twelve months, was a cabin. A temporary structure that had received none of the love and care the tree had. It had arrived flat-packed on the back of a truck and been built within an hour. It hadn't escaped people's notice that there were an inordinate number of pieces left over. They were probably just spares.

From inside this temporary structure came a deep, foreboding voice. A terrifying rhythmic drone that would have sent living beings to hide under duvets while wishing they'd thought of installing a light switch underneath their pillows.

"We can build a snowman in the meadow and pretend that he is—"

"Your Highness?" Mortimer interrupted.

"Ew, no, definitely not Your Highness."

"Um, Majesty?"

"Grim is fine, absolutely fine. I don't like all this pomp and ceremony."

"It's the Bleakest Day celebrations. Every year we have all of this... ceremony."

Death sighed and shook his arms so that his robe jiggled. "I know that, Mortimer, but it still makes me feel... icky."

"Icky?" Mortimer said. "That's an interesting

choice of words."

"Bah, Angel of Death, the end of all things, the unavoidable, indecipherable ruler of Gloomwood, who stands aloft above all others in the afterlife, the Grim Reaper himself, blah, blah, blah. It gets quite tiresome. I do not need to feel important. What I need is to remind everyone else that they are important."

"So that's what Bleakest Day is?"

"Mortimer, what is important to you?"

"I want to be good at my job."

"Why?"

"Because..."

"You are not your job. You are a good man who wants to help people, who wants to make the world better for people because it makes you feel worthy. Wouldn't it be nice if, instead of wanting to be rich, or 'the best', or the most popular, we all just wanted to make each other happy?"

"That's... yes, it would be."

"But nobody wants to hear that. So instead, I stand in front of everyone and give a vague statement which always means 'Be nice to each other', but everyone hears what they want to hear."

"You don't sound like you want to do it."

"Maybe I don't, but I'm trying to do something worthy... to be good at my job."

"Oh."

"Oh indeed."

Mortimer was pacing the room as his anxiety levels grew with each passing moment. On the few occasions Death made a public appearance, he usually showed his skull for a moment and then vanished once more, as if he had bent space and time to be there. It was only in the last few months that Crispin Neat had shown the truth of things to Mortimer.

As the third assistant to the manager of the Office of the Dead, Ralph Mortimer was the second most important bureaucrat in the city. Crispin Neat was the head of the Office of the Dead—and Mortimer's boss. For reasons that had never been fully revealed to Mortimer, the first and second assistants to the manager of the Office of the Dead seemed to be permanently on leave, absent, or in locations unknown. That left Mortimer as the manager's right-hand man, and Crispin Neat was the man who controlled the city of Gloomwood.

The Grim Reaper ruled with the grip of the house guest you keep a plastic cup for as a joke. Only not really as a joke because you know they'll drop an expensive glass if you give them one. His leadership style was not so much *laissez-faire* as 'Leave me alone'. Long ago, he had accepted that creating Gloomwood might not have been his greatest idea and that death had been easier before the public engagements.

"Explain what I do again," he said to Mortimer.

"Um, you mostly sit in your office reading bad paperbacks—"

"What I do for the ceremony, Mister Mortimer."

"Of course. It'll be just like last year and, uh, most years. You will say your speech, and then everyone will sing the song. Then we set off some fireworks. Sometimes you do a fire trick with your scythe."

"Oh yes, the fiery scythe thing. Always risky. Remember that year—"

"Everyone remembers the year you burned your robe, sir, yes."

"Mhm. See, that's why we don't have social media here. Imagine the videos."

"I… don't know what any of that is."

"Mortal things, Mister Mortimer. Fascinating, destructive, terrible mortal things."

As Mortimer paced, he could hear the sounds of people outside. In amongst the cursing and shouting from those desperately trying to decorate Dead Square was a more pleasant sound. It was a choir that seemed to consist mainly of pabies singing festive tunes.

Bleakest Day was the one day of the year when pabies, those who chose to remain as children regardless of their age, were happy to play their part. Something about the sound of children singing merry songs did things to people. It made people… less unpleasant.

"Aren't we here quite early?" Death asked.

"Yes," Mortimer said. He hesitated for a moment. "The reception area is filling up with media types, film crews, presenters. You know how they all carry on. Mister Neat thought it would be best if we were here in advance in case anything should go wrong."

"He thought I'd wander off and mess everything up, didn't he?"

"No, of course not."

"I'm Death, Mister Mortimer. One of my many skills is being able to see through veils, like the weak facade of a lie meant to spare my feelings."

"Right."

"...We could go for a walk though."

Morgarth

"How much?" Blunt said, leaning forward in the back seat of the taxi to get nearer to the transparent screen, although he knew it didn't make him any easier to hear.

"It's on the meter, mate. Don't act like it's daylight robbery," the driver said.

"It bloody is."

"Can't be. It's nighttime."

"Come on, you can't be serious."

"Bleakest Eve night. What do you expect? I'd rather be at home with the wife settling in to watch the Grim Reaper and getting hammered on mulled wine, forcing another piece of chocolate into my face even though I feel sick."

"Alright, time and a half maybe, but that's—"

"Take it up with the Office of the Dead, fella. They make the rules, I just follow them. It's triple time. Are you working?"

"Well… yeah."

"Right, I'll give you a receipt. Give it to your boss and they'll reimburse you, won't they?"

"I'm my boss. Well, I've got a partner."

The driver let out a snort of laughter without turning around. "Listen, mate, if you're out working on Bleakest Eve and your 'partner' isn't, then it sounds like you might actually have a boss."

Blunt said nothing and handed over the nails, emptying his wallet. He slid out of the car and tried to put the snide taxi driver's brief lecture out of his head as he looked up at the warehouse. Taking a taxi here hadn't been his first choice. The canal boats had stopped running an hour ago to make way for the celebrations, and getting a bus that ran on time on Bleakest Eve was about as likely as a visit from an angel telling you they've made a mistake and you're supposed to be in Heaven.

Inside the warehouse, the demons had attempted to make things seem festive. Blunt wanted to scowl about it, but it was difficult to be filled with rage at the hypocrisy of it all when he would have to direct that rage at an army of dejected soft toys. They might be demons, he thought, but it was hard not to feel sorry for the little bastards.

"Ah, Blunt," Morgarth called from her position near the top of a dead tree. She had contrived to get herself tangled in a string of fairy lights. "You couldn't, maybe, um…"

"Let me help you there," the detective said, reaching up to untangle the blue furry dinosaur before putting her on the ground. "You shouldn't let people pick you up. It's demeaning."

"We don't *let* people do that. If one of us was stupid enough to be picked up by someone, I would expect swift and violent retribution. I was *asking* you to. Some of us have a little of our previous powers remaining. The voice is the main thing. Would you like to hear?"

"No. I remember well enough what the voices can do."

"Most of us lose that ability. I expect we all will. Now, you have some news about our friends?"

"Some." Blunt nodded as he followed Morgarth towards her tiny closet of an office. "Not all good."

"Ah. I do too. They invited me to identify a body today."

"I know. It wasn't a demon though."

"You know? Well, you are a detective, after all. How could you tell? Was there some dust on my tail from the scene?"

"Eh? No. I was told by a contact I have. What do you mean, 'dust on your tail?'"

"That's how they do it on the television box. We just watched—"

"Television isn't real, Morgarth. Pretty sure your lot invented it, actually." He closed the door behind them as Morgarth climbed onto a cardboard box.

"Right, quick news," Blunt said. "I met two demons who have got themselves jobs. The octopus is working in the kitchen at Pallbearers on good money. It's a good job. The other one is stacking shelves in a corner shop, also not a bad way to earn a living."

Morgarth nodded too quickly to hide any excitement. "Jobs, may the wound forever fester and spread. That is great news. I will tell the others."

"Right. While you're at it, I've got some bad news. I can't find your other demons."

"Ah, one has returned. Vellmar."

"Vellmar?"

"One of the six elite demons. They attacked her."

"Is she hurt?"

"No, no, I just said she's one of the six."

"So she broke out some of that demon magic and—"

"She shouted at them and they ran away."

Blunt nodded. "Demon magic."

"That wouldn't have worked for the others, and Vellmar, well, we were lucky it was her. When she told me, Garglemier—"

"Who's Garglemier? There are too many bloody demon names."

"Another one of the six. He said the same thing happened to him in the middle of the day."

"Was it near a restaurant called Carlini's?" Blunt asked, pulling the notepad from his pocket. "Existential Avenue?"

"I don't know—"

"Is Garglemier a little pink squirrel or cat?"

"I think he's a beaver. We're not very good at animals."

Blunt couldn't help but grin. "You're an army of stuffed animal toys, and you don't even know what animals you all are?"

Morgarth shrugged her tiny shoulders. "We're an army of torturers, tempters, connivers, punishers, and fear-mongers. Not many of us learned much about the flora and fauna of the mortal world, detective. We are... lost. Adrift."

He wiped the smile from his face. "Sorry. I shouldn't laugh—"

"Don't apologise. Laughing at us is preferable to hating us or cowering in fear. People despise us, and we haven't got a defence because we were terrible. Though we were never terrible to these people. They just imagine we're evil. We have only ourselves to blame. Of course, we could decapitate some of them. Perhaps tear them limb from limb, but I understand that is frowned upon."

Blunt swallowed as he watched the burning irises in the googly soft toy eyes burn a little fiercer. "I don't think that would be a good idea. It definitely wouldn't make you more popular."

"What if we pulled the right people's heads off?"

Blunt couldn't help but smile. "How would you decide that?"

Morgarth sighed. "It is needlessly complicated here. The grey is messy."

"The grey?"

"In between the light and the dark, the edge of the shadow, the edge of the penumbra. This place." She flapped her dinosaur arms. "You are an infinitesimally small decimal, a fraction so tiny that it ought never to have deserved consideration at all. If we had been better at pushing you, tempting you, every single one of you would have joined us in Hell."

"Hold on," Blunt said. "Maybe if you hadn't pushed us, we would have stayed in the light. We might only be here because you pushed us out of the 'good place'."

"There's not one good place, there are many. We are not to blame for you falling from grace."

"But apparently you are to blame for us not going to Hell?"

"You're right, of course. Perhaps we should be proud we aided in creating this place."

"Did you?"

Morgarth looked around the room, her head tilting to one side. "No. We're not responsible for anything because we didn't have free will."

"Just following orders isn't a very good defence—"

"Orders? Detective, they weren't orders. Our nature compelled us. We were slaves to the thoughts of Beelzebub. Now things are different. We have a choice."

"Do you? I thought you didn't have free will."

"The line is blurry. We didn't have free will, but we had some autonomy."

"That is free will."

"Is it? For example, you are currently on a mission to find out if demons are being taken by someone."

"Technically, all I'm doing is a terrible job of looking for decorations. Honestly, I don't know why the... um, client didn't just ask me to pop down to the corner shop and fill a basket with tinsel and other crap."

"Ah. That is your prime goal. You are on a

mission with everything you're doing. You have the choice to abandon that task, though. Everything you do while working towards that mission is your choice, but the choice to abandon the task is also yours."

"So you could do what you liked, but it had to be 'on mission'."

"That's oversimplifying it, but yes. We could not deviate from our mission as Beelzebub's servants."

"I suppose a henchman has to do—"

"Please don't call us henchmen."

"Sorry. Uh, minion?"

"So much worse. Can we talk about who's doing this?"

"If someone is doing this," Blunt interrupted. "We don't know for sure if it's—"

"I have two respectable demons—"

"Isn't that an oxymoron?"

"—who have both escaped near abductions, and several others are missing."

Blunt let out a sigh and lifted his hat. He patted down his pockets with his other hand, looking for a cigar.

"No smok—"

"I'm quitting, anyway."

"No, detective, we're demons. Smoke doesn't bother us. I was saying there's no smoke without fire."

"Yeah, well, I've made mistakes before, and I'd rather not get burned again. So maybe rein in the conjecture until I get a little further."

"The exorcists are behind this, and they are framing us in the act. There are stories floating around that demons are turning up places just to wreak havoc, to spread misery, that we're here to take Gloomwood to Hell. The people of this place want to keep us as we were, and we will take action if needed," Morgarth said, her voice deepening.

Blunt's hands curled into fists as he felt the hairs on the back of his neck rise. Fear was blooming within him and threatening to choke off his rational mind.

"Stop it, Morgarth. I'm on your side. If you and your demons charge at the exorcists without proof, you'll only end up doing what everyone expects, and you'll lose. You're not an eight-foot-tall demon with impenetrable fireproof skin anymore." As Blunt spoke, his voice grew quieter, and he finished with a tremor to his words.

Morgarth, her red pupils enlarged and glowing with intensity, let out a long slow breath with a whooshing sound. "Sorry, detective. I'm teaching others to be mindful of how we interact with people, and here I am losing my temper. We'll wait for more news, but I'm quite confident in my reasoning."

Blunt felt the warmth returning to his fingertips and a flush rising in his cheeks. All the biological responses to fear leaving. Everything a living body would do. Though when you're dead, it's all just psychosomatic.

"Don't worry about it. It's not like I was scared, it's just this cheap off-the-shelf body."

"You're talking to me about 'off-the-shelf bodies'?"

BUSINESS TALK

What lies under the tree?
What lies under the tree?
Gifts for me, gifts for me
That's what's under the tree
What's wrapped up in a bow?
Wouldn't you like to know?
Gifts for you, gifts for you
All wrapped in a bow
Because Bleakest Day's for spending
Empty out your pockets
Show you care for others
By buying socks and lockets
Spend, spend, spend, buy, buy, buy,
What else can you do after you die?

The Retailers Association's annual Bleakest Day awards party was always a merry affair. For them, this was their most profitable time of the year. There had never been any pretence about Bleakest Day being a plea to consumers to spend all of their hard-earned money. The Retailers Association leaned heavily on marketing, guilt, peer pressure, and the public's susceptibility to the myth of 'bagging a bargain'.

Every year, they gathered together to tell people how much they had raised their prices by in the weeks before Bleakest Eve so they could pretend they'd slashed prices. Which was exactly what Trevor Slather was doing as he held the attention of a table of his peers.

"Seven hundred nails for a clock radio, slashed to a hundred for the Bleakest Day sales. How much did it actually cost? Guess! Go on, guess!"

"Um, seventy nails?" asked a man with an eye in the centre of his forehead.

"Hah, try seven."

"Oh, that's unbelievable, you rip-off merchant."

"I am, I really am!" Trevor said as they fell about laughing.

Nobody likes the Retailers Association. They didn't even like each other. The party was an excuse to get drunk, mock the public, and sneer at their competition. Which was why, on this particular Bleakest Eve, there were very few toymakers present.

In fact, there were only two. The first was the owner of Gloomfields, who produced the Sally Sugar and Barry Buff toy ranges. The other was the owner of Toywood, which produced the Grimly toy cars and building blocks and the Raven Squad toys based on the popular television show, which was clearly a thirty-minute-long advertisement for more toys. Compared to most toymakers, they were vast companies—the elite.

And right now, they were very unhappy.

For the first time in forty years, they had taken a seat together and were in hushed conversation about ideas for diversifying. Soft toys were out, but the future still had opportunities. Board games had been big sellers, as had memorabilia. Plastic models, ornaments pretending to be toys, had prevented sales from being too disastrous, but there was a worry.

"What if he lets more creatures in and they end up looking like plastic toys?" the first man asked. "Can you imagine? What if a load of angels revolt and ask for asylum and he makes them all into Sally Sweet and Barry Buff dolls? That's the entire range out of the window!"

His colleague was a suited, bespectacled man who appeared to have all the joy removed from him daily. It was as if someone arrived every morning to remove it with the aid of a large syringe and a handful of bitter pills to replace it. His name was, ironically, Colin Sweet.

Colin leaned forward. "I shouldn't say this, but I have a plan in motion."

"A plan? What is it?"

"It's a step-by-step process for getting from A to B, like instructions."

"I know what a plan is, Colin, you arse. What is your plan?"

"We all know that only the Grim Reaper can bring newcomers in. So, we'll just stop him."

"Stop the Grim Reaper? That's... that sounds

like treason to me."

"What? No, don't be daft. I just mean, stop him thinking about doing it again. Making sure the whole demon thing is a one-off. Maybe make the whole thing into a bit of a disaster."

"Get rid of the demons, you mean?"

Sweet shrugged. "Doesn't bother me if we do or don't, but I definitely don't want toys to be in the line of fire if this ever happens again."

"Okay... yeah. All above board, right?"

"Well, I'm not getting my hands dirty, if that's what you mean. You in?"

"In?"

"Yeah, if we do this right, we can buy up all the other toymakers while things are going wrong and corner the entire market."

The man he was talking to took a long drink from the pint glass he was holding. "Why are you cutting me in?"

Sweet smiled. "If I buy them all, it's going to look suspicious. Plus, nobody likes a monopoly. There are even laws against it. If we're both buying them, though... well, it just looks like opportunism. Can't blame us for taking the opportunity. It's good business."

"So you're telling me to buy up some of the small businesses?"

"Telling you? Not my place to tell you anything," Sweet said. The corners of his mouth twitched as if he wanted to smile, but his muscles were too weak to allow it. "But trust me, after all this, we'll be rid of the demons, and it won't ever happen again."

"Cuddly toys will be back?"

"In a big way."

The Presents of Demons

Sarah carried the box with both arms wrapped around it. She struggled through the doorway to the warehouse, almost tripping over the sill as she couldn't see her feet. Demons walked towards her until she dropped the box with a bang near the edge of the sea of blankets beneath the glare of the strip lighting.

"Hello, Miss Von Faber," a demon rhino said. "What's with the box?"

"Apparently you have some friends," Sarah said. "You've got a present."

Morgarth and Blunt came out of the tiny office and joined the growing circle of demons standing around Sarah.

"Why do I feel you've just brought a bag of sweets into an orphanage?" Blunt asked.

"It's the strangest thing. I got a phone call from a Hope who runs a toy shop. He was closing up for the night when a man came in and bought a few last-minute bits and pieces. The shopkeeper said it was the customer's idea."

"Are you building suspense?" Morgarth asked.

"Not deliberately," Sarah said. She reached into her lab coat and pulled out a scalpel. Her various pockets contained everything from magnifying glasses to sample tubes and plastic pipettes, even blank microscope slides, and, in one pocket, a coil of rubber hosing because… you never know when it might come in handy.

She drew the scalpel across the top of the box, slicing through the tape holding it together. As she unfolded the top of the box, demons crowded forward to peer inside.

"What is it?" one asked.

"Clothes," Sarah said. "Clothes from toys. The Hope said that things had been pretty quiet since… Anyway, he sold up his toy shop today. Said it was a stroke of luck and wanted to share his good fortune with someone." Sarah stopped talking and looked around, pausing when her eyes met Blunt's.

"Oh," Blunt said. "I see."

He turned to Morgarth and nodded away from the demons who were already poring through the contents of the box and sharing them out with childlike excitement.

"What is it?" Morgarth asked as they walked away from the group. "Is it a trick?"

"No," Blunt said. "At least, not an evil trick. It… pains me to say it, but it's actually incredibly kind. The fella who sent them is going out of business because nobody wants to buy toys from him."

"Why would—"

"Nobody wants the toys because nobody knows if they're toys or demons. This bloke sent you these clothes after pulling them off the toys he was trying to sell because he can't sell them, and… well, he doesn't blame you. He thought he could help."

"I don't understand why he would do that. It must be a trick."

Blunt swallowed. Unexpected kindness was something he had discovered wasn't a rarity among the people of Gloomwood. There was something beneath the layer of cynicism and apathy that raised its head when it was least expected. As if the kindness of humanity could only be seen from the corner of your eye.

"It isn't a trick. It's what people do. Sometimes when things are bad for you and you don't see any way to fix it, you try to fix something for someone else."

"Hoping they will help you?"

"No. I mean, yeah, sure, that would be nice, and maybe there's a little karma mixed in there, but no, that's not it. Helping someone else can remind the person doing the helping that not everyone is a bastard. That's the secret to helping other people. If you do something good, then you know for sure that good things must happen."

Morgarth nodded. "And everyone knows that?"

Blunt laughed. "No, nobody knows that. I don't even know that, and I'm telling you. It's a secret that we all forget the second we turn back to everything else that's facing us."

"You look upset."

"Shut up, Morgarth, and get yourself a new t-shirt."

The demon looked at Blunt for a moment, shook its head, and walked away. Sarah passed it, walking in the opposite direction.

"Is it a trick?" Sarah asked.

Blunt shook his head. "Don't think so. It's too obvious. Think the fella was just being kind."

"They don't know what that means, do they?" the scientist said, looking at the demons.

"Absolutely not."

"Is someone kidnapping demons?"

"Definitely. I just don't know who. Or why."

"The exorcists?"

"You were at the crime scene earlier?"

Sarah nodded, then shook her head. "It wasn't a crime scene. There's no law against torturing inanimate toys. It looked more like someone was doing some bad craft work."

"No law against it yet," Blunt said. "But it sounds like it was pretty close to a hate crime."

"Yes."

"Who sent the clothes?"

"Why?"

"He got the idea from someone. Someone who was doing a lot of chatting about demons and buying toys. Like, maybe someone who wanted to send them a message?"

"Oh. Don't you think that's a bit of a leap?"

Blunt frowned. "I've got another lead to follow up first, but it can't hurt to look."

"Blunt, you know I don't want to interfere—"

"That sounds suspiciously like the words of somebody who's about to interfere."

"It's just that you seem to be focused on the demons... I thought the case was about the decorations."

He nodded. "Yeah, you might have a point. Panderpenny will have my guts for garters if she finds out I'm more worried about the demons than I am about finding the missing decorations. Weird thing is, I'm doing what the client told me to do."

She smiled. "You big softy. Your, um, client, gave you an excuse to help the demons. You don't think they're really linked?"

"Honestly, I thought it was tenuous before. Morgarth gave me the list of pink demons. There's nearly a hundred of them. I can't narrow that down, and none of them has hooves. The setup of a demon was pretty weak, but why bother? There's something joining the two together. If I chase the decorations, I'll probably find out who's kidnapping the demons… or it could just be a coincidence."

Dead Greetings

The crowd cheered as Mortimer tried to pull the curtain back across the window through which the Grim Reaper was peering out.

"I really don't think that's a great idea, sir."

"I just wanted to see how many people were here. There's a lot."

"Yes, sir, isn't there usually?"

"Yes. That's why I was checking. If there weren't many people, it would have been unusual, and we would all have felt foolish if we'd not realised until the last minute."

If there was ever a man who believed in prudence and preparation, it was Ralph Mortimer. Because of this, he could find no fault in the Grim Reaper's logic.

"I will check again shortly," Death said. "Let's try not to tussle the curtains this time. It doesn't look good for either of us. Curtain twitching, I mean."

"But every time you check, everyone gets overexcited, and you know someone will end up getting trampled or something."

"Ah, the trampling tradition. A very important part of Bleakest Eve."

"Tradition? They're accidents, horrible accidents where people are seriously injured and suffer."

"No they don't."

"They don't?"

"Certainly not. It's like a raffle. If you're lucky enough to get trampled, then the city will pay for a brand-new, top-of-the-range body. Not from the government body shop, either. They get scraped up and taken to Burke and Hare's in a wheelbarrow to have any body of their choosing. It comes out of my pocket."

Mortimer once again reminded himself that he was in a room with Death and nodded. "I didn't know that. Even so, it's not the nicest thing to experience."

"No, perhaps not, but people seem to like it, and there are worse things. Did you know I've been to Hell?"

"I did not."

"It's fascinating, boiling, but not a nice hot, like, say, the Caribbean. It's more like a dry roasting oven hot, only what's cooking is people. I used to go quite a lot, but it's not good for the old bones. Drying. Especially when you don't sweat." He lifted his arms like a chicken. "No glands, you see. Oh, but you do, of course. You're dead."

"Yes, sir. Everyone is dead."

The Grim Reaper nodded. "It's wonderful, isn't it?"

"It is?"

"Of course. Everyone being dead means there's none of that fear of dying, no fear of me."

"Is that… is that why Gloomwood exists?"

"No, that would be ridiculous, Mister

Mortimer. Creating an entire afterlife existence just so that people wouldn't fear me? Hah! Could you imagine... ahem. So, how long until the big show?"

"About two hours, sir."

Grim tapped his index fingers together. "Mister Mortimer, how do you think people would react if we cancelled Bleakest Day?"

"Cancelled it, sir? You mean in the future?"

"Yes. It would be strange to declare previous Bleakest Days to have been cancelled, as they've already happened. I suppose we could tell everyone they should never mention them again, but no, I was considering the ones that have not yet happened."

Mortimer nodded. "Why do you ask?"

"Are you avoiding my question? That doesn't seem very fitting, considering I'm Death, and you're, well, you."

"No, no." Mortimer raised his arms, his eyebrows scaling the top of his head and trying to clamber into his hairline. "I simply meant... You have me worried, sir, your lordship. I think people would be very upset."

"How upset?"

"People really like Bleakest Day. Thank you for doing it. We're very grateful."

"Oh. I see. I wasn't really asking for compliments... never mind. I think I'll just read for a bit after one more quick..."

Death threw aside the curtain again and waved to the crowd, who let out a roar of appreciation.

What neither Grim nor Mortimer could see was the small group of soft toys that were placing signs around the cabin. The signs said things like 'Down with Death' and 'Power to the People.' They also couldn't see the confused looks on the faces of the members of the public as they watched the toys.

Their observations could be described as 'wary', which is the sort of watching people do when they want to see what's happening but wish they weren't so close to it. It's not the same as rubbernecking because that's from a safe distance, but it's quite similar.

An astute observer, of which there were none, might have spotted that none of those demons had glowing red eyes.

The Priest

He had borrowed money from Sarah. It was embarrassing, begging for money from his girlf... lady... from whatever Sarah was to him, but he didn't have an alternative. Urgency had taken hold as midnight drew closer.

"Seventeen nails," the taxi driver said.

"Seventeen? Come on, it's Bleakest Eve," Blunt said. "We've barely gone five miles."

"True, but I had to drive to get you. People always forget that, don't they? It's a one-way trip for you, but not for me. Now I've got to drive home."

"Seventeen? Look, I've only got fifteen on me, and I had to borrow that."

"Are you serious? There's a meter. You could've stopped me at fifteen and walked the rest of the way. Now my meter says seventeen, and I have to turn that in to the office when I get in. Am I going to have to put in my money to pay for your bloody laziness?"

Blunt stared at the rear-view mirror, where he could see the look on the driver's face. It wasn't anger; it was shock.

"I'm sorry, I wasn't looking. Hang on. I might have some change." He took off his hat and reached into the sacred compartment reserved for phone money. He counted through the change and made up the extra two nails. "Look, I'm sorry, it's all change, like proper change. This is emergency phone money. That's got you covered, right?"

The taxi driver reached into the tray and counted out the change. "Yeah, thanks. I mean, it's what you owed, but… thanks, anyway."

Blunt nodded and opened the door. As he stepped onto the pavement, the driver wound down the window and leant out.

"Oi, mate, here." He held out a hand, and when Blunt put his palm out, a handful of change dropped into it. "I'm sorry. Bleakest Eve is rough, but it's two nails. Who has a tantrum over two nails on Bleakest Eve? I'm going home. You look like you might need these more than me."

Before Blunt had time to argue, the taxi was disappearing into the mist, its red brake lights the last thing to fade away.

Lights on wreaths made of dead sticks hung on the lampposts that lined the street along the avenue. This was an affluent part of the city—not dripping in money, but comfortable.

Blunt walked along the pavement. The festive music being blared out in households changed as he passed each home, as if somebody was impatiently flicking through channels, but everything had the same theme. The 'M' on a glowing sign hanging over the middle of the street flickered and died. 'ERRY BLEAKEST DAY'.

It was cold enough for his breath to form a cloud of condensation if he breathed out, but only if he focused on exhaling. As time had gone by, the subconscious autonomic function of breathing had faded. His breaths were smaller than they would be in a living person. This, he had been told by Sarah, meant he was settling into being dead. She'd meant it as a comforting thought, but it hadn't set him at ease. Being dead wasn't all it was cracked up to be.

A brief phone call from Sarah to the man who had delivered the box of clothes to the horde had garnered enough information to provide Blunt with a lead. It wasn't much, but his plan was to follow this to a dead end and then tear the Artificer a new one.

"A vicar," Blunt mumbled to himself. "If anyone is going to be an exorcist, it's going to be a vicar. Should've started with the church…"

The vicar lived in the rectory of a church in the middle of the street. It would've suited Halloween if Gloomwood celebrated it, which they did not because it offended its ghosts, ghouls, and mythical monsters… and everyone was dead.

The church had put more than a little effort into making the building festive. A large animatronic plastic model of the Grim Reaper, in his Bleakest Day purple and green patchwork cloak, let out a hollow laugh every few minutes. A dead tree stood behind it, dressed in decorations and purple, red, and green lights.

Blunt took the steps up to the main doors and pulled them open, expecting an empty interior. He gawped at the rows of people inside, swaying to the sound of a large organ and singing along.

"Bleakest Eve service," he said, shaking his head. "Of course there would be."

A woman dressed in a thick purple woollen jumper with a grinning crow and the words 'It's caw, caw, caw-ld outside' on it handed him a piece of paper and a chipped mug filled with mulled wine, which he took with a forced smile.

"Happy Bleakest Eve," the woman said.

"Thank you, and to you. I'm looking for the vicar."

"Oh, he's just done the service, and now he's over there," she said, pointing to one side of the church, where Blunt could see the vicar greeting members of the congregation.

Blunt thanked the woman again before making his way across the church. With every step, he had to mutter the words "And to you" or "Merry Bleakest Eve to you."

Eventually, now somewhat exasperated, he came face to face with the vicar.

"Happy Bleakest Eve," the vicar said. He was tall and lean, his hair was cut in a short back and sides that made Blunt think of the military, and he had the face of a goat.

Blunt had made the effort to remove his hat, which he now tucked under one arm so he could reach out to shake with his free hand.

"Nice to meet you, vicar. My name's Augustan Blunt. I was hoping to have a minute of your time."

"Of course. I always have time to speak to a parishioner."

"I'm not, uh, a parishioner. I'm a private investigator."

"I see. I hope this is nothing serious."

"Me too, me too. Is there somewhere quieter we could talk?"

"Oh, I see." The vicar looked around the room and directed Blunt towards a curtain, which he pulled aside to reveal a door.

Upon passing through the doorway, Blunt had the sense they had stepped into the vicar's home. Photographs lined the walls, and paperbacks filled a bookshelf at the end of the corridor.

"Excuse the mess, I was planning on seeing all visitors in the church itself. So, you're an investigator, a detective?"

"There's some debate about that," Blunt said. "I don't mean to be abrupt, but I think time may be an issue here. I need to know why you bought all those things from the toy shop today."

"Do you? That sounds like something that would be my business. Can I ask what it is you're investigating?"

"Missing people."

"Missing... What would that have to do with toys?"

"You were talking to the shopkeeper about demons."

"I'm sure that's something many people do. I don't mean to be rude, Mister Blunt, but I have quite a lot of guests here tonight, and Bleakest Eve is quite an important night for me."

"I don't understand. Is it a religious thing? I thought it was just a celebration of, I don't know, being dead?"

"Yes, that's pretty much it. It's a celebration of being dead and free and being thankful for each other, as well as the Grim Reaper, of course."

"And that's religious?"

"It can be. We give thanks to our Lord."

"God?"

"Hm, God can mean many things to many people. I'm happy to discuss this with you, of course, more than happy. Perhaps you'd like to come and see me another time?"

"Sorry, look, I'll cut this short. What are the toys for, and are you kidnapping demons?"

"I beg your pardon?"

"I'm going to need the complete story and quickly because either you're an evil sonofabitch or you're wasting my time."

The vicar shook his head.

"I see you're in the festive spirit. It's quite simple, really. Bleakest Eve is crushing the toy-making industry. The independent businesses, anyway. Now people are buying fewer toys, and those who are are buying them from the big companies. The church is trying to encourage recycling. Toytown has been kind enough to offer to recycle toys. They put out a call for specific ones, those awful duck masks. Do you remember Tuck the Duck?"

"Sounds like a rhyme waiting to happen."

"Yes, well, it seems other people felt the same way. So, toy shops are stuck with hundreds of masks that nobody bought. I took some of my parishioners' charitable donations and spent them in toy shops, hoping that some owners would at least be able to have a pleasant Bleakest Day. It also means we might be able to forget about that horrible duck business."

"You did what?"

"Please don't tell my parishioners I spent their donations on toys. They won't understand."

"Haven't you got a roof to repair?"

"How did you know that?"

"Every church has a roof to repair." Blunt shook his head. Another dead end. He turned to leave, then stopped himself. "Why were you talking about demons?"

"It was the strangest thing, actually. The fellow I was giving the masks to had a few demons with him. I have a leaflet asking for the masks around here somewhere."

The vicar started leafing through various pamphlets on a coffee table in the hallway.

"Here it is. See? 'Get off the naughty list: Bring your Tuck the Duck masks to be recycled by the big man himself, and he'll know you've been good.' Quite clever, and recycling is important."

"Even in the afterlife?" Blunt asked, taking the leaflet.

"Especially in the afterlife, detective. We might be here for a lot longer than we were alive."

Firestorm

Morgarth was pouring tea. Death himself had taught her the importance of tea.

"Morgarth," he had said, "when the world is crumbling and there is nothing but a single tiny rock upon which the last of all existence remains, you shall find me there. Sitting with my feet up on a table, not unlike this one, with a cup of tea in one hand and a good book in the other." A cup of tea, it seemed, was the glue that could hold everything together, whatever the circumstances.

When you are as short as Morgarth, tea making, cooking, and anything involving the lifting of objects is best done as close to the ground as possible. Morgarth's 'shelf' was two planks of wood on top of one another, and she reached up to pour hot water over the tea bag. Tea bags were an acceptable form of heresy here in Gloomwood, although Morgarth could definitely sense the paper in the tea once it was made.

Morgarth added a drop of milk but no sugar. Sugar was evil, and she was evil enough already. She lifted the mug in both hands and blew across the surface of the tea. This, she believed, was part of the process. Then she took a sip and felt her furry tongue burn.

Something was incorrect about her process. She turned to look at Sarah, who was sitting in a chair against the wall of the warehouse, a mug balanced upon one of its arms as she leafed through sheafs of paper.

"Is the burning tongue—"

"You're supposed to wait for it to cool," Sarah said without looking up.

"I see." Morgarth placed the mug back on the 'shelf' and turned back to Sarah. "I believe the phrase is, 'Don't you have a home to go to?'"

Sarah picked up the mug by her side and took a sip. "I do."

"Ah, well, that's good."

Silence rolled in on a chariot with a pink neon light strapped to it that flashed the word 'awkward' repeatedly.

Morgarth picked up the mug once more and again attempted the ritual cooling. She took a sip and this time found it did not burn. This, she supposed, was when it became comforting.

The next challenge she had observed less often, but as she was to give a lesson to the rest of the demons tomorrow on tea drinking, she needed to practise.

She tried to unwrap a packet of biscuits, a challenging task given her tiny furry T-Rex arms, until Sarah intervened. The scientist unwrapped the packet with a precision that was unnecessary and, if considered for too long, a little creepy.

"I don't like to go home. It's empty, dark and quiet. I'd rather stay here and stay busy. It's what people do."

"It is?"

"It's called avoidance, or denial. If I go home, I will have to consider all of this." She waved a hand at her face and body.

"I'm confused."

"The disappearing in and out of existence thing."

"Are you conscious when your head goes, or do you just not exist?"

"I remain here. It is only the physical aspect that vanishes. When my head goes, it's a bit like an out-of-body experience."

"Oh, yes, we do this to mortals sometimes. You know you can remove a limb, and because it still feels like it's there, you can torture the phantom limb."

"I did not know that. Fascinating. How does that relate to what happens to me?"

Morgarth shrugged. She held the biscuit in one tiny claw and looked down at the tea. She dunked it and held it before her.

"Integrity appears to be complete," she said with a nod. "Miss Von Faber, if you know you are in denial, how can it be denial?"

"Well, as long as I'm busy, I can pretend it isn't a problem. We're all different. This city is a melting pot of the weird and wonderful. I know a woman who is a tree. She is the only tree that isn't dead in the city, and yet she's dead. Isn't that peculiar?

"Then there's the fact that people, the establishment, don't like me because I am an example of an experiment gone wrong. You know they don't think I'm technically a post-mortal person anymore. They all wonder where I go. Am I even fully dead?

"The problem is that you cannot apply logic to the way an individual's mind works. The way people work is that we have a constant battle inside of us."

Sarah crouched on one knee beside Morgarth with a biscuit in her hand. She dunked the biscuit in her own tea, taking a little longer over it than the demon had.

"Structural integrity intact," she said as she lifted it out.

"I don't understand." Morgarth looked at Sarah's biscuit, then back at her own, her eyelids dropping as she stared at it before dunking it once more. "Integrity intact!"

Sarah looked at her own biscuit and then at the tea. "We're full of contradictions. I know I am in denial, just as you know you are unwelcome here, but we will convince ourselves otherwise until we can deal with it. It's preparation until"—she dipped her biscuit, and as she lifted it out, half of it fell into the mug—"we weather the storm or collapse, our integrity breached."

Morgarth nodded, but as she opened her mouth to speak, the warehouse burst into chaos.

The large roller shutters exploded inwards as a van smashed through them, skidding to a halt while demons ran on padded feet, or whatever means they had, towards the walls.

"Evil little bastards!" a voice shouted as

figures piled out of the van with buckets and water pistols. They began firing and throwing their pails of water everywhere, yelling a chorus of shouts and chants as they splashed the interior of the warehouse and any demon that got in their way.

"Down with evil!"

"Begone, foul demon!"

"Down with evil!"

Sarah walked towards them and stopped four meters from the front of the van.

"Are you finished?" she asked, raising her voice loud enough to be heard but without shouting.

"Demon supporter! We're here to exorcise these foul Hellspawn and anyone associated with them!" A man ran at her, brandishing a baseball bat.

Sarah stepped to one side and grabbed the back of the man's coat as his own momentum carried him forward. She dug her heels in and leaned back just enough to spin him around and throw him at the front of the van.

"You can all leave now," Sarah said, looking around the room, "or, well, you're trapped in a warehouse with nearly five hundred demons." Then she unleashed a grin, ghoulish beneath the white strip lighting. "And something else."

"Demon sympathiser!" another figure shouted, running towards Sarah.

"Yeah, nobody likes electronic music!" someone else yelled, spraying Sarah with the water pistol. "Burn in holy water!"

"Sympathiser, not synthesiser Derek, you

bleedin' eejit!" said a man holding a struggling lion teddy bear in one hand. There were several lions in the demon cohort. This one was green with a purple mane.

"Put her down," Sarah said, and she vanished, suddenly reappearing by the man's right ear. "Or I will make you."

The man cast the demon to one side with a yelp. "What kind of freak are you? Next worst thing to a demon! Not surprised you're—"

Sarah's right hand vanished. When it reappeared, it was protruding out of the man's chest. There was a popping sound that seemed to come a moment after. Then there was a crunch that came with a wail that made even the demons flinch.

As if the screaming was little more than background noise, Sarah withdrew her hand and wiped it on her coat. There wasn't much in the way of gore.

"Next?" she asked.

"But he put the toy down!" a man holding a water pistol in one hand said as he pulled down his mask.

"Oh? Silly me." Sarah said.

Red Herring

"Yeah, okay, I feel pretty silly, but there's no need to rub it in, you big beardy bastard," Blunt said, fighting a smile.

"Kidnapping demons!" The man let out a burst of thunderous laughter from his dominant position at the head of the table. There was so much food and drink on it, it looked like they had specially arranged it for a festive photo shoot. Which, as they were in a department store, made sense.

Along either side of the table were demons. Cats, squirrels, and rabbits in a rainbow of pastel and neon colours. Each demon had a mask hanging around its neck.

"You took demons from the street?" Blunt asked.

"Yes! Of course I did! Where else would I find them?"

Everything the man said was loud, enthusiastic, and bordering on obnoxious, but he said it with such good humour, it was infectious.

"You could've advertised."

"Advertise! Advertise, he says! Well, I did advertise. I advertised for experienced salespeople wanting a bright new opportunity where they could make good money working from home!"

Blunt rolled his eyes and let out a sigh. "That sounds like a scam."

"It does?" The man's bottom lip hung out for a

moment as he considered it. "Why would that be a scam?"

"Sounds like a pyramid scheme. Or one of those jobs where they pay you for what you do and it always ends up being far lower than expected for loads more work."

"I don't understand."

"It sounds too good to be true, and there's no detail. It's a terrible advert."

They were sitting in what Blunt could only call a grotto in the middle of a large department store. Themed music blared from speakers in the ceiling, but the shop was otherwise empty of customers, having closed up hours ago.

"Well, there's no need to be mean about it," the big man said, removing the pointy hat he wore on his head, complete with bells, and placing it on the table. "It's not been easy, you know? I was down and out on the streets, giving my possessions away. I'm not much of a salesperson. Then, boom! Out of nowhere, the idea hit me. Calling people up to sell them things on the telephone—"

"It's called telesales, and everybody hates it."

"Telesales? Never heard of it. I'm calling it the targeted wealth acquiring telephony system. It will be—"

"You can't call it that!" Blunt said. "You realise what people are going to shorten that to, what the acronym is? I mean, it's apt, but it's definitely not a good idea."

"Acronym? I don't really do acronyms."

"Ugh. It's telesales, or telemarketing, and it's been around in the mortal world for a long time. How long have you been here?"

"Hm." He looked down at his green felt clothes, white cuffs and collars, and his enormous belly, looking like a bowl full of jelly. "How long have I been here? I think it was when they started making me dress in red. I don't really remember. Anyway, isn't it rude to ask?"

Blunt nodded. "Yes, sorry, it is." He looked around at the demons staring down at the table, resolutely refusing to look Blunt in the eye. "What about you? I've been running around this city, spending a fortune on taxis, and your friends in the horde have been worried sick. Can you imagine that? Here you are in a bloody grotto with…" Blunt looked at the man in green with white trim and too many bells and shook his head. "Ugh, I was about to accuse somebody of kidnapping you when in reality you're just too bloody selfish to tell anyone where you are."

A demon bunny rabbit looked up at Blunt and pulled her mask up over her face. "It wasn't like that," she said in a voice that definitely didn't belong to a demon.

The big man leapt up and moved around the table with unexpected grace. He placed a huge hand on the shoulder of the toy rabbit that had spoken.

"Look," the bearded man said, pointing to the mask. Dangling from it was a series of buttons, and the big man leaned forward to press one. "See what a difference this makes? Say something, Donder."

"I thought you were Trem?" Blunt said.

"We… we have alternative names," she said in a different voice. It was the voice of a kindly neighbour, the friendly receptionist, the lady who offered you the change you were missing for your bus ticket home, the manager who knew you were just having a bad day and told you to go home and get some rest. "They're more… user-friendly."

"That's… that's incredible," Blunt said. "And the names, yeah, I've heard of places doing that to make people more comfortable. I mean, it's questionable, but then who's going to think they're talking to a demon? Brilliant."

The big man let out a hearty laugh. "We were trying to get the fit right, the sound right, and the business model right. We could only do one at a time. If we went back now and it turned out it only worked for a few lucky demons, we'd have everyone hoping for a future as fellow twa—"

"Customer service representatives," Blunt interrupted.

"Right," the man said, squeezing the rabbit's shoulder. "Customer service representatives, and it might not work. Then what would we do?"

"You could have told them you were safe, at least," Blunt said to the rabbit. He looked up at the rosy-cheeked man. "You told them to keep it a secret?"

"It would be cruel to give them all hope and then discover it was a fluke. Plus, we needed to get supplies. Tuck the Duck masks, for example."

"And now?"

"Well," the big man said. "I have a thing for the grand surprise, the flourish on the big day. I have many more masks, but, due to recruitment problems, I haven't managed to get them all done. It's a busy time of year in the grotto." He waved his hands around, showing off the gaudy decorations and fake snow.

"You honestly expect me to believe you're him?"

"Well, there's the rub. Nobody believes he's him, or I wouldn't be here, would I?"

"That's just confusing," Blunt said. "So, where are the others? And what about the van and the whole dead inner child thing?"

"Ah, the company bought that van," the big man replied with a chuckle. "I quite like the slogan, personally."

"You're not one to judge that kind of thing, trust me."

Blunt looked around the room. Decorations hung from every available space, but nothing screamed 'These are the Grim Reaper's'.

"These all yours?" Blunt asked, knowing the answer already.

"The walls?"

"The decorations."

"Yes. Well, they belong to Toytown. They've done a wonderful job with the grotto, don't you think? Between you and me, I think this whole Bleakest Day thing is just an excuse to celebrate Chri

—"

"Don't say it."

There was something off about this scenario, but considering who the big man was claiming to be and the absurd idea of a festive dinner that literally looked like a teddy bear's picnic, Blunt couldn't put his finger on the problem.

"Right," he said with a shrug. "Guess it seems this is a kind of… bleakest miracle thing? Demons getting fresh voices, you pulling yourself back up from the gutter… I suppose this is what's supposed to warm a man's heart."

There was that laugh again. It was almost the reverse of a demonic voice, the way it washed over Blunt like a wave of soothing cheer. The big man waved his arms around, gesticulating at the expanse of the enormous department store. There must have been more sale signs than there were things to buy.

"Just business, but when business is good, everybody wins."

Need a Ride

The big man in the green fur suit had insisted that Blunt use the phone to let Morgarth know she didn't need to worry about the demons.

It turned out the demons already had enough to worry about. After the third time Morgarth had dropped the receiver because of her slippery T-Rex hands, Sarah took the phone off her.

"Are you okay, Sarah? Did the demons protect you? Are you going to call the police?" Blunt asked.

"Them protect me? Um, sure. The police? The only thing the police will ask is why they sprayed us with water and not something flammable."

"That's a little harsh. Sowercat called you into the crime scene earlier. He's trying to turn the corner—"

"The chief isn't a monster, Blunt, just the people who work for him, and I'm pretty sure that on Bleakest Eve, they've already got a full house for the night. So it'll be some poor soul on his own at the station while everyone else is at the Bleakest Day ceremony or getting drunk, or both."

"They can't—"

"Augustan, they most certainly can. If you want to do something unlawful, right now is a great time to do it."

"Does everyone else know there's virtually no police tonight?"

"Probably."

"Then what's stopping people from rampaging through the streets?"

"…Festive spirit? That's not the point. I've got a group of inebriated exorcists here who were sold 'holy' water by someone who must've been laughing all the way to the bank."

"There's no such thing as holy water in the afterlife."

"Exactly. So they're out of cash, have broken their van, and are now surrounded by nearly five hundred demons who aren't too impressed with them. Oh, and one of them is trying to claim that I have to pay for new ribs."

"Why?"

"Apparently if you break them, you pay for them. They were new."

"Well, he should've thought of that before he attacked a warehouse full of demons. Tell him he's welcome to take the case to court. I'll get Ursula to be your mediator. She's never lost a fight."

"Oh, thank you. I wasn't asking."

"You never ask, Sarah. It's not how you do things. Now, the van?"

"It's just a white van, nothing exciting."

"Right. Well, that's one lead down the drain. Listen, I'm going to need a ride. Is your car working?"

The other side of the phone remained silent, and Blunt peered at the receiver.

"Sarah, you hear me?"

"Yes, yes, I heard you, and yes, it's working."

"Brilliant. You're going to need to pick me up fast. I think I'm being played here."

"Played? How?"

"Just hurry. I'll meet you at the scene with the toy from earlier."

"I can pick you up. I just have to go get the car."

"Never mind then. I don't think we've got that time to waste. Just get there, and I'll meet you there."

Blunt hung up the receiver and turned to face the room. The telephone was in the dining room. As he looked back at the table, he realised he was looking at a large elderly gentleman having dinner with a group of soft toys. "Only in Gloomwood," he muttered, shaking his head.

"Right," he said, addressing the man in green as he walked back towards the table. "Could I borrow that van?"

"No, unfortunately not. It's being used. I used to have a sleigh, but there aren't any reindeer in this place. Unless…"

He looked at the demons around the table.

"Absolutely not," Blunt said. "I am not being dragged around on a sleigh by bloody toys. I'd never get there on time."

"Wait," the man said, standing up. He pushed his chair back, then stepped to the right, gesturing at something behind him. "Now, this belongs to the shop, but as long as you return it, I'm sure they won't mind."

Blunt's scowl settled across his face as he saw the mode of transport being proffered. The natural frown lines he had fostered through life had been carried through to death and had only grown more defined with every day of post-mortal humiliation.

Blunt sighed dejectedly, sensing he had little choice, then disappeared from the grotto, grabbing the offered transport on his way.

The big man in green waited until he heard the side door slam before turning to the demons around the table.

"Well," he said, with none of the mirth that had bubbled through his voice before. "It would have been easier just to crush his skull, but apparently, he has a role to play."

"Let us go," Trem said, standing up in her chair.

"I will, don't worry. When the time is right, I'll let you all go... and it will be glorious."

The Car

The car was a bone of contention with Blunt and Sarah for a simple reason. It had been his.

When Ursula Panderpenny had put an offer on the table to set up the Panderpenny agency, Blunt had been furious. Outwardly, it had been because he didn't 'need' a partner and didn't want to work for someone else. Sarah, who had seen through Blunt's quite simple facade, knew that it had actually been about money.

There was no way Blunt could afford the buy-in that Panderpenny had been asking for, and it was a generous offer. Sarah had also known that Blunt would never ask to borrow money from anyone, and no self-respecting bank was going to fund Blunt, given his public reputation.

Sarah had made noises about needing a car and, through the careful orchestration that takes place between couples who both know exactly what the other person is doing, suggested buying Blunt's.

It was not a car she enjoyed driving. It was brutish, loud, and fast. The suspension was too hard, and it growled like a tarmac-chewing beast when she was crawling through traffic.

The reality was it barely ever moved now that she held the keys and instead spent its days parked behind the apartment building she lived in. When Blunt had asked if it was running, he had really been asking when the last time she had driven it was.

She swerved around a slow-moving car that was curb crawling. It was that kind of neighbourhood. Then she sighed as she found herself held up again, this time by a cyclist weaving unsteadily along the road. The bike was pink, with streamers on the handlebars.

It took her a moment to recognise the figure in a coat wobbling on the bicycle. Riding it, hunched over and puffing like a steam engine, was Detective Blunt, trying to direct the bicycle and hold onto his hat at the same time.

Sarah rolled down her window as he drew up alongside. "Nice bike."

Blunt turned, and the bike lurched dangerously close to the car. "I was in a hurry."

"So you stole a bicycle off a little girl?"

"I didn't steal it, and it was all there was. Who cares anyway? It's around the corner, right?"

"Ditch the bike and hop in."

"Can't, borrowed it. See you in two." Blunt lifted himself on the seat and attempted to put on a burst of speed. It made little difference, and Sarah, making no effort to mask a fit of giggles, awkwardly sped up.

Turning the corner, Sarah saw the Gloomwood police had decided to go overboard on the crime scene tape. It still barred the main entrance to the building, a tall narrow structure in a row of similar apartment blocks, each one of which had four storeys and a basement. A few broken strands of tape fluttered from either side of the doorway, incongruous against the lights hanging from lamppost to lamppost. From the apartments above, the sounds of drunken revelry and several songs all playing at once filtered down to the street.

Blunt stepped off the bicycle and into a large puddle that had formed in a pothole in the road. He carefully stood the borrowed transport on its kickstand as Sarah climbed out of the car.

"Don't say another word about the bike," Blunt said, holding up a hand. "Why's the place all taped up? I thought they decided it wasn't a crime."

"Are you asking why our friendly neighbourhood police officers decided not to tidy up the mess they made?"

Blunt nodded. "Yeah, fair enough. Shall we?"

Sarah withdrew her scalpel from her pocket and sliced through the tape in one smooth motion before stepping over the threshold into the building. "Why are we here?"

"I should've come here before. I put it to one side after hearing from you and Morgarth— and my... contact. I was too hung up on the van when I should've been looking where Morgarth and everyone else was pointing."

Sarah led the way down the stairs to the basement. "The exorcists?"

"Just because most of them are nothing but whining complainists."

"Complainists?"

"It's a word."

"I don't think it is. Anyway, you were saying?"

"Well, every group has outliers. Ones who believe a little too fervently. The attack on the warehouse, that was by a bunch of exorcists?"

Blunt pushed a door open and fumbled for a light switch. Sarah followed close behind.

"A handful of idiots who had been drinking together in the Rusty Guillotine. Most of them felt pretty stupid when they sobered up and were offered tea by a bunch of friendly toys."

"Hah, that'll teach them," Blunt said as the light flicked on. "Wow, this is creepier than I thought."

"It seems worse now."

Red paint was daubed over the walls, saying, 'Thou shall not kill, thou shall not steal, thou shall not...' in thick, haphazard brushstrokes. Six toys surrounded the toy nailed to the table, all cut open with foam and stuffing bursting from them.

"I told you it was weird. It's..."

"Hellish?" Blunt finished for her as he flicked through a book lying on a small table by the doorway. The table was too short to be an altar, but someone had clearly placed it there to act as one. "This is a book on fairy tales. Do you know anything about the Kalli... Kallikantzaroi? That's a mouthful."

"They're goblins, or gnomes. They're related to... you know, the winter festival. Obsessed with cutting down the tree of life."

"Why would anyone be reading about that?"

"They're always up to something stupid at this time of year."

"Hah, yeah, well—"

"Blunt, they're here in Gloomwood."

"What? But they're not real... Is everything anyone ever believed real?"

Sarah shook her head. "I don't know. Are we real? It's Gloomwood. If someone living believed in something, it can exist. Those little gnomes definitely do though, horrible bunch."

"So they did this. Why would they do this?"

"It's exactly their sort of thing. Why would anyone steal decorations?"

"Because they're more than decorations."

"What are they?"

"Something bloody powerful. Other than that, I've no idea. I don't even know what they look like."

"Ah, it's your first Bleakest Day. The decorations go up every year on the tree. They're snow globes and stuff, but they're swirly and purple and they glow. They're pretty and highly thaumaturgic."

"You mean magical, don't you?"

She pulled a face. "You know I don't like that word."

"No time for a bit of magic?" Blunt said with a half smile and a lewd waggle of his eyebrows.

"Don't get your hopes up. Your wand is remaining holstered."

The detective shrugged, then reached into his inside coat pocket to pull out a pen. He clicked a button on the side, and a light on the top started glowing.

"Speaking of magic wands," he said.

"Cute."

Blunt looked at the penlight and considered it for a moment. "I guess you'd prefer the term thaumaturgic wand."

He pointed the light at the toy pinned on the table, then inspected the ones hanging from the ceiling. "The stuffing's been taken out of them. It's like someone's cut them open and hollowed them out. Weird."

He reached forward, a grimace on his face, and pulled one toy towards him. It was attached to the ceiling with a rope and a coat hanger. With care, he turned the fluffy, eerily deflated toy dragon around.

"Look at this. It's a zip."

"It's broken," Sarah said.

"Which might explain why it's been abandoned." Blunt looked around from toy to toy, pointing at them. "The others are all knackered as well. There's a hole in that one. That one's got no material in the mouth... These are suits."

"Disguises? Who would want to dress up like demons?"

"Someone who wants demons to look bad? I mean, that's pretty bloody obvious. If I was going to dress up as someone to incriminate them and make the public hate them, can't do much better than literally wearing them as a suit, can you? Bloody genius, really."

Sarah shook her head and stepped across the room to pull open a cupboard. It was disappointingly mundane. A single plate, bowl and mug next to a shelf of own-brand supermarket cereal and a carton of milk. On the shelf below was a pile of newspapers.

Blunt walked over and grabbed the top newspaper, then the one beneath, and the one beneath that. "These are a few weeks old."

"There's nothing here but foam and fur. There aren't any actual demons either. Just toys."

"How can you tell?"

"Morgarth said I'd know if a demon had been killed in here."

"What's that supposed to mean?"

She shrugged. "Probably means we never want to see it."

"There's got to be some kind of clue in there. Wait, what's that?" Blunt pointed towards a small box.

"A sewing kit?"

"Doesn't that seem a little odd to you? This is a clue."

"That's a clue?"

"I'm the detective."

"You know," Sarah said, "Sowercat said they all called you the defective detective down at the station."

"Liar."

"Why'd you say that?"

"Too many syllables in that name for the

Gloomwood police. I know they all just call me Detective C—"

"What's this?" Sarah interrupted as she picked up a piece of paper from the floor. There was red paint splattered across it. "Some kind of test?"

"Let me see." Blunt reached out for it. He took the paper and turned it over in his hands. "One old knacker."

"What?"

"That's what's written on the top. It's an answer sheet… from a pub quiz. Guess that points somewhere."

"The idiot exorcists wanted to be taken back to the pub."

"Back to the Rusty Guillotine?" Blunt held up the answer sheet and pointed to the top right corner, where there was a logo of a guillotine with a beer barrel where a person might be placed. "Seems unlikely this is a coincidence."

Demons Unite

"What do you mean, protest?" asked Clive, one of the six former elite demons, now a blue and purple spotted dog with a pink collar and long, flapping ears. It was a sign of how things had changed that he was grateful to be a dog who walked on two legs rather than four.

Morgarth was standing in a circle of demons in the centre of the warehouse, which was now lit only by candles after the holy water attack had shorted out the electrics. It was cold, and many of them were wet and tired, but they were demons—misery was to them what blue skies and sunshine were to most norms.

"Yes, protest. Like the demon union did."

"Ugh, the union." Clive looked around the room. "I suppose many of you supported the union?"

"This is not the time to divide us, Clive," Morgarth said. "We were in a unique position in Hell. Here, we are all equals."

"So we're in the union?"

Morgarth's tail waved behind her, and she tilted her head to one side. "There are just over five hundred of us in a city of people who have already begun fostering hatred towards us. We have a reputation that makes people fear us, and we now"—she held up her tiny arms and looked at them—"look like this."

"They *should* fear us," Clive snapped.

"Fear us and employ us? Fear us and help us integrate into society? Do you think Miss Von Faber fears us? Hates us?" Morgarth asked.

The dog shrugged and folded its arms. Morgarth told herself that being jealous of someone being able to fold their arms was pathetic, but it didn't stop her feeling it.

"Morgarth," a furry tortoise said as it stepped forward. "How do you suggest we protest? In Hell, we impaled those we tortured and carried them aloft while we marched in front of the palace, throwing excrement in its direction while refusing to work."

The dinosaur nodded her head. "Thank you, Deceivious. We will do something very similar but with signs instead of victims, and probably not excrement." There was a palpable sound of disappointment at her announcement, but the demons nodded. "We shall make signs and march upon their large public gathering, this Bleakest Day event."

"Can we go home?" a man sitting in a wheelbarrow asked. He was one of the men who had crashed their van into the warehouse. The demons had since put him into a wheelbarrow on account of his broken legs, though nobody wanted to own up to how he broke his legs, including the man.

The demons had also given all the men a cup of tea. The tea, Morgarth had explained, was important in calming the situation. Most of the men were now approaching sobriety and a change of heart and were watching the demons from a corner of the warehouse.

"You're not prisoners," Morgarth said to the wheelbarrow man. "Miss Von Faber said something about your reproductive organs being on your heads. I'm not sure why that makes your brain malfunction, but apparently it means you cannot use it fully. As an act of kindness, we're accepting that you were inebriated and foolish."

"Really?"

"Some of us would like to skin you and then roll you in salt," said a demon in the body of a unicorn.

"Yes," Morgarth said. "We *would* like to do that, but as decent citizens of Gloomwood, we won't. Perhaps you could remember that next time you decide to paint us as inhuman monsters."

"But we are inhuman monsters," a toy hedgehog said.

"I know. But I don't want to confuse things further. We're being bigger people."

"But we're tiny. They're much bigger."

"Yes. Miss Von Faber said that doing this makes us bigger people."

"Are we going to grow?"

"No. I asked. She said it's internal growth."

"Are we going to explode?"

"No. I don't think we'll grow very much."

TO THE GUILLOTINE

"So, is it over?" Sarah asked while Blunt pulled the seatbelt across him.

"Oh yeah," Blunt said, "I mean, that's the demons found. That'll do. Half the job done, so that's a win."

"There's no need for the tone."

"Don't even start. It's definitely not over," Blunt said as he slapped at his pockets in search of a cigar.

Sarah put the car in gear and pulled away from the curb. "We're really going to a pub this late on Bleakest Eve?"

"We're following a lead."

"You think this is all coming from the Rusty Guillotine?"

"The idiots who attacked the horde came from the same pub as this quiz sheet did. I want to know if they have a sewing club."

Sarah nodded as they stopped at a traffic light. "You're being sarcastic." She turned a dial on the radio, and festive music broke out before a DJ silenced it, talking about the buildup to the Bleakest Eve celebrations. "I can see it from their perspective."

"From the exorcists' perspective? That's very diplomatic of you. I wouldn't have thought you'd have much patience for that way of thinking."

"That way of thinking? It's about looking at perspectives, considering the data."

"It's not okay for me to say it, though, is it? That the exorcists might have a point? People would tear me to shreds. Again."

"No, it's fine in this context. I mean, the way you say it isn't usually right, but this time it is. Nobody likes change. Everyone has something to fear. People used the same way of thinking to justify Hope bashing. The entire Gloomwood police, for example. They didn't hate Hopes and Dreams, they hated the fact that they might show them up, that things were changing, so they focused on the differences rather than the similarities."

"Tribalism."

"If you want to call it that."

"It's over-simplifying it, but yeah. Create a group mentality, give them a common enemy, blame them for all the suffering, fill in the gaps with half-truths and lies. Get people riled up enough and you can just say things like, 'I heard demons hypnotise people to make them believe they can be trusted. If you hear anyone supporting them, then they've been possessed. They're blackmailing the Grim Reaper. It explains everything, and if anyone disagrees, they're ignorant, or in on it.' Then you've got yourself a group of people who are fighting the good fight against an evil, insidious plot, even if it's a pack of lies."

Blunt finally found a cigar and extracted it from his pocket. From another pocket, he pulled out a lighter.

"Don't smoke in the car," Sarah said as she pulled to a stop.

"It's Bleakest Eve. Give me a break. Anyway, it was my car. I've smoked in it loads of times."

"I know, and it took me weeks to get rid of the smell. We're here anyway." She turned the car off, the radio died, and the engine rattled into silence. Over the clatter of hail on the car roof, festive music blared out of the doors of a pub across the road. A man wearing a purple Grim Reaper costume was on his knees with one hand on a lamppost, giving the pavement a splash of colour with the contents of his stomach.

"Wait here?" Blunt asked as he clambered out of the car.

"As if I've nowhere else to be," Sarah said. "How long should I wait?"

"Eh? As long as it takes for me to find out who's been dressing up as demons or making the suits."

"I meant before I come in. In case you get in trouble."

"Pfft. This is a pub, my spiritual home," Blunt said before slamming the passenger side door and walking across the road.

He walked around the drunk hanging onto the lamppost but tipped his hat towards him. "Merry Bleakest Eve."

"Is it?"

Burn

"What's that smell?" Mortimer asked.

"Don't look at me. I'm a skeleton," Grim said, looking up from the paperback he was leafing through.

"I'm sorry, I didn't realise you couldn't smell anything."

"I can smell perfectly well. I meant I can't produce a smell. Now that you mention it, though, there is the smell of cremation."

"Cremation? You mean burning?"

"Yes. How else would you cremate something?"

"It's just… it seems a little specific."

"Everything is about perspective, Mister Mortimer. In your existence, burning things in general is more common than cremation, but in mine, not so much. I mean, does a bird see someone falling from a building and say, 'look, they're falling' or 'look, they're flying'?"

Mortimer stared at Death, he who brings the end, and nodded. "I suppose that's one way to apply logic."

"Exactly. What is that smell?"

"I think what's being cremated might be, um… the cabin."

"I think you're right. Which means this could be our cremation. So don't just stand there. We need to leave."

"If we go outside, the crowd will go crazy."

"Yes. That's quite terrifying. Almost as worrying as being burned to a crisp. I'm not a big fan of fire, Mister Mortimer. Fireworks, on the other hand, are lots of fun, but they aren't for another hour."

"Maybe someone started things early?"

Flames burst through the floor of the temporary structure in the opposite corner from Mortimer and Grim. The fire licked against a pinboard and leapt onto paperwork attached to it. Within seconds, it was climbing the walls, and billowing smoke filled the small, box-like building.

"I wanted to use one of the new inflatable buildings," the Grim Reaper said. "Probably wise that we didn't. Shall we leave?"

Mortimer looked at the growing flames and back to the Grim Reaper, who appeared indifferent to the imminent danger. It was hard to tell, though, as his skull never really showed expressions unless he drew eyebrows on, and Crispin Neat had asked him to stop doing that.

"Yes, we had better."

"Lead on, Macduff," Grim said, grabbing his scythe and standing to his full height.

"Right." Ralph Mortimer, third assistant to the manager of the Office of the Dead and least qualified bodyguard to the Grim Reaper he could imagine, put his hand on the door handle. "You know, technically, that's a misquote. It should be 'lay on', not 'lead on'—"

"Fascinating. You realise my robe is about to catch fire… again."

Last Orders

Blunt took a seat at the bar and waited for the landlord to notice. When the large man behind the bar poured a pint of ale into the tankard without even looking at Blunt and placed it in front of the detective, Blunt let out a cough.

"Who are you?" the bartender asked as if he was surprised to find a customer there, despite just serving him. He was broad-shouldered with a shaved head and a nose that told a tale of a violent past.

"Stan," Blunt replied.

"Stan? You look like that detective that used to be in the papers."

"That's me."

"But his name's Blunt."

"I have a first name, too. It's Augustan. People once called me Stan."

"Ooh, Augustan is it?"

"No. I literally just said that." Blunt shrugged again. "You got darts?" he asked, looking around.

"Hang on," the bartender said, placing a hand on top of the tankard. "You haven't paid for that."

"What do I owe you?"

"Two nails."

Blunt pulled his hat off his head to sift through the emergency phone money once again and found himself feeling grateful for the festive spirit of the taxi driver earlier that evening. As he slid the coins across the bar, the big man behind it raised his eyebrows.

"Low on funds?"

"Bleakest Day. Stuff like this sucks the cash from you, right?"

"True enough. What brings you here?"

"Someone told me we have a similar outlook on things like demons."

"Oh, here we bloody go. Now it makes sense. I don't want to hear anything about it. Maybe I shouldn't be so surprised. Didn't you get in trouble already for the things you keep saying? You want to talk to Dan and his mates about that. They're all in bed with the exorcists. Why do people think this is the place for stuff like that? It's just a bloody pub, not ground zero for conspiracy theorists."

"So you're not with us?"

"With who? There's no bloody 'us' or 'them'. Have your drink and bugger off." The bartender pushed himself off the bar to serve a woman who was shouting something about another round.

Blunt squashed his hat back on his head and turned around. Leaning his back against the bar, he surveyed the room.

It reminded him of the living world. People laughing and joking, many of them worse for wear. There was a camaraderie that didn't exist most of the year round.

Bleakest Day, he thought. *Maybe it does do something.*

A woman with short bleached blonde hair and

a cigarette hanging from her bottom lip staggered towards him. "Well hello there, buy me a drink?"

"I'd love to, but I just spent the last of my cash."

"Oh, all spent, are you? That's a shame."

Blunt forced his eyes to remain still while they begged to roll. He forced a smile onto his face. It was hard to tell if she was incredibly drunk or had crawled out of a vat of embalming fluids. Either way, it wasn't a pretty sight.

"Heard you talking about demons. I don't trust 'em, you know."

"No. Seems you're not alone there." Blunt lifted his pint. "Heard Dan was the man to talk to."

"Dan's all talk, hasn't got the stomach to really get involved where it matters. Should've seen it when Bertha told him he was a wannabe."

"A wannabe?"

"Yeah, Dan hated it. Right after giving a speech about how we need to stand up and make our voices heard about the demons. Bertha doesn't say much, just shuffles by and mutters about pretend exorcists being all talk and no action."

"Well, I heard Dan and his mates tried to storm the demon's place and sprayed them with holy water. Sounds like they took action after all."

"Bah, idiots. Anyway, enough about them. What about you and me?"

"I'm actually interested in sewing," Blunt said, deciding that the woman was probably too drunk to care that he hadn't even made an attempt to segue into the topic.

"Sewing? What are you on about?"

"Sewing. I heard it's big around these parts."

"You're a weirdo," the woman said before taking a drink from a bottle. She slammed it down on the bar and wiped her mouth on her sleeve, from elbow to wrist, in a perfect example of how not to be dainty. "But, now you mention it, a lot of this lot used to work in the toy factory down the road. Used to be run by a bunch of pabies, but they shut up shop when the demons came to town. Ain't nobody buying soft toys now."

"Oh yeah? Surprised nobody's dressing up in them and pretending to be demons," Blunt fixed the woman with a cold, hard stare. It was a stare he'd long practised, literally in front of a mirror, prepared for exactly this sort of moment. This was when something would crack, when the real villains would crawl out of the woodwork, and he'd know he was on the right track.

The woman sneered. "Ew, you really are a weirdo. Gavin wanted to buy my worn pantyhose the other night and I thought that was perverse, but you really are a freak. Ugh, bugger off."

"Um, right," Blunt said, stepping away from the bar with his pint.

A crowd was gathering around a television mounted above a gambling machine in the room's corner. Blunt gave the woman another smile and walked away. A thud behind him suggested she'd finally succumbed to gravity, but he didn't risk turning and potentially being drawn into more awkward flirting.

He swallowed the last of his drink before depositing the empty tankard on a table and walking outside. The man he'd seen on the way in was sitting with his back to a lamppost, fast asleep. As Blunt passed him, he noticed a bottle of something that smelled like petrol in the loose grip of the drunk.

"You don't want any more of this, do you?" Blunt asked.

The man's eye's flickered for a moment, then fell shut. "Nah, s'alright, you have it."

Blunt lifted the bottle and prised it out of the man's fingers. He slipped it into his long coat pocket before crossing the street quickly as the rain intensified.

Sarah rolled down the window as he approached. "Are we ready to go?"

"Not yet—"

"You need to hear what's on the radio."

"I need to check something first. Follow me in the car and keep the engine running."

"What's going on?"

"Just get ready."

"But the radio—"

"Get ready."

Whale, Whale, Whale

Juanita couldn't help herself. She'd followed the others like a sheep. Easily drawn into their anger and frustration. Bleakest Eve brought people together. They'd all been drinking, celebrating.

Then this had happened. There was only one thing for it. They would march against the demons, arm in arm. It didn't matter that the demons were scary, that they were Hellspawn. They were Gloomwood, and, well, there were a lot of them.

A man dressed in a tracksuit that should have been consigned to the annals of history some time ago bumped into her and she whirled around. He had a piece of wood in his hands, a makeshift club.

"Uh, sorry," he said, looking up at her.

"It's fine. Your club is too thin. It will snap with the first blow, leaving you defenceless," Juanita said.

"Oh. Thank you, um, miss?"

As dead gods go, Juanita wasn't the most imposing, but she was close to it. Nine feet tall with the head of a whale—a little smaller than an actual whale's, of course—and three tentacles where a human's arms would be. Beneath her dress, she had the body of a large slug. It was a nice dress.

"Uh, miss?" the tracksuit-wearing man said.

"Yes?"

"Would you mind if I walked with you?"

She let out a laugh, a coquettish giggle. "You

little flirt."

"Um, yeah, if you like."

"Okay, but you need to get a bigger club than that and promise to protect me from the demons."

"Protect… you… yeah, right, course."

The Kallikantzaroi

They had boarded up the windows and doors, so not a crack of light escaped from within. Despite what people might say, they were quite handy when it came to DIY. Of course, the fact that they liked to break into people's houses to practise the fine art of home improvement was irrelevant.

A thin layer of green fur made it look like they were glowing, and their small bright yellow eyes, pointed ears, and sharp pointy teeth meant they stood out in the day. Not that the Kallikantzaroi cared. They preferred to sneak around at night. Their cloven feet were quiet and softer than they appeared, and they always worked as a team.

Inside the factory, fairy lights covered the walls and an array of decorations, many of them crafted by their own hands, covered every surface. The furtive little creatures moved with speed around the room, pulling the stuffing out of toys and pulling on the leftover 'skins' to see if they fitted.

Standing several feet taller than even the largest Kallikantzaros was Elric Jackson. He was a tailor by trade who, two weeks ago, had been overjoyed to be visited by helpful gnomes who ensured he finished an urgent order for wealthy clients just in time.

Of course, it had come with a catch.

He was now shackled to a table, trying to operate a sewing machine as the little green gnomes screeched barely comprehensible instructions at him. The long chains imprisoning him rattled around his feet.

"I said a horn, not a honking horn, a pointy one. I'm supposed to be a terrifying unicorn toy. Where are the teeth?"

"My zip broke again, can't you use press studs instead?"

"The eye holes are in the wrong place… or maybe it's my eyes, but I can't move them, so fix it."

Elric pressed down on the speed control pedal. The sewing machine was noisy, but it did nothing to drown out the sound of the music.

He worked because the deal had been simple: work hard until Bleakest Day, and then the bargain is complete. He wasn't sure what would happen then, but if he didn't do this part, then he knew there would be pain. The big bearded man had promised it, and he had been neither friendly nor jolly, but he had promised that he would know if Elric had been bad or good and that he better be good, for goodness' sake.

The Kallikantzaroi were annoying but neither violent nor aggressive. Elric found them needy and whiny. There was constant festive music on repeat, and the only food they offered him was Bleakest pudding, or Bleakest cake, to be washed down with mulled wine. His work-rate and quality had suffered, but the little green gnomes didn't seem to notice.

There came a hammering at the door, and the

gnomes froze. One of them reached out a gnarled talon of a hand and turned off the music.

"Oi! I could hear music. Open up in there!" someone shouted from the other side of the door. "I've got some toys I need to get rid of, figured this would be the place."

The gnomes shared a look of confusion until one of them—Elric couldn't tell them apart—looked in the tailor's direction.

"You," it said. "Answer the door and tell them to go away. If you do it wrong, we'll... we'll tell our boss."

As threats went, it was vague, but Elric's terror of the behemoth of a man who had shackled him to the table haunted him. He stood up, the sound of the chains around his right ankle far louder than they had ever seen before, and shuffled towards the door.

Elric grasped the handle and looked around for guidance. None was forthcoming. He took a breath and opened the door with his best fake smile. Standing in the rain was a man in a large coat and a hat.

"Can I help you?" Elric asked.

"Are you the tailor?"

"Um, yes?"

"Did you leave a bunch of torn-apart soft toys in a basement apartment on Penance Road?"

"Ah, yes. I was doing some work on them. Wait, why were you in there? Who are you?"

"I'm a private investigator, name's Blunt. Can I

come in?"

"No."

Blunt looked the tailor up and down. Elric knew he would appear panicked, uncomfortable, maybe even terrified. Part of him hoped it would be noticed, and part of him hoped it would be blamed on Bleakest Eve frivolities.

"Would you like to step out here?"

"I... can't."

"You can't, or you won't?"

"What difference would it make if I was out there or in here?"

A loud clattering sound came from behind Elric, and he winced.

"Who are you with?"

"Are you the police?"

"No."

"Then you should just leave."

"Are you suggesting that if I was the police, you'd like me to stick around?"

"That's not what I said."

"I'm going to come in, if that's okay with you."

"It isn't it okay with me—"

Blunt put his weight on his back foot and kicked the door, knocking the tailor over. The scrawny man in his week-old clothes, covered in red wine stains and crumbs, lay sprawled on the floor as Blunt stepped over the threshold.

Small green creatures with glowing yellow eyes backed away from the door, making a strange chattering noise. The inside of the factory looked like they had converted it into a mockery of a slaughterhouse. Dismembered soft toys were lying around the place with their 'skins' hanging from the ceiling.

"Well, what have we here?" Blunt said.

Elric watched as a small green figure stepped towards the newcomer. The detective glanced down at its feet and frowned.

The gnome pointed a finger at the man. "It looks like we've got one nosey person and twenty of us," it said.

"My name's Blunt," the man said, as he reached into his pocket and pulled out a cigar. After patting himself down, he found a lighter, and, after a few puffs, managed to light it, letting out a long plume of smoke.

He nodded. "Yup," he said before taking another pull. "Lots of you strange little green people hanging around where there are lots of toy costumes. You like a bit of dressing up, do you?"

They gnomes drew closer as it became more obvious that Blunt was on his own chattering like birds.

"I'd be a little less brave if I were you," Blunt said. "My partner is in the car just waiting to call in reinforcements."

The chattering sound came again. Elric new it was laughter. It looked like Blunt did too, as he smiled.

"Reinforcements come in the form of demons, just so you know. I imagine they'll be very pleased to find out that someone's been dressing up as them and giving them a... well, an even worse name."

Perched on the table to the right of the detective was a sewing machine. Elric watched as Blunt noticed a chain affixed to one table leg, and he followed the chain with his eyes back to the tailor's left ankle.

"Oh. So you're keeping prisoners now?"

The closest figure in green sneered. At least Elric thought it was a sneer. They were ugly to begin with. "You're not leaving here—"

"Woah, now," Blunt said, lifting a bottle out of his pocket. He held it in one hand and his cigar in the other. "I'm going to disagree with you there, my little green friend. You're all going to take a step back, or this place, and your pretty new suits, are all going up in flames."

Elric found himself crouching, cowering while the detective took a step forward and another drag on his cigar, exhaling as he walked towards the table with the sewing machine.

As Blunt neared the edge of the table, he placed the bottle on top of it. Then, with a smile at the nearest of the Kallikantzaroi, he lifted the table and kicked the chain away from the table leg.

The gnome-like creatures hissed, but Blunt snatched up the bottle and began walking backwards until he reached the doorway. Elric looked up from where he was crouched down on the floor and the detective looked back at him with a half smile.

"Everyone stay calm," Blunt said. "I'm going to take this fella with me, because it's Bleakest Eve and he really shouldn't be working, and we can all forget this ever happened."

"He's not finished," a different Kallikantzaros snarled.

Blunt waggled the bottle so that a little of the potent booze inside sloshed out onto the floor.

"I think he has. Up you get, fella." He placed the cigar between his lips and bent down to pull Elric up by the crook of his left arm.

"I can go?" Elric asked, confused.

"No," a gnome snapped.

"Of course he can. No prisoners here, are there? I mean, that might cause me to drop my cigar in shock," Blunt said, rolling the cigar between his teeth as he spoke. He hauled the Elric up and pushed him through the doorway, letting him fall into the street.

The detective remained inside, just out of the rain, and took another drag on his cigar.

"You're not supposed to inhale. It's supposed to be about the flavour, but to be honest with you, I can't tell the difference from one cigar to the next. I'd probably be better off with a cigarette," Blunt said between puffs. "But a cigar looks better, and I'm dead, so it isn't like it's going to do me any harm."

As he spoke, a car rolled towards where Elric cowered, its engine so loud it almost drowned out the sound of the rain and Blunt's voice.

"Anyway, what was I saying?"

"Leave, take the silly sewing man. We have what we need."

"Do you?" Blunt asked. As Elric leapt into the open car and slammed the rear passenger door shut. Blunt took one more long drag on the cigar. The end of it glowed bright orange.

Then he flicked it into the air, threw the bottle hard at the ground, and dived into the car as Sarah kicked the front passenger door open. It hit Blunt in the face, but despite his cry of agony, he tumbled into the passenger seat, and Sarah hit the accelerator.

They pulled away in first, for too long, before Sarah remembered to change gear.

Behind them, smoke billowed out of the factory doors.

So Much Worse

Sarah had been listening to the radio when she'd seen the tailor stumble out of the factory door. It was a small building with dark alleyways on either side in a neighbourhood where the boarded-up buildings were the ones that had been looked after.

Something about his wild-eyed look, and the way he was pulling a chain behind him, told Sarah he was the victim in whatever was going on. She'd told the man to get into the car and then watched until Blunt turned and launched himself at the vehicle, prompting her to kick the door open as flames burst into life inside the factory.

The aim had been to allow Blunt to land in the car and speed off to safety. That's how it works on television, at least. Instead, the door had collided with Blunt's face.

As the detective climbed into the passenger seat, she put the car in gear. The tyres squealed against the asphalt as she locked the wheels into a u-turn. Before Blunt could pull the door shut, they were already heading towards the canal.

"You could've killed me," Blunt said. He held a hand to his forehead, where there was a dent. For a mortal person, it might have resulted in a gushing head wound, but Blunt didn't bother with getting any more than the minimum synthetic life lubricant, blood.

"Sorry, I was trying to help," Sarah said. Her

hands gripped the steering wheel as she stared straight ahead.

Blunt rubbed his head and pulled his hat down to cover the mark. "Never mind. That should slow down those creepy gnome things."

"The Kallikantzaroi," Elric said from the back seat.

"Yeah, that's one name for them, evil little bastards."

"That's what they're called. Thank you for getting me out. How did you know I needed help?"

"You looked like you were about to collapse from exhaustion and you were scared, but not of me. As a rule, if someone opens the door to me and they're more scared of something behind them, there's something wrong."

"You're not that scary," Sarah said with a snort.

Blunt shook his head, ignoring her. "So, they kidnapped you to make toys into costumes so they could impersonate demons?"

"They've been at it for a few days. They go out in the suits and come back cackling. It's fun for them. They love the mischief, but they're not that evil. Just stupid and scared."

"Well, I'd feel more guilty about setting the place on fire if you weren't showing classic Stockholm syndrome."

"You're going to have to tell me what that is later," Sarah said.

"So why are they doing it?" Blunt asked.

The tailor grabbed the back of the chair and pulled himself forward. "Because he tells them to," he said. "He's terrifying."

"Who?"

"The big man."

"The big man? Hang on. Big bushy beard, belly like a bowl full of jelly, hands that look like they could twist off the top of a man's skull so he can drink what's inside?"

"Yes." Elric slapped Blunt's headrest. "That sounds just like him. Thinks he's Father Chri—"

"You bloody idiot, Blunt. Stupid, sodding..."

Sarah grimaced as she pushed the car through its gears. "I think you might want to hear what they're saying on the radio before you beat yourself up too much."

Detective Blunt snapped his seatbelt in place just as Sarah swung the car around a corner, lifting two wheels off the ground. When they were driving in a straight line again, Blunt leaned forward to turn the radio up.

"Why, is it going to cheer me up?"

"No, definitely not. It's just silly beating yourself up for whatever this is when it's so much worse. So, so much worse."

Blunt grunted and listened to what was being said over the radio.

"*—have released video footage claiming responsibility for what must now be assumed to be an assassination attempt on the Grim Reaper. We are speaking to officials about the correct terminology to* *use and are aware that assassination might not be appropriate. At this moment in time, we're unsure if this is a faction among the demons or if the demons behind this attack speak for all demons. Professor Gupta, as one of Gloomwood's foremost experts in criminal behaviour, do you believe this is the action of a rogue element among the demons?"*

The next voice that came over the radio was deep and confident. *"No. I'm not an expert on demons, but... they're demons. So, I have to assume they're inherently evil."*

"Some would say that's prejudice," the presenter interrupted.

"Yes. It's a fine line between prejudice, stereotyping, and using evidence to put a theory in place. Remember, I am an academic."

"So you can explain how you've concluded that demons are inherently evil and are probably all in this together?"

"Absolutely."

"Okay..."

"What, right now?"

"We are live."

"Oh, well... they're demons, aren't they?"

Blunt pulled his hat off and tossed it onto the dashboard with an exasperated sigh.

"Now people will claim that the expert has given an opinion on it, so they're following the science," he said as he wiped rainwater from his face. "It's just one bloke who claims to be an expert. Where's the other side of the discussion?

Where's the actual evidence? Where's the demon spokesperson? This is going to be a disaster."

"It's a setup," Sarah said.

"Of course it's a bloody setup. Do I look like an idiot to you?"

Sarah risked a look in Blunt's direction. The glow of streetlights flashing through the rain into the car didn't help visibility, but she took in the detective in one glance. Slumped in the passenger seat. Head bowed as he checked his pockets once again for a cigar.

"I'd rather not answer. I'm going to check on Morgarth and the others. I need to make sure they know what's going on and get them ready for what comes next."

"Who is Morgarth?" Elric asked from the back seat.

"She's the leader of the demon horde."

"Um, is there any chance I could go… somewhere else?"

"I'll drop you at Aunt Agnes'. It's on the way."

"What did you mean by what comes next?" Blunt asked.

"History repeats itself."

"That's fun and cryptic. Forgive me for not having read up on my Gloomwood history too much."

"It's not just Gloomwood. Happens to mortals too. People are going to attack the demons."

Blunt nodded. "I need to find the decorations."

"The decorations?"

"Whoever is doing this is trying to pin everything on the demons, but where are the bloody decorations? It's like someone is waiting for some kind of big fanfare, some kind of... oh crap..."

Blunt's voice trailed off as he picked up the next news item on the radio.

"We're hearing reports of an attack on the demons earlier today from a group of people claiming to be exorcists. Our sources suggest these exorcists came from a gathering at a public house called the Rusty Guillotine. We called the Guillotine for comment. Their landlord suggested we seek Augustan Blunt as a prominent figure who stands against demonic terrorism. Detective Blunt, our listeners will remember, was instrumental in two high-profile cases in the last twelve months, one of which involved demons. It looks like people might follow his rallying call after this incident."

"Rallying call?" Blunt said. "Did they just suggest I'm the leader of some anti-demon movement? It's been two minutes since I was there."

"It sounds like that. Wait, there's more..."

"Hello, caller, you're live on Ether ever after. I understand you spoke to Augustan Blunt earlier today?"

"Uh, hello, long-time listener, first-time caller. Yes, he came to our house today asking questions. Disturbing people on Bleakest Eve, but I think it was about demons. He said he was working, trying to protect people."

"So you think he knew about the terrorist

demons?"

"I think he was trying to stop them. I wasn't very nice to him, but with everyone being so anti-anti-demon, I suppose we needed someone who wasn't afraid to do the right thing."

"So you think he's a hero?"

"Well… I guess he is. He was fighting the demons when we all wanted to say they were fine—"

Blunt reached out and turned off the radio. He let out a groan. "That little bastard who called me a tosser. Right, drop me off at the fire."

"That's the opposite—"

"You said it's a stitch-up, and now I'm being made to look like some kind of anti-demon exorcist. Here I am running around the city asking about demons—"

"—with people saying you were trying to stop something like this happening."

"Exactly."

"It doesn't make sense. You can just deny it. Tell them what's really going on."

"Confidentiality."

"Who am I going to tell?"

"It's not you I'm talking about. Client confidentiality. It's Panderpenny's agency, and she's a mediator. A lawyer. So there are contracts and… I can't tell people I'm looking for things for you-know-who," Blunt said with a pointed look over his shoulder. "I shouldn't have told you. If it goes public, well, Ursula's going to use every letter after her name to make sure I take the blame."

Prepare to March

Sarah could hear the noise from inside the warehouse before she stepped through the smashed shutters. In one corner, the remaining members of the drunken attack on the building were in varying states of extreme distress. All of them were covering their ears, many in the fetal position, sobbing.

She glanced around and couldn't help a grimace slipping across her face. For a moment, she flickered like a neon light, her entire body snapping in and out of phase with reality. If it got out that they had tortured the exorcists, it wouldn't help what was coming.

In the middle of the room, an argument was taking place.

"Well, they aren't here, are they?" a furry toucan was shouting in full demonic voice.

Sarah, despite her condition, was not immune to the effects of the demonic voices, and she felt a wave of nausea roll over her as she drew closer.

Something about flickering provided her with a kind of resilience to the worst effects, but as she got closer to the clamouring voices, she experienced dread, guilt, regret, and remorse for things she had shaken off long ago. The flickering worsened, and she held her hands up in front of her face, watching them appear and disappear.

"Please stop," she said, but the demons couldn't hear her over their bickering. "Stop!" she shouted, and though many ignored her, Morgarth spotted her approaching.

The little blue dinosaur gestured at her to cover her ears, then she shouted.

"SILENCE!"

Despite doing her best to defend against the power of the demon's voice, Sarah knelt on the ground. She pitched forward for a moment and tried to stop herself from retching. She failed.

After Morgarth's exclamation, the demons' argument fell to a low hubbub and then stopped.

"Look at what you've done!" Morgarth waved a hand towards Sarah, then to the figures in the room's corner.

"They're going to come for us," the toucan said.

"They might. If they do, we will remind them we are demons, and if we want to harm them, we can be far more imaginative than a simple fire." Morgarth stared at the toucan until it lowered its head. "Those men need to leave, and we need to have a sensible, reasonable discussion about our next step. First, though, we will make tea."

Sarah struggled to her feet while Morgarth was talking and looked at the demons. She'd seen the same look on the faces of men, women, and children, even gods and nightmares, hopes and dreams. It was the face of someone dealing with rejection, with hopelessness, with the dawning realisation that they were in the hands of forces they couldn't control.

"Tea?" asked a bear wearing a red and white dress.

"Yes," Morgarth said. "Everything's better with a cup of tea, isn't it, Miss Von Faber?"

"You're absolutely right, Morgarth."

"We didn't do it, Miss. Nobody here was involved," the toucan said.

Sarah nodded. "I didn't think you did it."

"It must have been one of the ones who left," the toucan said. "Walking out on us and then doing this. Traitors. I bet it was Jarg, or maybe Bacter… Or Trem. She just left. She was always a conniving—"

"This isn't helpful, Gozar," Morgarth said. "Why don't you help me make some tea?"

"Some little green gnomes have been impersonating you," Sarah said, "and they work for someone who thinks he's something that mortal children believe in."

Morgarth, and a room full of demons, stared at Sarah Von Faber, who flickered, then vanished… except for her shoes.

Wet Blanket

"—It looks like the Grim Reaper and Ralph Mortimer have escaped from the burning building unscathed!" Leighton Hughes pronounced. "Mister Mortimer, the third assistant to the Manager of the Office of the Dead, looks a little shaken but is here to speak to us. We're pleased to see you're safe, Mister Mortimer. Can you tell us what happened?"

"Um, yes, the building caught fire."

"Do you know what caused the fire?"

"It appears to have come from outside the building, so I'm afraid not."

"What happened in the building?"

"Well, we saw a fire… and then we left."

"It sounds quite stressful. What were you feeling when you noticed the fire?"

"Well, I was holding a mug, so… I was feeling dishwasher-safe ceramic."

"I meant emotionally?"

"Oh, it wasn't a special mug."

Behind the camera, Dennis the fly waved two of its hands, then said, in a Scouse accent, "They've cut away. Left us at 'dishwasher-safe'."

Leighton's hand holding the microphone dropped to one side. "What else could they have cut to? This is literally the biggest—"

"Someone's claiming responsibility," the fly said.

Ralph Mortimer, who had been backing away,

hoping to escape the limelight, paused.

"Who?"

"You can watch it in the back of the van," Dennis said, "with… um, him."

The three of them hurried around to the back of the news van. Inside, sitting on top of a very expensive piece of recording equipment and struggling to stop banging his head against the roof of the van, was the Grim Reaper.

The de facto ruler of Gloomwood was watching a small colour screen of the live broadcast from the news studio. He looked up as the reporter, cameraman, and his erstwhile chaperone arrived. The rain was getting heavier.

"Mortimer. Very well done," Grim said. "Miss Hughes, unlike Mortimer, I was feeling a paperback novel, if it's of interest. According to your colleagues, demons have claimed responsibility for setting fire to the shed thing."

"You mean the temporary building?" Mortimer asked.

"You say tomato. It seems quite unlikely to me that demons would do this. Nevertheless, it seems all hell is about to break loose."

The three standing outside the van, soaked through and nervous, nodded solemnly.

"I said, 'all hell is about to break loose,'" Grim said. "It's funny because they're demons and… I suppose it's not really the time for jokes. Wait, don't quote me on that, Miss Hughes. There's never a bad time for jokes."

"Technically—"

"Technically, your very existence depends upon me. Have any of you seen Detective Blunt?"

"Blunt?" Dennis asked. "You mean that fascist who always has his fingers in the near end of the afterlife?"

"Yes," Grim said. "That's who I mean."

"Do you think he's responsible for this?"

Mortimer, Leighton, and even the Grim Reaper laughed. Well, the Grim Reaper's shoulders moved up and down as he projected an aura of merriment.

"Can you imagine?" Leighton said, still laughing.

"Blunt? Plan something?" Mortimer added.

A loud cough came from behind the fly, Leighton, and Mortimer.

"Ah," the Grim Reaper said. "We were all just making fun of you."

Blunt's hat poured water onto his right shoulder like a miniature gutter. He eyed Mortimer, Leighton, and Dennis standing in the rain.

"You're all hilarious. Let's all laugh at Blunt, but you're still going to want me to clean up this mess, aren't you?"

"Calm down, Blunt," Leighton said.

"Yes, detective," the Grim Reaper said. "After all, they thought they were laughing at you behind your back."

"That doesn't actually help, your, ah, lordship," Mortimer said.

"No? But he wasn't supposed to hear you? If you wanted to upset him, you'd have said it to his face. So there was no intent to be cruel. It was just a joke at his expense, in his absence. Isn't that preferable to being mocked to your face, detective?"

Blunt shrugged. "You're right. It's preferable to be punched in the face by accident than on purpose."

"See?" Grim said. "So we're all friends. Right, will you clean up this mess now?"

"What?" Blunt said.

"That *is* why you're here, isn't it? Or are you actually leading the fight against five hundred stuffed animals?"

"No. Obviously I'm not… Wait, you were expecting me?"

"One day, I'll explain why you're always stuck in the middle of these things, detective. It will give you a chuckle, I'm sure."

"It's not a coincidence?"

"Oh, you already know? Well, that's disappointing."

"So, what's the plan?" Leighton asked.

"We need to find some demons."

"So you *are* a demon hunter?" Dennis the fly said.

On the Fly

"Dennis, for the last bloody time, just play the video," Blunt said to the cameraman.

"Fine, but it's not called a video," the fly said.

"I swear to God—"

"Blasphemy," Dennis said as he turned a cog on a mechanical device.

"—I will swat you—"

"Offensive."

"—with a giant rolled-up newspaper."

The fly stood up, leaning forward a little in the confines of the van, and put two of his four arms on his hips.

"Extremely offensive. Why do you expect people to help you when you speak to them like this?"

"That's a reasonable point," Blunt said. "Now, are you gonna press play?"

"You don't press play—"

"You know what I mean. You call me offensive, but you are deliberately winding me up. You understand exactly what I mean, and you're just trying to make out that you're some kind of technological guru because I don't know the right words. The reason I'm being offensive is because you're being a smug bug about it."

Dennis folded his upper pair of arms and hit the 'go' button with his lower left hand.

Wavy lines coalesced into an image on a

bubble-screen monitor hanging from a metal bar on the ceiling. On the screen, sitting behind a desk, was a soft toy. It was staring into the lens of a camera.

"Citizens of Gloomwood," it said. Its mouth flapped open and closed, not quite in sync with the words. "By now, you will have witnessed our attack upon the leadership of your failed afterlife state. We are sending this as a warning. Bow down to the demons, or we shall unleash the true terror of Hell upon you. We shall deliver never-ending eternal torment, the likes of which you have never seen. Without the iron hand of Beelzebub to control us, we will be free to pursue all means to exact righteous retribution for your sins. Submit to our position as your new rulers, and we will allow you to remain in peace. The choice is yours."

The recording switched to a logo of a horned circle surrounded by flame before it ended.

"Are you kidding?" Blunt said.

"What?" Dennis asked.

"I said show me the video of the demons taking responsibility. Not, show me a terrible impression of a demon talking rubbish. Have people started taking the piss already? Doesn't 'too soon' apply in Gloomwood?"

"What are you talking about?" Leighton asked. She was leaning against the corner of the van.

"What he's saying is that wasn't a demon," said Grim, still perched on a piece of recording equipment.

"It's a sodding puppet," Blunt said. "And not

even a very good one. That's really what they sent? That was a recording of someone with their hand up the backside of a toy. Which, in the mortal realm, was quite a popular pastime but now looks… disturbing."

"Like a corpse marionette," Leighton said as she scribbled on her notepad.

"What are you doing?"

"Taking notes for the story. Don't you take notes for your investigations?"

Blunt let out a huffing noise, then pulled out his own notepad. He scribbled down the words *puppet*, *demonising demons*, and *misdirection*. Then he sighed. In his experience, it was always about misdirection.

"We've got green gnomes impersonating demons, and that was obviously a puppet, and the public is lapping it up. Where are we not looking?"

The door to the van opened. Outside, Ralph Mortimer was standing with Chief Sowercat and four constables.

"We're ready," the bureaucrat said.

"Well," Grim said from the far end of the van. "Let's get this party on the road."

Blunt groaned.

"Is that not the phrase?" Grim asked.

"Yes, but it's… Never mind. Right, Leighton, you're with me. Dennis, buzz off."

"Offensive," Leighton and Dennis said.

Cabin

The torched cabin made ominous creaking sounds as Blunt took careful steps across the floor. He froze as the boards beneath him let out a groan. Something snapped beneath his feet, and he waited for a moment before moving on, wincing with every step.

"What are you looking for?" Leighton asked.

"I don't bloody know. Evidence that it wasn't demons?"

"What does that look like?"

Leighton was standing in the doorway, her notepad in one hand and a pencil in the other, watching Blunt inch towards the far corner of what the fire had left of the cabin.

"The Grim Reaper asked if you could see if he'd left a book in here—"

"I'm not hunting for a bloody paperback book in the remains of a fire. Especially not when I might fall through the floor at any minute. There are probably steel rods just waiting to impale me underneath."

"Waiting?"

"It's a turn of phrase," Blunt said. He reached as far as he was comfortable walking and peered down into a pit of burnt remains. Beneath the cabin, it was dark, wet, and reeked of burning plastic. "There's nothing here."

"Mortimer said the fire came from under the

floor in the far corner. That's where the demons were running from."

Blunt turned, took his hat off his head, and used the forearm of his sleeve to wipe his forehead. It left a sooty smear behind.

"Yes, Leighton, I know what Mortimer said. I was there as well. They were clearly more of those green things dressed up as demons. Or toys. It's confusing. Now, would you like me to levitate over to the far corner, or shall I reveal I have the abilities of a spider and just walk across the wall?"

"Sorry, just trying to help. I wrote it down," she said, tapping her pencil against her notebook.

"I wrote it down too. Writing stuff down isn't difficult, Leighton. Stop acting like it's some kind of virtue."

The reporter turned to look behind her, where a small crowd had gathered outside. "What are you looking at?" she shouted. "You can watch it all on the news later!"

Blunt cautiously walked back towards her. "Not very Bleakest-spirited of you."

"I've been doing fluff pieces about Bleakest Eve since first thing this morning. Filming people preparing for the festivities. My Bleakest Day spirit has long since been summoned back across the mortal veil."

"How long before the main event?"

"Well, this delayed it, so probably an hour. Maybe two?"

"And I've still got three missing demons and

an arson attempt to deal with."

"Misdirection?"

"I know it's misdirection. Something's going on elsewhere. I said that before. If you're only here to quote back what I'm saying, why are you here at all?"

"You asked me to come. Why did you ask me?"

Blunt shrugged and mumbled something she couldn't quite hear.

"What?"

"Because you're not the worst investigator I've met since I died. Happy?"

Leighton smiled. "Yes. So no clues?"

"Nothing up here. Underneath were some footprints and a button placed right next to where the fire would begin."

Leighton put her notebook away. "You sound unsurprised."

"You sound unsurprised," Blunt said in a poor imitation of Leighton.

"Well, that's mature."

"It's too obvious. A bunch of demons put up signs, caused trouble, and then set fire to the cabin? They're malicious dark creatures who entrap humans through smoke and mirrors, not idiots."

"Demons?"

"No, tooth-bloody-fairies—" Blunt said as his foot fell through the floor. "Sonofabitch," he shouted as he pulled it out, tearing the bottom of his right trouser leg.

The rip revealed a black sock with embroidered decorations and a message that said,

'Hands off my baubles'.

Leighton couldn't take her eyes off the sock.

"They were a present," Blunt said. "And the only clean pair I had."

"They're… cute."

Blunt made a growling noise as Leighton ducked to the side to let him step out of the cabin.

"They set it up so it looked like I was hunting demons. Then, by coincidence, this crap attempt at an assassination takes place, and a puppet claims responsibility. Come on, Leighton, you're a journalist. What do we look for?"

"The heart of the story?"

"Piss off. We look for the money. Who's benefiting from all of this?"

Leighton shrugged. "Someone who wants everyone to hate the demons? That's loads of people, though. Everyone hates them. Maybe the exorcists, or the developers who wanted the warehouse that the Grim Reaper put them in, who are blatantly funding the exorcists."

"Argh! Of course. The demons will have to leave the building because everyone knows where they are. Otherwise, drunken idiots will go down there demanding furry toy heads on sticks. So they leave, and the building will be 'accidentally' set on fire."

"That's a bit of a stretch—"

"Would you stay where everyone knew you were if the entire city wanted your head on a stick?"

"You're head-on-a-stick obsessed."

GNOME SWEET GNOME

The toy suits had burned up in the fire faster than the Kallikantzaroi had expected.

"That was dangerous," one of them said. The others, six of them, looked at their feet, then away.

Eventually, one of them broke the silence. "Funny though."

Their snickering cleared the air.

Nobody had paid any attention to the little gnomes as they walked through the crowd away from the fire. All eyes had been on the perilous situation that the ruler of the city had found himself in and where the demons had disappeared.

Short green gnomes with glowing yellow eyes were simply different, not unusual. The melting pot of Gloomwood society contained many similar creatures, pixies and brownies, tree gods and creatures of darkness. In relative terms, the Kallikantzaroi didn't really stand out as exceptional.

They walked in a line snaking through the crowd towards the stage.

"Next step?" the last gnome asked. They

passed the question forward in a whisper. "Next step, next step, next step, next step, next step?"

"Get a saw for the tree," the lead gnome said over his shoulder.

"Saw for the tree... saw forth tree... south forntree... sew fourteen... so fourteenth... snow fort bee."

"What? Do we build one?"

With quick hops they ascended the stone steps leading to the rear of the tree. They slipped beneath the scaffolding platform, covered in black fabric, that the tree was standing upon. The back of it, which faced towards the Office of the Dead, had not been decorated to quite the same standard as the side facing the crowd.

To the side of the tree was the small stage for the Grim Reaper's speech. Further to one side, the remains of the temporary building continued to smoulder.

Beneath the platform, where they had hidden it before suiting up to implicate the demons in their assassination attempt, was a large, two-handled saw.

Save the Horde

Blunt crunched the gears in Ralph Mortimer's car, and the Grim Reaper's chaperone, standing outside the vehicle on the driver's side, winced.

"Sorry, Mortimer," Blunt shouted out the window. "Your clutch is a little"—Blunt grimaced as the gear stick juddered in his hand and the car protested, squealing, as he put it in reverse—"sticky."

Mortimer tried to say something, but the car was already moving.

In the passenger seat, Leighton was scribbling notes down on her pad. "So where are we going?"

"To the warehouse the demons were sleeping in."

"Because you think they're going to be attacked?"

Blunt nodded. "Well, they're accused of being traitors to the entire city. That announcement has gone out on every channel possible. We need to tell them to get out of there."

"They won't have worked it out?"

Blunt threw the car into a turn too quickly. The driver's side wheels lifted from the road for a moment and slammed back down, bouncing the detective and reporter around inside.

"Of course they will. Sarah is with them as well."

"So what's the rush?"

"They might choose to stand and fight, which is exactly what the bastards will want them to do."

Leighton gave up trying to write as Blunt made another sudden turn, hammering the horn, and her pen tore through several pages of her notebook.

"And you're going to stop this attack?"

"No, I'm not a bloody superhero. I'm going to get Sarah out and then tell them to run, to get their furry little backsides out of there and hide."

She put the notepad back into her coat pocket and straightened out her hat. "You're going to convince them to run?"

"Obviously."

"Will it work?"

"Probably not, but I can't just leave them to it, can I?"

Leighton shrugged. "I couldn't, but you don't even like them."

"Oh, this again?" Blunt said as he swerved between vehicles. "I don't like anybody, Leighton. In case you hadn't noticed, this place isn't filled with the moral and upstanding members of the dead. They all got to go upstairs."

"It's not Hell either—"

"Yeah, yeah, I've heard that one before. I don't mean to point out the obvious, but not going to Hell doesn't make anybody a saint."

"Not going to Heaven doesn't make everyone a sinner."

"We're all sinners, Leighton."

"You're saying Gloomwood is for the damned?"

"No. Well, yes. The Grim Reaper pretty much told me we're all grey, morally grey. We were weighed up, and neither side wanted us. Heaven, Hell, whatever else there is, nobody wanted us, so we're not the good guys. The demons, well, Hell didn't want them either." Blunt took his eyes off the road to fix her with a stare. "But none of us are the good guys."

"Watch the road," Leighton said. "I see it differently."

"You can't see it differently. It's fact. It's what Death himself said."

"Yes," she said, stopping another rant. "But he didn't say why, and he didn't say it was over. Maybe we're still being judged."

"Well, if that's the case, we're all completely buggered."

"I suppose I'm just surprised you're worried about the demons."

"We're going to get Sarah. Maybe we'll help the demons, although"—Blunt grinned—"it's not them I'm worried about, Leighton. It's the rest of us."

Thugs

"Eric," said a man in a builder's hat.

"What?" asked Eric, who was also wearing a builder's hat.

"Do you think they'll eat us?"

Eric shook his head. "Don't think they can. I mean, they're all toys now, right? Toys don't have digestive systems. They're all fluffy as well."

They were standing side by side in a row of people dressed in yellow hats and overalls. The hats offered no protection against any kind of injury as they'd all come from a novelty costume store, but they'd been told to wear them. Eric and his friends weren't builders; they were thugs.

Thuggery is a longstanding Gloomwoodian profession, so much so that there were now courses available for those looking to pursue a career in thuggery. Eric had only recently completed his level 4 advanced thuggery qualification and was proud to have been invited into the thuggery training institute as an entry-level instructor.

Of course, that was just a daytime thing. He still had to work nights like all the other thugs, but he had high hopes and was working on developing a home thuggery training course for entry-level thugs.

"Eric," the man beside him said. He was much more junior in the thug world, and Eric had already needed to help him with his technique for slapping a cudgel menacingly into one palm. Being menacing is trickier than people think.

"What is it, Darren?"

"Doesn't it seem strange that they booked us for this gig before that thing happened with the Grim Reaper?"

"No, Darren. It does not. As a thug, it's important that we always act professionally and that we are ready for anything. That fire is a fortunate coincidence for us. Nothing better than having a legitimate reason for carrying out acts of violence. I think it's a bit of a Bleakest Eve miracle. Personally, it's nice to be on the side of the right."

"Course," Darren said. "I mean, thugging for the good of the people—"

"It's always for the good of the people," Eric said with a shake of his head. "You're a person, I'm a person, and we do things to get paid, ergo, everything we do is for the good of the people. We're the people."

"What about the people who we hurt?"

"Oh no, they're not the people, they're idiots."

"Oh," Darren said. "That's a relief."

Behind them, industrial lights were turned on and engines thrummed to life. The roar of mechanised behemoths filled the air as the full might of the crew was revealed. A pair of excavators flanked a bulldozer, and behind them waited a pair of large tipper trucks.

"Right then," Eric said, slapping a cricket bat into his gloved hand.

"Oh, nicely done. That was an intimidating thwack."

"It's all about the receiving palm, Darren. Open, slightly curled, and with a good connection between the fingers—"

A squeal of tyres interrupted their conversation as a car, an old estate hearse, bounced over a curb and came hurtling towards them. It spun wildly as it drew nearer.

"Run!" Eric shouted.

But the realisation came too late. The back end of the car, spinning through a hand-brake turn, hit a level 2 thug, sending him flying through the air to be impaled upon the upraised bucket edge of one excavator.

Detective Blunt stepped out of the car, which had finished facing the now scattered and confused line of men, and held onto the driver's door of Ralph Mortimer's car..

"Now, what's all this then?" Blunt barked.

A Blunt Arrival

Eric eyed the man behind the car door. All the lights made it difficult to see anything more than a silhouette, though it looked like there was someone in the passenger seat as well.

The fake builder's hat now felt ridiculous on his head and he looked around him, waiting for someone to respond, but nobody did.

Behind him, making the occasional plea for help, hung a man in overalls on the end of one excavator, part of it protruding from his stomach.

"Can somebody get me down? This is quite painful."

In the vehicles were thugs who also had construction experience, which was less common than people realised. The row of thugs standing in front of him were mainly amateurs, hobbyists, or those working through the ranks. For the first time that evening, Eric wished he hadn't achieved his level 4 qualification.

"Um," he said, his mouth drying up. "We don't seem to have a stooge around."

"What?" the man by the car shouted. "You need to speak up."

"We haven't got a stooge to do the talking bit."

"What are you on about?"

"I'm a level 4 thug, but we're only supposed to deliver one-liners. What you're looking for, in this kind of situation, is a stooge, or our employer."

"Eh? Are you telling me there's a henchmen hierarchy?"

"We don't use that word," Eric shouted back. "It's not inclusive. A thug can be a man, woman, child, god, demon, anything you want. It's a good career choice, no matter what your background is."

The man ducked his head back into the vehicle. While Eric couldn't hear what was being said, he got the impression that it involved a lot of swearing. The man hit his head against the top edge of the doorframe as he ducked out of the car again, knocking off his hat. It took a moment for him to find the hat and stand up straight again.

"Right. Who's in charge?" he shouted.

There was the sound of shuffling and quiet coughs as everyone around Eric looked away from him. He rolled his eyes.

"We had a stooge, a little green bloke with a lisp, but he hasn't turned up yet. So, strictly speaking, I'm the most senior thug, but you're not listening. I'm not qualified to enter a discussion with a third party. You need a stooge or someone from our employers. That's how it works. There're rules to follow."

"What's the difference between a thug and a stooge?"

"What's the difference?" Eric said. He looked around him, shaking his head. "Honestly, that's just plain ignorant. Do you know how hard thugs work? To compare us with a stooge... well, it's an insult. A stooge is just a mouthpiece, a talker. They wouldn't know an honest day's work if it hit them with a crowbar. A thug is a highly skilled physical profession, but a stooge, well, anyone who can talk can be a stooge."

There was a cough from behind Eric.

"Though you can get stooge qualifications too, I actually—"

"Not now, Barbara," Eric snapped.

"Look." The figure slammed the car door and started walking towards Eric. "If you're saying you can't talk about things, that's fine. I'll just wait, parked here, until you get someone who can."

A murmur went up and down the line of bludgeon-wielding thugs.

Eric smiled. "That's the thing, though. Because we're not contracted to negotiate, or do the whole overarching villain speech reveal, or discuss terms, or any of that, it means we don't have to wait and listen either. I mean, one of the first things you learn in thuggery 101—that's the first class in level-one thuggery—is that thugs don't consider consequences."

The man stopped walking several feet away from Eric, well out of the reach of the weapons held by the row of thugs before him.

"So, no consequences? But you're all still standing there while I've parked my car in the way?"

"You're right," Eric said. "Appreciate the reminder. Okay, thugs, beat the crap out of this fella, then we'll move the car and demolish the building. Same plan."

He looked around and nodded. The thugs began walking towards the car while Eric, and the two thugs on either side of him, looked at Blunt.

"So, anything in particular you'd like us not to break? I mean, we avoid the face. It's just courtesy. Ah, before we get started, here's my card."

He reached for his 'utility belt' and clicked a button, causing a business card holder to pop open, from which he withdrew a business card. He held it out for the man to take.

"Um, thanks?" the man said, stepping forward to grab it before taking an extra step back.

"No problem. Any time you need a thug, big or small, just give us a call."

"Okay."

"Okay," Eric said with a nod. "Fists up then. Nobody likes to hit someone who's unprepared."

"Hang on," a figure next to Eric said. They looked like they was made of stone.

"What is it now?" Eric snapped.

"Isn't that Augustan Blunt?"

"Yes," the man said, removing his hat. "It is. Look, I know the pabies and I have a history, but—"

"I'm not a pabie," Eric said, holding up his hands, the cricket bat raised in his right. "My designation as a pre-adolescent-bodied individual is irrelevant while I'm at work. We don't do that here. We're thugs, nothing else."

"Oh, right."

"Now, there's clearly been some confusion here. Leave the car alone!" Eric shouted to the group approaching the car. "It's Detective Blunt."

"I don't understand."

"Honestly, my bad. This is exactly why we need good stooges," the boy said with a sigh. "You probably want to go in and arrest a few of the demons before we knock down the building. I mean, we're here on business, but you're a proper demon-hating fascist type."

"Hang on—"

"Oh, no judging here. If I haven't been clear enough already, the number one rule in thuggery is being non-judgemental, open-minded, and inclusive."

"I got that, thanks," Blunt said. "To be clear, you're being non-judgemental about my apparent… um… hatred of demons?"

"Exactly."

"So, I can go in the building?"

"Yup. Need any backup? We're going in soon anyway."

"No, thanks," Blunt said, placing his hat back on his head before tipping it at the boy before marching towards the building.

"See that, Darren?" Eric said. "That's someone who would make an outstanding thug. He's got natural thuggishness written all over him."

Dead Ready

The Grim Reaper was sitting in the back of the television van, reading a paperback book he normally kept sequestered somewhere in his robes.

Suddenly, he closed the book with a snap and looked up. Leaning against the closed van doors, still dripping from the rain, was Ralph Mortimer.

"What's wrong?" Mortimer asked.

"I have a bad feeling."

"A bad feeling?"

The Grim Reaper stood, hit his head on the ceiling, muttered phrases that only an ancient being who traverses time and space really understood, and stooped.

"We have to begin the ceremony."

"But it's been delayed because of the fire," Mortimer said.

"At the expense of seeming overly dramatic, Death waits for no one."

"But you're the one who said we had to delay it."

"Apparently, I don't even wait for me."

"So Death… doesn't wait for Death?"

"…"

"Sir?"

"How about, 'Death always runs on time?'"

"Shouldn't we go?"

"Yes, we should," Grim said. With a balled-up skeletal fist, he reached up and rapped on the panel that separated the driver's cabin from the rear of the van.

A muffled voice answered, "Yeah?"

"Time to go."

"Okay, but there's a crowd and they're getting rowdy. I can get you closer to the stage, but it's going to be slow."

The engine thrummed into life, and Grim and Mortimer braced themselves.

"Are you ready?" Mortimer asked.

"I'm ready, are you?" Grim asked.

"Um, yes, but I'm not doing anything."

"Oh… right."

Empty Nest

Blunt ducked through the shattered shutters and peered into the warehouse. There was a single lightbulb flickering on the other side of the vast space. The lorry from the earlier attack still blocked the entrance.

He squeezed down one side of it, his back pressed against the grinning face of the cartoon cannibal chicken as it gorged on its own family in a single-shot horror story for the ages. The former occupants of the lorry must have been removed, presumably in wheelbarrows.

A large abandoned warehouse, complete with toy paraphernalia inhabited by demons, was not where Blunt wanted to be on the darkest night of the Gloomwood year. He gritted his teeth while patting down his coat. A cigar wasn't just deserved right now, it was required. Its glow would warm the unsettling cold that was sinking into his bones.

Then, echoing around the warehouse, came a sound that froze him to the spot. The only thing preventing him from sprinting back out of the door was the terror of moving and drawing attention to himself.

Bleakest day,
Darkest night,
Shadows sleep,
No sky this night,

Rest in peace,
Give up the fight
Just once a year,
all will be right,
To one and all,
Death shines a light.

"Who's there?" Blunt said when the song ended and he had gathered enough of his senses to speak.

Something rustled to his right, and he turned. He wished for more light as he peered into the darkness.

"I'm not here to hurt anyone. I'm Detective Blunt. I was here earlier today. Come on, you all know who I am."

Laughter came out of the darkness.

"Don't you know who I am?" The voice echoed around the empty warehouse. "Don't you know... who I am?"

"That isn't what I said."

"That isn't what I said," said an unfamiliar voice, a growl that made Blunt's hair stand on end.

"Alright, smart arse, enough of this," Blunt said as he strode into the middle of the warehouse, kicking the occasional blanket, mislaid piece of toy clothing, or assorted junk out of the way until he was standing beneath the lonely lightbulb. "Right, well, the place is empty except for some creepy little weirdo who isn't brave enough to come out and face me."

"Hear us," the growl came again.

Blunt balled his fists and tried to shake the panic that was taking hold of him.

"Hear us," came another voice, wheedling but filled with menace.

The detective stumbled on something and fell, catching himself on all fours.

"Hear us." The voice of the singer came from close by.

He turned his head and forced himself to move.

"Enough of the voices. If you were all here, you might win, but none of you are Morgarth. How long do you think your voices are going to keep you safe when there's a small army of thugs outside?"

From out of the shadows, walking on four tentacles while four more wielded knives, came a furry octopus.

"Jargle?" Blunt said. "You came back?"

"Where are our brethren?" the octopus asked as it approached.

Blunt shifted himself to a sitting position, raising his hands, palms open, in the demon's direction. "I was about to ask you the same thing."

"You hate us."

The voice came from Blunt's left. An elephant approached, a hatchet grasped in its trunk.

"Phil? You're here as well? I don't hate you. Take a minute to breathe, or whatever it is you do. Did you see the sock puppet? It didn't even have glowing eyes. Someone's lying about you. There are a load of gnomes who have been dressing up like you. What makes you think they're not lying about me? Look at this, I came here on my own to help you all," Blunt said. He was still sitting on the ground as he turned his head from one demon to the other. "Who else is here?"

"I am," came an ominous voice, "and I assure you, Detective Blunt, Morgarth has nothing on me."

Stoogeless

Even without a stooge to demand they 'attack', 'show 'em who they're messing with,' 'teach them a lesson', or any of the other fifty-seven specified directions in the thug handbook, there was only so long they could wait without taking action.

"What are we going to do?" rumbled a voice behind Eric.

"Why are you asking me?"

"Um…" The voice grew a little softer. It belonged to someone who closely resembled a brick wall. They weren't made of stone or bricks; it was more something to do with the way they moved. It was difficult to recruit people with exceptional bodies to be henchmen. They often took offence when asked. "You're in charge. I think."

"What?" Eric looked around as panic took hold. "I don't want to be in charge. Being in charge is not what a thug does. Denial of responsibility is crucial. It's in the mantra."

"It wasn't me, guv," a chorus of voices said. "I was just doing what I was told. They started it. I need this job and thought I would be fired if I didn't do it. Please, sir, I had no reason to believe there was anything untoward happening. I was only defending myself."

Eric nodded. "See?"

"Yeah, but…" the wall said.

"Fine." Eric shrugged. He cleared his throat, looked into the distance, then shouted towards the warehouse.

"I believe our bosses would expect us to go into the building to ensure it is safe. We are just doing what our employers would expect us to do. It is a matter of health and safety."

The thugs all took a step forward, brandishing their weapons of choice.

Thugs frowned upon guns and knives. Thugs, so the rules went, are about hand-to-hand contact for the up close and personal individual attention the discerning client expects. Guns are for amateurs. They're also quite ineffective against the dead. Instead, thugs formed two camps on armaments: the improvisers and the purpose-made.

Eric was a firm believer in the improvised weapon camp, but Barbara, the brick wall-like woman who had labelled Eric their leader, favoured the more modern variety. Her knuckledusters, brass and polished to a shine, were custom-made for her slab-like fists. As she stepped beside him, Eric looked at her hand and let out a 'tut'.

"Don't pretend you haven't modified your cricket bat for thugging," Barbara retorted. "I know a reinforced bat when I see one."

"It's not reinforced," Eric snapped. "I've just repaired it a few times."

"Repaired it with a metal rod through the handle right up to the end?"

Eric shook his head. "It's a classic everyday

object."

They walked towards the building. Their swagger pronounced a resounding message stating they were confident, prepared for action, or, as the guide termed it, 'a proper Billy Big Bollocks'. Which, now that Eric thought about it, was unnecessarily masculine. He'd have to check with the admin team if they'd had the full sensitivity check on that one. It was probably just a throwback to an older time. Eric was hot on rectifying inconsistent messaging. Thuggery was well-known for stamping down on that kind of thing, and Eric loved a good stamping, especially if something snapped.

As they approached the large warehouse doors, which looked like a van had driven into them, Eric considered his position. Could he move into stooging? Very few stooges had experience as a thug. He'd be very well qualified. Stooges were struggling in terms of enrollment numbers, and he knew he held the respect of most thugs.

He stopped in his tracks, and the others did the same. They were working as a unit now. It was the best way to do things. Fall in line with everyone else and minimise personal responsibility for your actions by behaving as a mob, then you can add, 'but everyone else was doing it'. That led to the holy trinity of thug deniability: plausible deniability, following orders, and everyone else was doing it. Perfect.

"Why have we stopped?" Barbara asked.

Eric pointed ahead, where Augustan Blunt

was squeezing through the gap between the lorry and the door.

"Just me," the detective said as he dragged himself out.

"Are you sure, because you—"

Eric cringed. "Barbara," he hissed, "what's rule number four?"

"Thugs don't ask questions?"

"And?"

"Oh." She nodded. "Sorry," she shouted towards Blunt. "Forget I asked."

"Right," Blunt said as he looked at the assembled thugs. The lights from the demolition equipment cast long shadows towards him. "Well, there's nobody here, but I know you've got a job to do, so I'll be on my way."

There was the noise of shuffling feet and a few nervous coughs, but no one said a word as Blunt walked away. Something about the way the detective had pulled his coat around his waist irked Eric, but he was a thug, not a stooge, so it wasn't his place to question him.

"Oh, do you want me to write a review or a testimonial or something?" Blunt asked.

"That would be fantastic. I don't think Toywood will want to admit to hiring us, eh?" Eric said.

"Hah," Blunt said. "Could you imagine that? Well, Merry Bleakest Eve!" the detective shouted over his shoulder.

The thugs, in unison, replied, "Merry Bleakest

Eve!"

"Eric?" Barbara said.

"What, Barbara?"

"He did already know that Toywood hired us?"

"Of course he did," Eric said. "I mean… he's a detective, ain't he?"

Hold Back the Horde

"Hold," Morgarth said as she faced the horde of soft toys. She held up one tiny T-Rex arm.

The toys were packed together from wall to wall in a narrow alleyway. In front of them, a small group of people had erected a makeshift barrier. Draped across the front of the barrier was a sheet adorned with the phrase, 'Demons, go to hell.'

The effect was somewhat dampened by the use of a festive tablecloth with candy canes and baubles around the edges. The barricade itself, erected in a hurry, was somewhere between a blockade and a celebration of the season, complete with a plastic Grim Reaper with glowing purple eyes dancing a motorised jig to the sound of a tinny festive carol.

"Go back where you came from!" a voice shouted before a bottle was launched from the other side of the barricade. It flew through the air, splattering dark red liquid over the demons until it landed on the head of a pink feline demon toy. It made a gentle thud, then rolled to the floor.

Morgarth could hear an argument break out on the other side of the barricade about only throwing empty bottles. The cat rubbed its head, then shrugged, unperturbed.

"We might do that," Morgarth shouted at the barricade, taking pains to minimise the demonic essence that turned norms into something Blunt had called 'quivering trifles'. "But we need to find out how. We need to do it safely."

That wasn't true, Morgarth knew. It was a lie, but then, she was a demon.

"Really?" the voice of the bottle thrower said. "So you're just going to go?"

"Well, we don't know until we find out if we can, do we?"

A muffled conversation began on the other side of the barricade, and she turned back to the horde. Hundreds of nervous soft toys looked back at her. In the glow of a flickering streetlight, their red eyes seemed brighter.

"Just wait," she said.

Patience is not a virtue shared by demons, though in fairness to the horde, virtues were not something they understood very well at all. When patience was called for, they preferred to think of it simply as waiting because, most of the time, they're the same thing, except with none of the messiness involved in the theological discussion of virtues.

"What's going to happen?" a unicorn asked.

"I don't know," Morgarth replied. "We just have to wait a bit longer and see."

"Right."

"It's Yargvel, isn't it?"

"Yes," the unicorn replied. "Do you remember everyone's names?"

"Yes," Morgarth replied. "I try to. I think it's polite."

"Ew," Yargvel said. "Wait. Are we supposed to

be polite now? Isn't that a good thing?"

Morgarth nodded. "It's all very confusing, but remember, we're not just the bad guys anymore."

"I know," Yargvel said as he kicked at a puddle. The unicorn's sodden feet splashed up filthy water. "It was just so much easier when we could just... torture things."

Morgarth shrugged. "It's not all bad. I mean, you're a unicorn now."

"I know."

"I don't think they realise—"

"They definitely don't. They think unicorns are nice."

"You don't even have fangs."

"I know. I get the impression they think a unicorn is just a horse with a horn."

"Ah... well, ignorance is bliss."

"Ironic, really. I went from being a demon to being a unicorn, which is probably worse, but they all think unicorns are nice and demons are horrible."

"Is that ironic?" Morgarth asked.

A white lab coat appeared by Morgarth's side. It floated in the air, and the rest of Sarah flickered in and out of existence until she was whole once more. She winced and gritted her teeth.

"Stay calm."

"We *are* staying calm," Yargvel said.

"You shouldn't be here," Morgarth said. "It looks like your... ailment is worsened by situations of high stress."

"Oh, does it?" Sarah said. "Well, thank you,

Doctor Dinosaur, for your diagnosis. I'm going to go and stand at the back of the horde in case they need help."

"You sound unhappy."

"Do I?" Sarah's face vanished, though her hair, a practical bob, remained for a moment. Beneath the coat, her sensible shoes flickered below black trousers. The arms of the coat lifted, waved in the air for a moment, then the ensemble marched through the horde.

"She seemed unhappy," Yargvel said, swishing his rainbow tail.

On the other side of the wall, they had reached a decision.

"Before we let you through," a masculine voice said, "can we just be clear that you're going to the Grim Reaper to find out how you can go to Hell?"

"We'll definitely be asking," Morgarth said. "But we can't promise we'll go because we don't know if we can yet."

"Yeah," another voice on the other side of the barricade chipped in. "Of course. I mean, if you can't actually go to Hell…"

"Then we can't go to Hell."

"Well, our signs would just look silly then."

"Oh," Morgarth said, looking around at the other demons standing beside her. "Well, we wouldn't want that, would we?"

"No. I mean, the signs have to be accurate. We'll keep them updated, and if you can't actually go… we'll change them."

"Great. Can we come through then?"

"Yeah," the second voice said. "Just before you do, though, would you find 'Demons go to Hell, metaphorically' or 'Demons aren't welcome' more intimidating?"

"Um..." Morgarth looked at Yargvel. "The second one?"

"Yeah. I mean, if you're going to put 'metaphorically' in there, it definitely loses the impact," Yargvel said.

"We think the second one," Morgarth said to the people behind the barricade.

"Great, thanks for your help," the voice said.

The furniture blocking the way shook as things on the other side were moved away until, eventually, the tablecloth was torn down and the horde could pass through.

Three's Company

Blunt watched while the thugs rushed the building. It wasn't quite the organised attack that they had given the impression they were launching. Having to squeeze past the lorry in the entrance meant they could only enter one at a time, which, when Blunt thought about it, would make them rather easy to deal with.

It was hard to make much out from beside the car. Heavy fog had descended upon them, and it was always thicker and soupier this close to the canal. Blunt cast a glance in its direction, spotting, even in this dire neighbourhood, that someone had thrown some lights up around the boat station. At this distance, they didn't look like lights. Instead, they looked like the menacing glowing eyes of something climbing out of the canal.

Bleakest Eve, he thought. *What kind of madness is this?*

His coat shifted, and he wrapped his arms tighter around his midriff.

"You're crushing us," a voice rasped, and he felt a chill that had nothing to do with the weather.

"Mind your voices," Blunt muttered.

When most of the thugs were inside the building, he opened the driver's door of Ralph Mortimer's comfortable, unremarkable car.

As he slid inside, he opened up his coat, and out fell a stuffed octopus toy, an annoyed-looking toy elephant, and Vellmar, one of the six elite guards who had left Beelzebub's side. She happened to be a furry hippopotamus.

Leighton, who had been waiting in the passenger seat, froze as the demons clambered across her lap.

"Don't talk to them," Blunt said. The detective fixed his eyes on the view out of the car's front window as he turned the key in the ignition. It started on the first try, and for a moment, he considered what it was like to have a car that you could rely upon. "There's nobody in the car with us. You're imagining it. Understand?"

Leighton followed Blunt's lead. She turned to stare out of the front window and let out a sound that she would refuse to admit was a whimper.

"So… nice weather we're having."

"Right, we've got a clue," Blunt said.

"Oh? That's good."

"It is, because this is getting too messy for my liking."

"There are demons sitting in my lap, Blunt," Leighton hissed.

"No there aren't. There are absolutely no demons here."

"Haven't got much choice," croaked Jargle.

Blunt let out a sigh. "Leighton, let me introduce Jargle, Phil, and Vellmar. Jargle and Phil are upstanding citizens of Gloomwood who have found work. Vellmar is still a demonic psychopath, though, so watch out for her."

"How dare you," Vellmar said.

Leighton instinctively moved to cover her ears, doubling over, then recoiling in terror as she found herself almost hugging the toys.

Blunt also found himself twisting away, hitting his head against the window before gathering himself.

"Vellmar," he said through gritted teeth. "Can you control your voice?"

The hippopotamus shrugged and let out a sigh. "Sorry, former mortals. I always forget the weakness of your constitutions. I have had quite a day, and my concentration slipped. Now, I am not *still* a demonic psychopath, thank you. I am a sociopath."

"Right," Blunt said.

Leighton was still staring out of the car window, refusing to look down. She had spent less time around demons than Blunt, and their voices, even subdued, sent a chill down her spine.

"I have information that might help," Vellmar said.

There was something familiar about the way the demon spoke, and then it clicked. Despite the attempts to distort the voice over the phone there was something unmistakeable about the sound of Blunt's inside informant. "Mufflemouth?" Blunt said with a gasp.

"Ah, I was hoping you wouldn't guess. Mufflemouth is a terrible name. Think of a better name."

"I can just call you by your name now the subterfuge is over. Why've you been helping me? How are you getting the information you've been giving me? And why the cloak and dagger informant bit?"

"I have been manipulating you to help the demons. That's what we do, manipulate."

Blunt nodded. "Do you think telling me that is going to make it easier to manipulate me in future?"

"Perhaps telling you that was part of my strategy."

"I… oh. Forget it. You've got information?"

"Yes. The Kallikantzaroi have been trying to cut down the Bleakest Day tree for years now. They're obsessed with it. Something about being the tree of life before they came here."

"Yeah. I've met them. They've been dressing up as you lot. Pretty clever idea that, actually. Almost… demonic."

Vellmar fell quiet.

"You also told me about the crime scene earlier today. To be honest, I thought you were Captain Sowercat putting on a stupid voice, but this makes a lot more sense. You've been helping them."

The hippo looked away from the octopus and elephant, who had both moved to lean against the car door.

"It seemed like simple mischief, and we're supposed to do jobs, aren't we? They paid me."

"Paid you to help them appear like demons?"

"When I realised what had happened, I went

back to the horde to tell Morgarth that we were being set up. I didn't want people to think it was me or the others who had found jobs. Before I could explain, those stupid exorcists arrived, and I thought it might be better to remain quiet."

"I don't understand what this has to do with the decorations."

"Maybe the decorations aren't important at all? Maybe it was all about the demons," Leighton said.

"So stealing the decorations was just a sort of test, something to… to put me on the case. They stole the decorations because they belonged to the Grim Reaper, and the Grim Reaper came to me because he knew I would keep his involvement quiet. Then when I go around the city—"

"Screaming, like a foghorn, that you're looking for demons. You realise you've just told them who your client is," Leighton interrupted.

"You didn't hear me say that," Blunt said to the demons. "I mean, I don't care how scary you sound. I'll shove my hand up your backsides and turn you inside out, clear?"

The demons nodded.

"When I went around the city looking for demons," Blunt continued, "it looked like I was hunting them down because I suspected something. So this whole thing has just been about making you all look evil."

"We are evil," said Phil, the furry elephant with huge pink eyelids and dressed in a sailor's outfit.

"Hang on," Blunt said. "Something isn't adding up here. What about the demons who were with the bloke who was dressed up as you-know-who?"

A Slow Death

The Grim Reaper stood on the platform in front of the Office of the Dead. A sizeable crowd had gathered to hear Death's speech. It was an annual event, one of the few times Grim directly addressed the people. Countless pundits would analyse his words afterwards to offer insight into the Grim Reaper's mindset.

Of course, none of them actually had any more insight than anyone else, but they spent a lot of time thinking about him, which qualified them as experts.

The intent of Grim's speeches and the nuances that were inferred from them were quite separate entities. So much so that he had stopped trying to say very much at all. It was much easier to let people imagine they were hearing what they wanted to hear.

"Are you ready?" asked Mortimer, who was standing to Grim's side on the platform. He wasn't particularly tall, which only made Grim's robed form even more imposing.

"Death is always but a moment away."

"Right… Does that mean you're ready?"

"It means I need a moment."

"Ah. Would you like me to warm up the crowd?" Mortimer asked in that special voice reserved for offering to do things while making it perfectly clear that the speaker does not want to do said thing.

"How would you do that?" Grim asked.

"I, um, I'd introduce you. Get the crowd cheering. Maybe tell a joke."

"Would you?"

Mortimer stared out at the crowd and the section reserved for the press. Unlike the media types who lingered less than a hundred meters away in the cosy confines of the Office of the Dead reception, where a temporary media circus had pitched its tent, these people were old-school. A motley bunch of seasoned journalists and highly paid paparazzi who were already snapping photos as if this moment might be the greatest historical occasion the city had ever known.

"Um, maybe?"

The Grim Reaper wore his gown of many colours on this one occasion of the year. It was a patchwork of pieces sewn together with obviously ragged and haphazard stitches, in some places frayed, and in others the finest embroidery. The pundits called it the quintessential representation of the city, a myriad of styles that, when combined, become something more beautiful still.

In fact, Grim had taken the original off a scarecrow and had added some sequins. Unlike the experts, he called it his lounging-robe, specially reserved for those days spent languishing on the sofa, an activity he hoped one day to try.

Taxi

"Where are we going?" Leighton asked as Blunt drove through the streets of Gloomwood. The festive lights worked with the gothic architecture to give it something approaching a cosy feel. Like Dracula had caught disco fever.

The rolling fog and the eerie quiet of the normally busy streets countered the effect in a way only Gloomwood could do. Having demons sitting on her lap and the Blunt sulking by her side weren't making things any more comfortable for Leighton.

"We're going to find the rest of the demons. I've got a terrible feeling about this."

"The horde," Jarg said as he stared down into the footwell of the passenger seat.

"Yes. Technically, they're the horde, but to be honest, I don't think that word is helpful."

Vellmar shifted in Leighton's lap. "It means the same as tribe, or—"

"It's got demonic connotations," Leighton said.

"We're demons," Jarg said. "Demons have hordes. It's a very common term. It's actually a mortal human term. In Hell, the word we use is difficult to say, and it might make your eyes explode or your blood boil. You do have blood, don't you?"

"Only a little. It's expensive," Blunt said.

"Oh. We'll try to get you some more."

"Very thoughtful of you." Blunt glanced

sideways. "Shit!"

He hit the brakes and dragged the wheel to the left. The car screeched in protest, then came to a stop. It rocked gently on its soft suspension for a moment.

Jarg looked at Blunt, large cartoonish eyes blinking. "Calm down," he said.

"Did you know that was going to happen?"

"It was right in front of you, and you weren't slowing down."

"It was right in front of you," Blunt said in a squeaky imitation of the octopus.

"I do not sound like that," Jarg said, his voice dropping to a demonic growl.

Blunt felt the hairs on his arms rise, and a shiver ran down his spine. Apart from Vellmar, the demons in the car were low on the demonic power chart, but they still had voices that filled him with dread.

Someone tapped against his window, jerking him out of his state of frozen fear. He wound it down, and a woman shoved her head in.

"You can't come through, there's a demonic horde rampaging through the streets," she said, staring at the soft toys on Leighton's lap, across from Blunt.

"They're just toys," Blunt said. "Its Bleakest Eve. They're a joke present for a mate. He's scared of demons. They look like demons, though, don't they?"

"Yeah. Here, aren't you that bloke from the

television who hunts demons?"

"That's not what I—"

Before Blunt could finish, the woman ducked her head out and was calling out to other people.

"We've got the demon hunter right here, that detective from the television!"

Blunt rested his forehead against the steering wheel and, with his face hidden beneath his hat, murmured, "Keep completely still and don't say a word, no matter what happens. That goes for you too, Leighton."

When he looked up, the barrier in front of him, which was mainly comprised of a skip and an old sofa, was being pulled apart.

A large man with a confident swagger, a large beard, and a helmet adorned with horns walked up to the window.

"Detective Blunt," the man said. "The path is open to you. May you slaughter many of the denizens of Hell. Should you wish it, you have my axe."

Blunt offered the bewildered smile of many a tourist meeting unexpected customs in an unfamiliar land. "Uh, thanks, but I'm not really an axe-wielding kind of guy."

"Hah! You have a sense of humour even in these dark times. I would have been proud to ride into battle at your side. Come now, my comrades and I have a thirst for demon blood—"

"I don't think they bleed, it's more fluff and foam."

"Then we shall sate our thirst for violence on their fluff!"

"It's only going to make you more thirsty."

"Yes, our thirst shall never be quenched until we vanquish them entirely. How right you are. We may not walk the halls of Valhalla—"

"Hold on. You're clearly some kind of Viking or Viking enthusiast, right?"

The big man shifted on his feet and leaned into the window a little more. "I am a Viking."

"That's what I said," Blunt replied, leaning away from the wild-eyed man.

"Who said I wasn't? Was it Deidre? Just because she didn't know me doesn't mean I wasn't a Viking, you know. There were lots of us."

"No. I completely understand—"

"Her group of Vikings must have done things differently, that's all. I can't know everything every group of Vikings ever did."

Blunt couldn't help but notice the man's accent had switched to something that suggested his origins were a lot closer to Lancashire than Denmark.

"That's very true. Look, I'm just going to drive on through. Thanks for taking down the barricade."

"But I offered you my axe."

"I told you, I don't need an axe."

"It means I'll come with you and fight by your side. The aid of a Viking should not be—"

"Right." Blunt lifted a finger and pointed it into the man's face. "How about you gather your most fearsome warriors and you can be my, uh, reserve troops. When the demons think we're defeated, you can rush in, our secret weapon, and rescue everyone like valkyries descending on the battlefield."

"That's not what valkyries do."

"Are you sure?"

The man leaned back and frowned. "Yeah, of course I am. I am a Viking."

"Right, well, you get the idea. I'll see you on the other side."

Blunt put his foot down, hoping to screech away. Instead, the car lurched forward and stalled. He restarted the engine while the bemused, possibly Viking, possibly Lancastrian man made a large double-bladed axe appear from behind his back.

The man put a large hand on the driver's door, where the window was still open. "Who are your compatriots, and why do you have those toys in your car?"

"They're decoys. They're just toys, but I use them to distract demons."

"That's clever, but it's underhand."

The car spluttered back into life, and Blunt slowly pressed down on the accelerator. The man kept pace as the car rolled forward, still with one hand on the door.

"You sure they're not demons? I mean, obviously you wouldn't have demons in your car by choice, but—"

"Nope, they're definitely pretend demons. I've

tested them."

"How do you test them?" He was jogging alongside the car now.

"You offer them cheese. Demons can't resist a good strong cheese."

"Really?"

"Yup. Right, gotta go stop another apocalypse now," Blunt said as he risked speeding the car up a little more.

Before he could wind the window up, he could hear the man yelling, "We call it Ragnarök where I come from!"

When they'd driven on a little further, Blunt turned to the two toys. "How're you decoys holding up?"

"He was not a Viking," Phil said.

Jarg revealed on of the knives he had hidden about his person. "Definitely not. I once tortured a Viking, and he tried to strangle me with his own intestines."

"Oh, delightful."

"One used to tear off his own ears and throw them at me."

"I remember him," Vellmar said.

Leighton, watching the demons in her lap, let out a cough. "Do you... do you miss torturing people?"

"Oh yes," Vellmar said.

Phil and Jarg sank a little lower on Leighton's lap.

NOT A HOPE IN HELL

Sven Spoons was a Hope. An interesting fact about Hopes is that their names all suffer from deliberate alliteration. Who decided they had to have names that all start with the same letter is a mystery, but it has stuck, despite many strongly worded letters from aggrieved Hopes.

The only time there had ever been a real debate about the issue was when Helena Harrison, who was not a Hope, complained that people assumed she was. It didn't go very well because she had no reason to be offended unless she was suggesting that people thinking she was a Hope was a bad thing, which Helena didn't, because some of her best friends were Hopes. Helena was a Hope-ist. She just didn't want to admit it.

Sven was proud of his Hopefulness. He lived in the neighbourhood known as the Styx with his wife Serena Spoons, who was not herself a Hope, though people thought she was because she'd taken his name in the old-fashioned way. They were happy in their humble terraced house with single glazing and a fancy electric fire that was only twenty years old. They had plastered festive decorations in every nook and cranny until they felt they could use the term 'festooned'.

Like everyone else, Sven had planned to spend the evening with his feet up, scoffing seasonal chocolates and nodding off to sleep in front of the Grim Reaper's speech before getting up tomorrow to unwrap the few presents he and Serena had scrimped and saved to buy.

That had been the plan.

"This isn't anything to do with us," Serena said.

"I'm not having it, Serena. I'm not having it."

"Sven. It's Bleakest Eve, can't we just enjoy it?"

"Exactly," Sven said, brandishing his finger like it was a sword pulled free from its scabbard, ready for battle. "On Bleakest Eve, the entire city is going after a small group of refugees."

"Refugees?"

"Yes, refugees. What else do you call a group of people who have escaped Hell and asked for help?"

Serena was standing in the space at the bottom of the stairs by the front door. On the wall hung an array of coats. Sven was sitting on the bottom step, lacing his work boots while she stood in a pair of Bleakest Eve pyjamas and fluffy bunny slippers.

"I don't understand what you think you're going to do."

"I'm going to stand in the middle."

"What?"

"There's going to be a reckoning, and I'm going to stand in the middle to stop it happening."

"On your own?"

"You could come with me."

"They tried to burn the Grim Reaper."

"Did they? All of them? One of them might have, maybe even a handful, but all of them?"

"It isn't safe."

"I'm not having it," Sven said again, raising his voice. He didn't direct it at Serena, but it wasn't not directed at her, either.

"That means nothing."

"I've been here sixty years, Serena. In sixty years, I've woken up every day knowing that some snide norm, or a big-headed god, might just decide that today's the day they treat me like crap because I'm not one of them. Waiting to hear the insults, 'You never lived anyway', 'Get a life', 'You've a face like a slapped arse'."

"That last one isn't about—"

"Well, enough is enough. If I don't stand up for them, I've no right to expect people to stand up for me."

"So, what you're saying is, you're standing up for yourself by defending the demons."

"I'm not defending them. I'm demanding people follow the rules."

"What are you going to do?"

"I told you. I'm going to stand in the middle and let the authorities do their jobs."

"The Gloomwood police?"

"The Office of the Dead. Mister Neat, and the bureaucrats, and the big guy."

"The Grim Reaper?"

"That detective, he's always banging on about truth and justice and making sure people get what what's coming to them."

"He's been hunting the demons."

"Has he?"

"Yes, love. See, everyone agrees—"

"Well, that just makes it even more important that I get out there and stand up for them."

A knock came at the door, startling both of them. What followed was a series of eye movements, nods, and improvised mime, which resulted in Serena ducking back into the living room and pressing herself up against the wall to avoid being seen in her pyjamas. This was despite the fact that she and Sven agreed it was ridiculous that she should hide as it was late and lots of people would be in their pyjamas.

Sven finished tying his shoelaces, straightened his Bleakest Eve jumper—the one with the light-up nose on the Grim Reaper—and pulled the door open. Six people were standing there, each dressed in similarly festive attire.

"Doreen? Derek? Nige? Bit late for Bleakest Eve singers, isn't it?"

"Sven," Doreen said. "We're, um, we're going to go down to Dead Square."

Sven nodded. "Aye? And why's that?"

"We, um, we think there's going to be trouble."

"Never picked you out to be trouble seekers. Well, except maybe you, Nige, but only when you've had a few."

There was a nervous laugh. The kind that starts and then dies halfway through when everyone realises it probably isn't something to laugh at.

Nige, who was sporting a bobble hat, which, instead of a bobble, had a carefully crocheted Grim Reaper complete with a plastic scythe, cleared his throat.

"Listen, Sven, we don't like this thing with the demons."

"Oh, hunting them, are you?"

Derek rubbed the back of his head and looked down at his feet. "No. We were sort of giving them a hard time—"

"We built a barricade and threw a bottle of wine at them," Doreen interrupted.

"Oh," Sven said. "That's not the kind of thing I want to be involved with. Thank you for stopping by—"

"It's not like that. We were just being idiots, but we realised we hadn't thought it through. We've no problem if people have made up their minds. The demons have never done us any harm, and we know what it's like to be treated like… well, you know what I'm saying. We're not making trouble. We'd just like to see things done properly."

"Standing in the middle?"

"That's it. We're going to stand in the middle."

"Right then." Sven nodded. "Serena—"

His wife stepped out of the living room and pulled a coat off the peg, pulling it over her pyjamas.

"Well, if you're *all* bloody going, I might as well join you. No point sitting here like Billy no mates."

"Oi," said Billy, who was standing behind Nige.

"But I'm keeping my slippers on," Serena said.

Teddy Bear's Picnic

Blunt rolled the car up the kerb and pulled to a stop. Heavy rain still hammered down on the car, and as the windscreen wipers stopped moving, the rain obscured their view.

They were parked outside the largest shop in the city. Despite the time of night, the lights on the decorations in the window still shone brightly.

"What's your plan?" Leighton asked.

"All these blockades have made this a nightmare. We should've gone on a bicycle."

"Do you know what's going on yet?"

Blunt still had his hands on the steering wheel as he shook his head. "I've got ideas, but it doesn't all make sense."

"Care to share?"

"Fine. Somebody wanted the demons out of that warehouse so they could demolish it. That bit's straightforward, but this all seems like a lot of effort to get the demons out of a building. I mean, they could've just bought a different building and asked the demons to move. You'd have moved, right?" Blunt asked the trio of furry fiends in Leighton's lap.

"Probably," Jarg said.

"There was a hole in the roof. It would have been nice to not have a hole," Phil said.

"Okay, so people are making you look bad, but they're also demolishing your warehouse. Now, the thugs mentioned Toytown," Blunt said as he pointed out at the huge shopfront.

"You know this is just one of their shops, not their headquarters."

"I know that. I also know that this is the only place in town that has a grotto, and who lives in a grotto?"

"People with not a lot of money, probably with high unemployment rates, usually minorities, like the Styx neighbourhood?" Jarg said, nodding as he looked at the others. "I read books."

"That's a ghetto," Leighton said. "A grotto is a small cave."

"Oh, in that case, witches, fire demons, pixies, elves, an unusually small dragon, troglodytes, hermits…" Vellmar said.

"Children who are raised by wolves?" Jarg added.

Phil raised his trunk and waved it. "Ooh, me, me!"

"Yes, Phil," Blunt said with a groan.

"What about a wraith, or a giant spider?"

"I've changed my mind. I hate demons," Blunt said as he stepped out of the car.

Leighton followed, but she closed the door on the demons and pointed at them through the window. "Stay," she said.

Blunt walked to the shopfront before he started marching around the building.

"Where are we going?"

"There has to be a side entrance."

"Why are we here?"

"Because whoever is behind all this has got somebody dressed up as you-know-who, and they've completely lost the plot."

"You mean, whoever dresses up as... the big man?"

"The big man?"

"That's what we all call him to avoid any kind of accidental mention of... that thing."

"Bloody Christmas. For Christ's sake, why can't anyone admit that it's just fake sodding Christmas?"

Leighton put a hand over her mouth. Took a breath. Then she put her hands on her hips and glared.

"Because, you arrogant arsehole, we're not celebrating that. Because we're all dead. Everybody here has died. The living people who died don't want to be reminded of it, the people who were never alive don't want to be reminded that they never had it. We'd just like to enjoy the feelings without all the reminders of what we've lost. Or never had."

Blunt froze. "Oh... I hadn't thought of it like that."

"You had a daughter. You had a wife. How were the holiday seasons after you lost them?"

Blunt nodded but said nothing. He looked down at his feet. "Right. I kind of get it. Like... city-wide denial?"

"Exactly like that. It's all just a huge marketing thing to make us buy ridiculous gifts."

He took a breath and continued walking down

the alleyway until he found a doorway. Next to it was a skip, and he opened the lid, rifling around inside before pulling out a brick.

"Strange thing to chuck in a skip," Blunt said with a shrug. He looked up at Leighton. "I'm sorry," he muttered before quickly turning back to the door and inspecting the lock.

Holding the brick in one hand, he attempted to smash the lock, but the brick crumbled after a single blow. "Bollocks."

"We're in a hurry," Leighton said. "Whatever you've got planned, we need to move fast."

Blunt nodded and broke into a jog back around the front of the shop. When he got there, he opened the car door and climbed in.

"You lot, get out," he said to the demons while pulling on his seatbelt.

"Where are you going?" Vellmar asked.

"Not far," Blunt said as he turned the ignition. The car started with a meek groan as the demons leapt out the passenger door. Blunt reversed out into the road until the headlights reflected back at him from the glass of the storefront windows.

"Sorry, Mortimer, hope your insurance covers this."

Then he put the car in gear and put his foot down.

Not so Jolly

"This will end badly for you," the stuffed toy said with a quack.

The big man's booming laughter rattled the cages.

"Oh no, no, no! It's already ended badly for me! I'm dead and trapped here, you idiot sock-puppet. You are hellspawn, evil incarnate, yet I can't escape your presence even when I've finally died. End badly? It has already ended, and it hasn't gone well."

"What happened—"

"Don't speak to me, foul demon. Your performances for that fatuous slob of a detective were satisfactory, and that's the only reason I haven't already pushed the button," the big man said with a snarl.

His white beard was streaked with dirt and oil from the hinges of the cages housing the demons. The big man stood by the open double doors at the rear of the lorry, inside which were the caged demons. Some of them had plastic duck masks attached to their faces.

The big man was leering at the cage nearest to him, holding a homemade device covered in brass buttons in one hand. He had wrapped it in tape as the plastic casing had burst at its seams, where tendrils of blue and red wires poked out. He waved it as he spoke.

"You hateful creatures ruined everything, and

now I have a chance at vengeance."

He jumped down from the back of the lorry and took hold of the doors, his enormous arms gripping the edges.

"Your existence will end here, demons. I can finally have peace by banishing you from this afterlife and then end it for all of us."

The doors slammed shut. Moments later, the lorry's engine rumbled to life.

"He realises we don't know who he is, doesn't he?"

"I doubt it," Trem said. "I think he's completely invested in the idea we're the reason he's miserable here."

"But we've got nothing to do with anything that happens here. We only arrived when Lord Beelzebub did," a voice from further within the lorry wailed.

"What's going to happen?"

Trem looked back into the lorry. Glowing red irises stared back at her, but otherwise there was darkness. The vehicle jerked from side to side, and the cages rattled.

"I think we will have a choice. Either do as he says, or we die."

"We can't die."

"We don't know if we can or not."

"We were never alive."

"Fine, maybe we can't die," Trem said. "But we can cease to be."

"That's not fair," a duck voice quacked.

"Oh, I'm sorry. I didn't realise things were supposed to be fair," Trem said. The quacking of the device attached to her face prevented the rage behind her words from being translated into demon tongue.

"Unfortunately for me, and for all of you," Trem continued, "we got into the back of somebody's lorry, and even though we're demons, we expected that to turn out okay. Now we've all got explosives inside us and these ridiculous duck voices."

"I don't mind the voice," a duck said. "The explosives are annoying, though."

"How do you know they're explosives?" another duck asked. They all sounded like ducks now.

There had been options, of course. They could all have had the ideal phone voice, a Scouse accent, or the voice of something called a Wookie, but the big man had decided the voices, and he'd felt the quack of a duck was the most humiliating.

Trem looked back into the lorry at the red eyes glowing in her direction. She didn't know why they were asking her for answers. They had exactly the same information as she did and had been prisoners for longer.

"I just want to check," she quacked. "We're all demons here, right?"

The glowing eyes nodded, and affirmative quacks confirmed it.

"Well, if we captured people, tied them up,

did some amateur surgery to them, and then drove them to an unknown location, what do you think we'd be using them for?"

The van filled with a chorus of quacks.

"Bombs!"

"Explosives?"

"Bio-weapons?"

"Mind-controlled assassins!"

"Those people who chase you down the street trying to do surveys?"

Trem shook her head. "Whoever said bombs gets a cookie."

"Really?"

"No."

"Is this a harness?" another demon asked.

Earlier, they had been clipped into something that jingled whenever they moved. It was a kind of backpack with bells on it. Until now, though, Trem hadn't considered that it might be a harness.

"Why would we need a harness?"

Grotto

The car smashed through the window but came to an almost immediate stop, throwing Blunt against the seat belt. The front of the car had buried itself in a display that included a polystyrene fireplace and a large dead tree, along with an excessive amount of wrapped cardboard boxes.

He took a moment to catch his breath and try to put the pain of whiplash to one side before unbuckling his seatbelt. As he opened the passenger door, shoving festive paraphernalia out of the way, the shop alarms were blaring.

Leighton climbed through the broken glass window, followed by the demons.

"Blunt, what are you doing?"

"Hurrying," he said as he fell out of the car. He scrambled to his feet, getting caught up in the tree as he did so, and swore as a row of fairy lights became entangled with his coat.

"Argh!" he shouted in frustration, before pulling apart the lights by snapping the wires. "Right, you three," he said, pointing at the demons. "Find the ladies perfume and makeup and all that stuff and pick up a really expensive-looking gift set. Leighton, we're going to the grotto."

The demons didn't hesitate, immediately scampering off into the shop. Leighton stepped beyond the display, turning to look at the front of Ralph Mortimer's car and shaking her head.

"Merry Bleakest Eve, Ralph."

"Never mind that," Blunt said as he followed her. "Which way's the grotto?"

"I'm guessing where all the signs are pointing?" Leighton said, indicating the many well-lit wooden signposts covered in fairy lights and fake snow.

"Right, we're off to the North Pole," Blunt said as he marched further into the shop.

Leighton sighed. "You were waiting to say that."

The grotto was the stuff of festive nightmares. If Gloomwood had gone overboard for Bleakest Day decorations, like a spider infestation across the city, then the nest they had spawned from was this grotto. Blunt stood by a sign that read 'This way to Faux-Santa'.

"How come this place can... you know, not pretend this isn't that special day?"

Leighton shrugged. "This is the toy section. I guess their marketing department decided if people were going to come to this, they didn't mind being reminded. They've never done it before, though. And I don't think it went down well." She pointed towards graffiti on one sign that said, in less than friendly terms, that Santa could... go away.

"Oh. Is that the general feeling on it then?"

"Pretty much. I'm guessing somebody got fired for this disaster."

Blunt turned to look at Leighton. "Maybe he got fired? Could this all be because of one disgruntled employee? People have done worse things."

"But why the decorations? How did he know where they were? Are you sure he has them?"

"Oh, I'm sure. I've been here before, remember, and he was laughing at me the whole time. I could've ended this right then, but I was stupid."

Leighton pushed her hair back behind her ears and straightened her hat.

"A jolly big man was being kind to a bunch of demons on Bleakest Eve. He told you he was giving them all a chance at a new start, and they backed him up. You're the most cynical person in the city, Blunt. If you fell for it, everyone else would have too."

"Yeah," Blunt said with a scowl. "A fair few people did." He thought of the kindly goat-faced vicar who was going to find out he had been complicit in kidnapping. "Come on, I want to know who this guy is and what he's planning, and I think we'll find it here."

"Why not at his house?"

Blunt pulled a piece of paper out of his pocket. The address given to him by the vicar. "I think this is his house, or at least he thought it was. It's the only address I have for him."

"That's weird."

"Yeah, maybe he was a method actor who took things too far." Blunt walked around the big table he had seen earlier. None of the food had been touched, and as he looked at it, he realised it was all exactly as it had been when he had visited. "This isn't actual food, is it?"

"We're not having the 'what is real' debate again. Because we're all dead—"

"No. I'm just saying, it's all fake." A large throne came next, with mountains of wrapped cardboard boxes on either side. Blunt stepped up to it and looked behind it. There was a doorway there. "Here we go. Prepare yourself. There might be a bunch of dead people behind that door."

"This is literally a city of dead people."

"You know what I mean."

Blunt pushed the door open, and it gave the sort of creak that was normally reserved for B-movie horror films. The alarms were still blaring, but as Blunt and Leighton stepped through the doorway, they became much quieter. There wasn't much light in the corridor beyond, and Blunt slapped the wall until he found a light switch.

As the strip lighting in the ceiling flickered on, he took a step into the corridor. It wasn't a long one. There was a doorway on either side and one at the far end.

"No dead people," Leighton said, her voice dripping with sarcasm.

"Give it a rest," Blunt said as he moved towards the nearest door. A sign on the front had a picture of a mop and bucket with 'Staff only' written underneath. "Recent experience tells me this isn't where cleaning things are kept."

"Despite the sign saying exactly that?"

"Funny, isn't it? It's almost like the sign tells you what's not in there. Want to bet?"

"No, open it."

Blunt looked over his shoulder at her to discover she was holding a small camera in one hand. "Where did that come from?"

"My pocket," Leighton said. "I'm a journalist."

"Yeah, a journalist, not a photographer."

"I'm branching out."

Blunt shook his head and put his hand on the door handle. As he opened it, he let out a groan.

"Well, that's hardly in the festive spirit, is it?"

Inside the room, there was a dentist's chair. Attached to it were various velcro and leather straps. An assortment of scissors, bobbins of thread, and sewing needles were spread out on the table next to the chair.

Leighton's camera made a clicking and whirring sound as she snapped pictures over Blunt's shoulder.

"Can you pause for a minute? Aren't you disturbed by this?"

"Yes. That's why I'm taking pictures."

"Hiding behind the camera."

"Yes. What's your point?"

"I don't have one. Wish I did, actually… What's that?" Blunt pointed to a table in the corner, on which sat a purple orb that gave out a dim glow. "Is that what I think it is?"

"It looks like it."

"What the hell was going on here? Why would he have this setup and the Grim Reaper's decorations? He couldn't have been…"

"You don't mean… That's just sick."

"That's got to be it. He's put them inside the demons."

"Why? What would it do to the demons?"

Blunt stepped into the room and walked across to the bauble on the table. He placed a hand over it and waggled his fingers before taking a breath and picking it up. His face froze in a grimace as he waited for something to happen, but nothing did.

"Are you okay?" Leighton asked. "It looks like you might have had an accident. There's a clothing section if you need it."

He turned to fix her with a glare. "These things are powerful."

"How?"

His lip curled as he looked down at the bauble in his hand. "I don't know, but they're inside the demons, and all the demons are marching to Dead Square. They've been stitched up."

Leighton stared at Blunt.

"Well, I thought it was funny," he said. "We need to get everyone out of Dead Square."

"How? Call in a bomb threat?"

"Yes, because that's exactly what this is."

Threat

"Miss Holt, there's a call for you," panted a woman in a knitted jumper as she tried to keep up with Lavender Holt.

"Unless it's a call from God telling me there's been a mistake and I'm supposed to be in Heaven, you can tell whoever it is to stick their phone up their backside and play Merry Bleakest Eve with their large intestine," Lavender snapped.

The Bleakest Eve address was a big event, but this year, everything seemed to be going wrong.

"It's Chief Sowercat. He says there's been a bomb threat."

"A bomb threat? No. He's mistaken."

"Uh, he said it's from a reliable source. Well, what he actually said was, 'It's from an absolute cockwomble, but if he's called it in, there's no chance it's not happening because he knows I'd love to let the lads kick seven shades of shit out of him.'"

Lavender turned to look at the woman still trying to keep up with her. She looked like she had been vomited straight out of a Bleakest Eve catalogue with her knitted jumper with the words 'We're gonna have a Grim ol' time' on it, pink perm, and horn-rimmed spectacles hanging from her neck by a candy-striped piece of ribbon.

"Ah, Detective Blunt," Lavender said with a sigh.

"You think?"

Being the Artificer, which was a title she had created herself and everyone else just seemed to go along with, was frustrating. People, she had long ago learned, choose the fastest route to stupidity.

Take, for example, the need to ask people to wear seatbelts, not to smoke while filling a vehicle with flammable liquids, or to write 'Caution: Contents may be hot' on hot drinks containers. These things exist because people are stupid. They choose to be stupid, and when they have been stupid, they blame their idiocy on other people for not assuming they are idiots. There is an entire system in place where people are financially rewarded because other people have 'unfairly' assumed them to have a level of intelligence they do not possess. All that is needed to access this system is a disavowal of any pride or self-respect and to give up any pretence of personal responsibility.

Right now, Lavender was looking at Deidre as a perfect example of this system. Deidre was, despite all appearances, very intelligent. Unfortunately, Deidre had ignored her own ability to make simple decisions and judgements and replaced it with three awful words: 'somebody else's problem.'

Here, it was Lavender Holt's problem, because Lavender was 'in charge'.

"Yes," Lavender said. "I think. You should try it sometime. Now, evacuate Dead Square."

"Oh... That's a good idea. How should we do that?"

Comes to Town

"Ho, ho, ho!" the figure in green boomed as the back of the lorry burst open, a ramp folded down revealing a sleigh covered in bells, lights and glitter.

Demons, eyes glowing red, dragged it forward as it screeched down a ramp from the lorry and across the cobblestones. Beneath the skis of the sleigh were wheels that looked to have been stolen from shopping trolleys. The sleigh bounced and juddered while the demons tried to pull it forward.

The enormous crowd around the huge fake tree covered in decorations let out a loud 'ooh' followed by a cheer as the big man himself, who so many recognised as the mythical festive figure, made an appearance.

The sleigh's skis made a sound like a thousand fingernails being dragged down a blackboard as the demons, too small and too weak, struggled to keep it moving in a forward direction.

"On Dasher and Dancer, on Prancer and Vixen, on Comet, Cupid, Dunder and Blixem," he snarled while cracking the whip in his right hand. In the other, he held a hessian sack.

"Merry Bleakest Eve, people of Gloomwood!" the man in green boomed. "Have you all been good?"

The crowd replied with a resounding "Yes!"

"Bullshit," he roared in a voice like thunder.

The crowd grew quiet, but alcohol and safety in numbers turned nervous titters into something more natural. Laughter, chortles and guffaws at the strange fresh addition to the Bleakest Eve celebrations. It was a joke. It must be a joke.

Beyond the members of the public waving half-empty bottles and festive flags above the heads of journalists wishing they had made a different career choice and the paparazzi weighing up the risks of moving to get pictures of the newcomer was Ralph Mortimer. Next to Mortimer, standing in deathly silence, the only type of silence he could make, was Grim.

"Well, the Artificer has outdone herself this year," Mortimer said. "It's not often we get something new. Is that Father Chri—"

"No."

"Oh, should we say Sant—"

"No."

"Saint Ni—"

"Absolutely not," said Grim. "Do you know something, Mister Mortimer?"

"Um, I know lots of things, but—"

"I don't think Detective Blunt is a talented detective. In fact, I think he might be quite a poor detective. Perhaps even the opposite of a detective. What would that be?"

"Um, someone who covers up crimes?"

"Yes," Grim said with a nod. "I will call him a crime cover-up-er."

Grim looked out at the crowd, which stretched out all around him, crammed right up to the stone steps leading up to the platform that housed the

Bleakest Eve tree. The huge dead tree was smothered in such a vast array of decorations that the boughs creaked and groaned as the wind picked up. It was to be expected. The threat of serious injury from a falling branch was a given, and having a dislodged glass bauble smash into your body was actually considered good luck.

"Mister Mortimer, please check with the Artificer that this is part of the celebrations."

Mortimer, never one to challenge the voice of authority, gave his best 'that's not weird at all' smile.

"Of course," he said.

As Mortimer walked from the stage, Grim looked up at the tree. Nobody else would notice the gaps—because they weren't really there—but he saw spaces where his purple orbs, snow globes and miniature purple present boxes that glittered with their own light should have been.

"This isn't how I expected this to go."

Saw it First

As always, it would be broadcast on television screens and described on radios as it unfolded in front of those present. The annual Bleakest Eve address, which marked the start of Bleakest Day, was about to take place.

To the right of the square, the man in green grew more frustrated as his sleigh refused to move.

"You lazy little bastards," he said. "This is taking too long!"

With a leap that belied his size, he jumped down from the sleigh and set about releasing the demons from their reins. "Come on, to the stage. This is perfect."

He began moving through the crowd. Their interest in the strange appearance of the sleigh and a character they were sure was supposed to be dressed in red was waning.

"Move," he bellowed, kicking aside a confused woman before smashing a brass bell across the face of a bobble hat-wearing man, knocking out several of his teeth. "You can either move, or I'll move you!"

The crowd, crammed into a tight space as it was, tried to create a channel for the big man in green and his cohort of demons who followed along behind, heads bowed. A tiger, a bunny, and an assortment of soft toys with glowing red eyes behind their duck masks that were displaying none of the festive spirit dragged their paws towards the stage.

"Are you part of the show?" asked a man with a permanent pair of antlers festooned with decorations.

"No," the bearded man said before swinging the bell once more and silencing the antlered interloper.

The commotion he was causing fed through the crowd, but as he had abandoned the sleigh, only those closest by could see the brutal swathe he was cutting through the crowd.

At the top of the stairs to the platform, Ralph Mortimer approached the Grim Reaper.

"Ah, it seems—"

"He's not part of the show."

"Yes, how did you know?"

"I am Death, Mister Mortimer. I have studied the interaction of individuals for time untold. Also, he appears to be assaulting members of the public as he is approaching us."

"I'll get security."

"They're already on their way."

Grim watched as a group of individuals wearing black coats with 'Security' written on the back of them snaked through the crowd towards the figure in green. As they got closer, they stopped, though it wasn't clear why.

"Hm," Grim said, tapping a skeletal finger against his teeth. "Where is Captain Sowercat, Mister Mortimer? I fear our security might be outmatched."

"Um, he's in the section with the Artificer, sir."

"Perhaps he should intervene?" Grim said, before a sound caught his attention.

The noise might easily have been missed over the crowd. Their shouts of terror at being attacked by the physical representation of the celebration that shall not be named mingled with the 'oohs' and 'aahs' of an audience who appreciated well-executed violence.

There are a few noises, however, that set off alarm bells somewhere deep in the consciousness of he who ends all others. One of them, understandably, is anything that sounds remotely like the sawing of bone.

Grim turned around to see six small gnomes, three on either side of a large saw, attacking the Bleakest Day tree. A seventh gnome appeared to be shouting at them.

"What in the trans-dimensional abyss do you think you're doing?"

"Cutting down the tree," the gnomes said in unison.

"Oh, you're the Kallikantzaroi, aren't you?"

"Cutting down the tree," they said again.

Two Doors Left

The room of horrors held no more secrets, so Blunt pocketed the bauble before leaving and pulling the door shut behind him.

"What now?" Leighton asked.

Blunt pulled a face at her. "What now? Investigative journalist?"

"Roving reporter now."

"Are you going to get in trouble for being here?"

Leighton's eyes opened wide. "I hadn't really thought of that. Yes, I think I'm probably fired."

"Again?"

"Again… It's going to be a great story, though. I mean, if you're right."

"If I'm right. Did that room look like something okay to you?"

Leighton tilted her head to one side. "We're in a big department store for a company that mainly sells toys. That might have just been a place where they repair or make soft toys."

"With restraints on a dentist's chair? How many toys do you know who try to fight back?"

"About five hundred?" Leighton said, giving a weak smile.

Blunt stepped around her and gripped the handle on the door opposite. He took an unnecessary breath and pushed down on the handle. The door clicked, and he gave it a little push.

Beyond was a toilet with a shower cubicle.

"Oh. That's a bit anticlimactic."

Leighton peered over his head and took a few pictures with her camera. "It's pretty disgusting."

"Yeah, but it's not horror-show surgery disgusting. Shall we see what's behind door number three?"

"Must we?"

"We really must. Do you want to go first?" Blunt asked.

"What, why?"

"Well, I don't want to be accused of being sexist."

"Oh, now you care about that? How convenient. Fine, step aside. I mean, I'll be fine with all that training I've had, all the fights I've been in. Look at me, you can tell I've probably tried to headbutt a shovel one too many times."

Blunt held up his hands in surrender. "Fine, fine. Hang on, what was that supposed to mean about your face? Did you mean my face? Uncalled for, Hughes, uncalled for."

Leighton waved Blunt towards the end of the corridor.

"Sarah likes my face," Blunt continued. "This is the face of a man who has lived, who has seen things. It might not be the prettiest face, but I wouldn't change it—"

"Because it's illegal?"

"I think you'll find I'm ruggedly handsome. Though perhaps more rugged than handsome. Now, are you ready?" he asked as they reached the last door.

Leighton took a step backwards as Blunt reached out for the door handle. He turned to look over his shoulder. "Where are you going?"

"I'm giving you space. In case you need to move quickly."

"More like a bloody head start if we need to run."

"Don't think I'd need it, to be honest."

Blunt gave her a grin. "I'm a lot quicker than I look, especially running away from things."

"I believe that. Are we going to do this?"

Blunt nodded, all joviality wiped from his face as he turned back. "I'm pretty sure we've already made enough noise for anything in here to know we're coming by now."

"Blunt!" a demonic voice boomed.

The cries of terror unleashed by Blunt and Leighton were irrepressible as they both panicked.

"Sorry," Vellmar said from the far end of the corridor. "It's worse in echoey places like this. We got you a gift set."

"You little bastards," Blunt said as he picked up his hat from where it had fallen on the floor.

"You scream like a child," Phil said.

"That was Leighton," Blunt said as he put the hat on and began searching his pockets for a cigar. He found one and lit it with a shaking hand.

Leighton said nothing as she stood up and straightened her coat. Her camera was on a strap around her neck, and she lifted it to take a picture of the three demons standing at the end of the corridor.

"Right," Blunt said when Leighton was finished. "Stay there. We just need to check this last room. Do not look in the other rooms."

"Why?"

"You might find it upsetting," Leighton said.

All three demons made strange squeaking noises, and it took a moment before Blunt recognised the noises as laughter. The stuffed toy form seemed to influence the demonic, menacing laugh Blunt had been expecting.

"Leighton, they tortured people for millennia. They can probably handle it. Try to focus on the fact that they're monsters, actual evil beings, in the bodies of furry little toys. If we had met these three six months ago, they'd have flayed us and laughed while they were doing it. We probably wouldn't have been able to look at them without screaming in horror."

Leighton nodded. "That's really helpful, Blunt, thanks. Now I can think about the demons behind me and the unknown in front of me."

Blunt shrugged, turned, and opened the door.

The room beyond it was a mess. Blunt had to put his shoulder against the door to push it all the way open, and as he flapped a hand around inside, looking for a light switch, he felt something sticky. When the light came on, a lone bulb swinging naked from the ceiling, it gave off a pallid glow that refused to reach the corners of the room.

"What's that smell?" Leighton said, pulling her coat collar over her face.

"It smells like vegetation. Like rotting leaves. Um... death?"

"That's what we've got," Phil shouted down the corridor. "Eau de Death, and it comes with lots of other little bits and pieces."

"It's De'ath, Eau de De'ath," Leighton shouted over her shoulder. "Why did they pick that up?" she asked Blunt in a much quieter voice.

"Present for Sarah. The one I bought her is back at the office."

"So you stole something?"

"I didn't. Those bloody thieving demons did, didn't they?"

"You're supposed to be the good guy."

"I am the good guy... for the big stuff. Look, I just drove a car through the window of this place. The alarms are blaring. Bleakest Eve will not stop looters from turning up, and it isn't like the police are going to be here soon. They'll probably turn up on Bleakest Day and arrest some poor idiot who got here too late. Why should Sarah be angry at me?"

Blunt stepped through the doorway and into the middle of the room.

"That's terrible logic," Leighton said, snapping pictures with her camera.

The room was a mess. On the walls were pictures, mostly crude, hand-drawn attempts at Father Christmas, or Santa Claus, or whatever people wanted to call him. They all depicted him in green instead of in his more modern red outfit. Against one wall was a bed that looked like it had broken in two when someone too large for it had tried to sleep in it.

In the far corner was a wardrobe, but the occupant of the room seemed to have been confused about its purpose; clothes lay in a mess inside it, but none of them were hanging up. All of them were made of the same furry green material with white trim.

"Definitely a method actor," Blunt said. He turned and finally identified the smell. It was coming from a tree. A realistic tree. An actual tree. "That's the smell."

"It can't be," Leighton said. "It's impossible. Unless…"

"Unless what?"

"Well look what's hanging on it. Are they Death's baubles?"

"They've definitely got that glow about them."

"They're bigger than I expected when you see them up close."

"Grow up."

"What?"

"Death's baubles, you know what you said."

"They're doing something to the tree."

"So they're magic decorations…" Blunt murmured as he crouched down to look at what the decorations were growing from.

"That means they're from outside of

Gloomwood."

"Well, I thought that was a given. The Grim Reaper's always bringing stuff from outside of Gloomwood."

"What?" Leighton snapped.

"Kidding, just a joke," Blunt said, slapping a grin on his face. "So, this big fella has the rest of the decorations. He knows they're magic—"

"Didn't Sarah say we should call things thaumaturgic because magic inherently means we can't understand it, but we have some understanding of these things, so it can't be magic?"

Blunt stood up and stared at Leighton for a beat longer than necessary.

"Fine," he said. "Look at this place. This bloke lives in a tiny room in a department store where he's the bloody seasonal entertainment. Do we really think he's behind all of this?"

"Well, he took the decorations, and there's the green gnomes who dressed up as demons—"

"Thanks to Vellmar," Blunt said.

"I said sorry!" the demon shouted down the corridor. "Can we move now?"

"No!" Blunt and Leighton both shouted.

"And there are the thugs at the warehouse, and the voice thing definitely happened. A device for changing the voice of demons." Blunt took a long drag on the cigar and blew smoke around the room. "The thugs said this place hired them, but nobody turned up to tell them what to do. Hiring that many people on Bleakest Eve must have required some kind of deposit, a down payment for their time. I don't think our big green bearded temp worker would have been able to slap down that kind of cash. It's not likely the little green gnomes are working for free either, even if they do hate trees. So who's paying for all this?"

Leighton nodded. "Follow the money."

"The people that own this place." Blunt looked up. "Four storeys of shopping, and most of it toys. They must hate demons. Soft toys are a big part of their business."

"And the Grim Reaper. He let them in."

"They've got the money for this sort of thing. And probably the skills to orchestrate everything. Set up the demons to make people hate them, turn the public against them. Not exactly difficult, as they're already hated. Just turn up the heat a little. What about the factory?"

"Prime real estate."

"Good point. Set the little gnomes off to set up the demons and incriminate them by stealing the decorations, then the arson attempt. Set off psycho-Santa with the decorations… Which means there's something else coming. Those other decorations are inside demons, Leighton. If they break… there's a tree here. What will happen to them?"

"We need to stop him."

"He does like a big reveal. He's all about that special moment."

"You mean he's going to Dead Square?"

"Where would you go if you wanted to make a

big statement?"

"It all makes sense."

"It does, and then there's this." Blunt pushed the door shut behind Leighton. On the back of it was a picture of the Grim Reaper with a large X drawn across him in red pen and a knife in his skull. Hanging from the knife was a piece of paper.

Blunt snatched it from the door. "Notification from the Office of the Dead, the Grim Reaper has decreed that Bleakest Eve should not be conflated with the mortal celebration of Christmas, or any other religious festival. For this reason, the Office of the Dead requires that you cease your 'Santa's Grotto' with immediate effect," he read out loud. "And beneath it, someone's written, 'Don't worry, Charlie, you'll get your own back. Stick to the plan.'"

"We have to stop him."

"We have to catch the bastards behind all of this. They've made me look really bloody stupid."

"And they're trying to destroy the Grim Reaper, the demons, and have set a lunatic on the loose with some seriously powerful weapons."

"Obviously, that goes without saying."

"It could've been said before you started whinging about looking stupid."

A knock came at the door, and Blunt opened it. Jargle the Exsanguinator looked up at Blunt, the other demons behind him. "What are we supposed to do now?" the demon asked.

"Where will the people behind this be?" Blunt asked Leighton.

"Um, if it's the owner of this place, then at the Retailers Association party. I covered it once, but it's just a load of drunk people boasting about conning the public out of money."

"Right." Blunt turned to the demons. "You're going to a party."

"You're sending them? Why not me?"

"I'm not sending anybody. I'm asking them to go. None of you work for me. Anyway, you're the one taking them to the party."

"What? What about you?" Leighton asked as Blunt stuffed the piece of paper into his pocket and took another drag on his cigar. He started walking down the corridor, followed by Leighton and the demons. "Blunt, what are you going to do?" she asked again as they stepped through the grotto.

The detective stopped in his tracks, looking at the display. "I'm going to go see a man about some decorations."

"How are you going to stop him?"

"I'm not. There's a whole horde who are going to be pretty bloody angry when they find out what he's done."

"Then why are you going there and we're going to the other place?"

"Trust me," Blunt said, dropping the cigar and grinding it out under one foot. "We need a... no, I can't say it, it's too cheesy."

"We need a Bleakest Day miracle?" Leighton asked.

Blunt let out a sigh. "I'm too dead for this sh—"

Here They Come

Morgarth and the rest of the demons walked, limped, crawled, slithered, and wheeled themselves across the cobblestones towards the crowd watching the ceremony.

The demons had never witnessed the event before, and so the sight of the Grim Reaper and several others dancing around the stage trying to catch some green gnomes with a saw seemed quite normal. The man making his way through the crowd while assaulting bystanders was unexpectedly novel.

The road towards Dead Square was downhill. If you carried on walking, you would reach the canal. The entire city sloped towards the circular waterway. A logical design in case the canal ever flooded. It also helped prevent too many accidents when the tentacles from beneath swarmed up the walls and caught unsuspecting pedestrians. There are yellow lines all around the towpaths, and it says 'Mind the gap' for a reason.

The lay of the land meant that the demons could see what was happening in the crowd, and when Yargvel the unicorn tapped Morgarth on the shoulder, she knew what he was going to say. "There're demons down there."

"I know."

"Did they get jobs as part of the show?"

"No, Blunt said they got jobs, but he didn't

really explain it. Something about sales and a big surprise."

"Well… it is surprising."

"We'll go ask them," Morgarth said. "We need to clear up this mess, and the Grim Reaper is here. People will listen to him."

So five hundred demons, in the form of childhood toys, sodden and filthy from their journey through the streets of the city, continued their march towards the crowd.

Run, Rabbit, Run

He ran.

In front of him, he pushed a wheelbarrow with two boxes balanced upon it. It was difficult to move with the extra layers and the head under one arm, but he managed. The cobbled streets threw the wheelbarrow around and the boxes threatened to tumble to the ground, but he kept running, telling himself over and over again, "You're dead, you do not need to breathe."

The rain lashed down, and the festive lights, so bright and colourful, were succumbing to the elements. Cheap electric fairy lights were shorting out under the rainfall that was turning to sleet. The ground was becoming icy beneath his feet, and he tried not to think about a single slip stopping him from getting there soon enough.

Nothing made sense, and when nothing makes sense, Blunt's best weapon was nonsense. He liked the sound of it, even if it was meaningless.

As he rounded a corner, he slipped and caught himself by grabbing hold of a lamppost.

"Woah there, fella," a voice called out.

A small group of people coming from the opposite direction paused while Blunt stood there, panting.

"Interesting outfit you got there," another of them said.

"I haven't got time for a little meeting for you

and your mates to weigh up the chances of kicking seven bells out of a man in a rabbit suit. So bugger off," Blunt said between ragged breaths.

The man held up his hands. "We're not out to cause trouble. What's in the boxes?"

"Nothing you'd want. Why don't you catch up with the demons and start abusing them instead?"

"Abusing them? Not us, mate. If that's your plan, I suggest you turn back now. We know what it's like to be on the receiving end. We're just planning on standing in the middle."

"The middle of what?"

"The demons and everyone else, of course."

Blunt looked up. "You're planning on standing in the middle? Why?"

"Seems like the right thing to do," another voice said.

"Right," Blunt nodded. "Carry on then."

"What are you planning on doing?"

"Me? Oh, I'm going to stop a man dressed up like Father you-know-who from attacking the Grim Reaper, unveil a plot by a bunch of green gnomes to incriminate the demons, and tell everyone that Bleakest Day is just a con by companies to make us spend our money."

"Oh," the man said. "Well, good luck with the stuff at the beginning. Everyone already knows the last bit, though, so don't bother."

Blunt nodded, then lifted the oversized head he was holding under his arm and put it on to complete his outfit as a pink rabbit in a nurse's uniform.

"Do my eyes glow?" he asked.

"It's quite hard to hear you with the head on."

"I said, do my eyes glow?"

"Oh, yup, you look like a huge demon," the man said, giving Blunt a thumbs-up. The small group behind him did the same.

Blunt returned the thumbs-up with the rabbit gloves and started running again. Before he'd taken two steps, he hit a stone, and the wheelbarrow tipped over. The boxes slipped out and crashed open. He started cursing under his rabbit head as the small group, one of them wearing a dressing gown, caught up with him.

Blunt looked up and tried to assess the little group. It took a moment, but he realised they weren't norms. There was something about the way they looked and the fact that they were walking from the direction of the Styx neighbourhood.

"You're Hopes, aren't you?"

"Have you got a problem with Hopes?" asked the man who seemed to be leading them.

Blunt shook his head, swallowed, and then said four words he hated.

"I need your help."

Moments later, he was running without the wheelbarrow. It was harder to run with the head on, but as he reached the end of the next street, he caught up with the tail end of the demonic horde. Behind them was a group of citizens.

Not everyone, it seemed, planned to stand in

the middle of things. As Blunt drew closer, he could hear the abuse being given to the horde.

"Bleakest Day is for people, not demons!"

"You don't deserve to be a fluffy fox!"

"Go to hell… again!"

In Blunt's opinion, the quality of insults was a woeful reflection of the quality of Gloomwood society's education. Which, he supposed, made sense. The Office of the Dead assumed everyone died with a certain level of education, which caused numerous problems because levels of education had changed a lot over the last hundred years.

At the back of the pack of demons, the less mobile soft toys struggled to keep pace with their limbed colleagues. As the citizens of Gloomwood, who were an eclectic bunch themselves, caught up to the demons, they began hurling more than abuse.

Blunt walked softly, which he found quite easy in his rabbit suit, and closed the distance with the growing number of angry Gloomwoodians. Soon, he found himself standing behind a creature with the head of a whale and a man who seemed to twitch with nervous energy.

"What do you think you're doing?" Blunt growled from within the bunny rabbit suit, trying to muster his best demonic voice impression.

When two ahead of him turned to look at him, they leapt backwards. The man tripped over his own feet and let out a wail of surrender, while the whale went on the attack, bringing down a stick on Blunt's head. The costume protected him from the worst of the blow, and the stick snapped.

Blunt raised his arms and waggled his fingers, making a sound that was normally reserved solely for the amusement of small children.

"Ooga-booga-ooga!"

The gathering of self-righteous demon-haters, finding a giant bunny demon on one side of them and an army of demons in front, was thrown into panic. They dispersed, the majority running past Blunt and into the night.

The braver few who were armed slapped weapons into their palms and began walking towards Blunt, but by now, the horde had noticed something—at least, the stragglers had—and turned, walking towards Blunt and those threatening him, almost all of whom were committed exorcists.

"You don't scare us, bunny," said a man with an extra pair of arms and a tattoo of a teddy in a noose.

"I prefer Thumper, or Bugs, at a push. Though I suppose you could call me Roger," Blunt said, trying to keep his voice demonic.

"Eh?"

"Don't bother talking to it," someone else said. "Let's just beat the stuffing out of it!"

That was when the soft toys joined the fray.

Blunt threw a punch, making some exorcists reconsider their actions, but when the demons swarmed over the men, he covered the mouth of the bunny head to stop him from being able to look out onto the world as Morgarth's words came back to him.

'Violence is about will, not strength.'

The sound of tearing flesh, weeping adults, and a chorus of demonic voices was too much. Blunt sank to his knees and covered his head until the screaming stopped.

When he felt a tap on his shoulder, he took his hands off his head. In front of him was a row of heads and, behind them, a stack of body parts.

"What do you say?" asked a demon rag doll with blonde wool hair and a t-shirt that read 'babe'.

"We're sorry for trying to bludgeon you," the heads said in unison.

"Uh, right," Blunt said.

The doll, which had two button eyes and a permanent smile, stared into the costume's mouth, and Blunt felt himself shrinking inside.

"Who are you, and why are you dressed up like a rabbit with red, glowing eyes?"

Blunt swallowed. His mouth felt like someone had spent a week in there with a hair dryer. "I was trying to make a point," he croaked.

"Did you succeed?" the doll asked as it hung on to the rabbit ears. Its feet dangled off the floor as it pressed its face against the black mesh fabric inside the mouth of the rabbit.

"Not yet. I need to get to Dead Square to show people how easily someone could dress up as one of you and incriminate you for a crime you didn't commit."

"And why would you help us? Why would they listen?"

"Um, have you heard of Augustan Blunt?"

"The one who stabbed us in the back. Visited us and then led the charge to treat us like animals, to hunt us. If we had him in Hell, he would scream for eternity."

"Yeah… Well, that's, uh, that's me. Hello."

"Blunt?" Sarah Von Faber asked as she flickered into existence from where a pair of sensible black shoes had been sitting on the cobbles.

"Sarah? You shouldn't be here."

"Where else should I be?"

"It's dangerous."

"You're an idiot, Blunt."

B TEAM

"This is ridiculous," Leighton said as she cycled through the streets of Gloomwood.

"But Detective Blunt—"

"Don't talk," Leighton hissed as she hopped off the curb and rode around a small group of people.

The small gatherings were made up of two different camps of people. Those who were celebrating Bleakest Eve and waiting to count in Bleakest Day were friendly. They waved and cheered as she rode by. The other type of group watched the news, carrying weapons, only some of which were makeshift, and 'readying themselves' for trouble because of the demons. In both groups, most people were avoiding a state of sobriety.

She bounced up a curb, and the handlebars juddered, sending a shock wave through her wrists and the basket attached to the front of the bicycle, where three demons were hidden under a blanket.

"What are we even supposed to do when we get there?" Leighton grumbled to herself. "I don't have any evidence. Just going to turn up and start pointing my finger at people? Say 'You planned this whole thing.' Yeah, Leighton, that's going to work."

She turned a corner and skidded to a stop. Further down the street, lit up by spotlights and displaying the second largest dead tree in the city, was Pallbearers nightclub and restaurant. Judging by the excess of black luxury hearses lining the street, the party was far from over.

The bike squeaked as she pedalled closer and took a left turn down an alleyway by the side of the nightclub. Out of the weak glow of the streetlights, she parked the bike, leaving it on its kickstand, and uncovered the demons.

"Okay, Jarg, which way now?" she asked the demon sous-chef.

"When Blunt came to find me, he must have come through that door. You can get to the kitchen that way. Can I wait out here? I don't want to lose my job."

"Jarg, if Blunt doesn't stop the big green fake Santa from using your fellow demons as suicide bombers, you won't have a job. Even if he stops that, the people who did all of this will still be around, and they probably won't give up. So you can stay here, but when you have no job and are being hunted by the rest of the city, don't say there was nothing you could have done about it," Leighton said as she offered a hand to the soft toy.

"Wish I had my knives," the octopus said as he slapped a tentacle into Leighton's open hand.

She lifted the demons out of the basket, trying not to carry them, but rather to help them, and then turned to face the door.

"If we get to the kitchen, I know how to get us into the party," Jarg said.

"Just get me close enough," Vellmar said with a wide hippo smile. It was threatening even though it really, really shouldn't have been possible. "I'll do the rest."

Leighton looked at the hippopotamus. It didn't look like it could do anyone any harm with its patchwork fur body and stumpy little arms. Its head was oversized, and its mouth contained nothing resembling a tooth.

"How?"

"Like the detective said. I've still got my voice."

"Oh," Leighton nodded. "How's that going to help?"

"I'll just ask them to admit it."

Leighton let out a sigh. Blunt had been clear. Just keep the party guests there and wait for backup.

Gnome Grab

The Kallikantzaroi were quick and determined. Before anyone managed to lay a hand on them, they had cut a gouge in the tree, but despite the wind, it was yet to collapse.

Chief Sowercat held a squirming green gnome in either hand while he barked orders at his officers to capture the rest. Mortimer had decided his efforts weren't helping anyone and watched on, helpless.

On one side of the stage, a woman in a festive jumper with a large pink mound of hair on her head and a clipboard in one hand waved at Mortimer. When she caught his eye, she mouthed, "Miss Holt needs you."

Mortimer nodded and disappeared offstage, running through the revolving doors of the Office of the Dead and into the building. They had converted the reception area into something between a party and a television recording studio. Radio and television crews recorded commentators talking about the evening's events, while their roving reporters stood outside in the worsening weather.

Wires crisscrossed the floor, and Mortimer had to play a game of hopscotch as he neared the central area, where Lavender Holt, the Artificer and chief organiser of the day's events, stood with Crispin Neat, the manager of the Office of the Dead.

"Mister Mortimer," Neat said, his dour features almost, but not quite, suggesting displeasure. For Crispin Neat, this was the equivalent of screaming obscenities into Mortimer's face. "A serious threat has been made, and we need to evacuate the square."

Mortimer tried not to meet the manager's gaze. "Right. Is this because of the green gnomes? The police aren't having much luck with the tree, and the man with the bells is getting closer to the stage. It looks like he has demons with him."

"We know, Ralph," Lavender said, waving a tentacle towards several screens. "We have a grotesque's eye view."

Mortimer nodded, catching her reference to the gargoyles and grotesques moving across the buildings around Dead Square with cameras to deliver aerial shots of the crowd.

"Look!" Lavender said, pointing at a screen which showed five hundred demons marching down the road leading into Dead Square.

"That one's huge," Mortimer said, indicating one of the demons. "I didn't think they got that big."

"The bunny," Neat said, unable to hide his distaste for the word. "We fear they have planned a larger attack. There has been mention of an explosive device."

"A bomb?"

"That's what an explosive device is."

"The problem is that the demons are now cutting off the only route out of the square," Lavender said. "Which means we are boxed in."

"We could bring everyone in here," Mortimer

said.

"That's the plan, Mister Mortimer," Neat said. "It must not look like an evacuation. We must maintain the festive atmosphere."

"But—"

"If those people run at the demons, do you believe it will end well?"

Lavender looked down at a clipboard and scribbled notes on it. "The optics would be terrible. The Grim Reaper would lose authority, and the Office of the Dead would suffer. By my calculations, the city would be in outright anarchy by noon tomorrow, and, in all likelihood, this building would burn to the ground. The city of Gloomwood would crumble, and all that would be left would be lots of dead people with nothing to do but torture each other. That's even if there is no bomb. If there is a bomb, well, it will happen quicker."

"Quicker than twelve hours?" Mortimer said. "The optics? Torture? They might be nice to each other."

Crispin Neat's right eyebrow twitched. "Have you met people?"

"Here's the script," the Artificer said, holding out a piece of paper to Mortimer. "Hurry. Give it to his Deathliness, it needs to be him, he's the authority. We need to create a distraction."

Mortimer grabbed the paper and made his way through the bustling media hub, dodging wires, cameras and people running from place to place while makeup artists tried to keep everyone looking fresh, or at least freshly dead.

He burst out of the revolving doors and ran across the platform, waving the paper. As he did, one of the gnomes ran at him, and he tripped, letting go of the script. Landing in a puddle of ice-cold water and sleet, it was soaked through in seconds. As Mortimer gathered it up, he realised the writing was smudged and illegible.

The Grim Reaper reached down, and without thinking, Mortimer took Death's hand. "Are you okay?" Grim asked.

"Yes," Mortimer said. Then he froze as he realised he was holding the skeletal hand of the Grim Reaper. It was no longer attached to the rest of him.

"May I have my hand back?"

"Sorry," Mortimer squeaked. "Um, we need to get everyone inside the building."

"I see. Is Miss Holt going to speak to them?"

"No… um, she says it has to be you to maintain authority. Oh, and it can't be an evacuation."

"I see."

"Here, there's a script." Mortimer handed the sodden paper to the Grim Reaper, who looked down at the smudged words.

"Do you know what it says?"

"Um, no. Maybe something about a party inside?"

"Oh, good idea."

Grim walked up to the microphone again and looked out across the crowd. The small group of demons and the man in green were now only a few meters from the stage. Further behind the crowd, the entire demonic horde was closing in, led by a large pink bunny.

"Citizens of Gloomwood, as it's Bleakest Eve and the weather is not what we hoped for…" Grim paused as laughter rippled through the crowd. "We thought it would be a nice thing to start a new tradition and open the Office of the Dead for all of you brave enough to come out tonight. It's warm and cosy inside and the perfect setting for our celebrations. Unfortunately, technical issues with our equipment mean the Bleakest Eve broadcast will take place indoors for the first time. There's even live music. You're in for a treat. Let's get our… groove on."

The problem with being a seven-foot-tall skeleton who embodies the concept of death is that it's difficult to come across as enthusiastic. So, although Grim was attempting to be as upbeat as possible, the crowd didn't quite get behind things in the way he had hoped.

Grim looked over at Mortimer as the crowd remained steadfast and unmoved. Mortimer shrugged, and Grim turned back to the crowd.

"There are also free drinks inside before midnight."

The crowd surged forward, streaming around the stage and through the revolving doors.

For a moment, at least, the man clobbering people with a bell and the strange group of demons had been forgotten. People ignored the gnomes bouncing around the stage, making the police look like some kind of clown show.

After all, there was free booze on offer and, among the cold, wet and tired crowd, a distinct lack of shame.

Going Downhill

"They're running away from us?" Morgarth asked the giant bunny by her side.

Blunt walked in time with the demons. The black mesh obscured his vision somewhat, but he could make out the crowd moving around the stage.

"They're going indoors because I called in a bomb threat. I'm not sure if there is one or not, but it clears them out of the way and hopefully means there won't be a fight. Can you see the man in green?"

On Blunt's left, a pair of black trousers, hovering a couple of inches above the cobbles, marched alongside them. Sarah had brought him, in costume, to the front of the horde. With that job complete, she had shrugged, "I'm struggling… I think it might be stress," and mostly vanished.

"Yes," Morgarth said. "He's still approaching the stage, and he's hitting people with a bell."

"Causing a right old ding-dong," Blunt said. Fortunately, nobody could see his face and his look of disappointment when nobody congratulated him on his quick wit. The mask also prevented him from seeing the look of disgust on the faces of many of the demons. A look of disgust on the face of a furry T-Rex is something to behold.

"The others are there," Morgarth said. She pointed a tiny arm in the stage's direction, but nobody noticed.

"The traitors," said Yargvel, the rainbow unicorn, marching beside Morgarth.

"No," Blunt said. "They've been kidnapped and tortured. I'm pretty sure that big green bastard has sewn baubles into them."

"That's just… weird, even for us," Yargvel said. "Sewing another person's baubles into—"

"Don't overthink it," Blunt said. "You're making it worse."

"And the attack on the Grim Reaper?" Morgarth asked.

"That was those little green bastards, only they were wearing costumes to look like you."

"And that's why you're dressed like a bunny?"

"Exactly. To help illustrate the point, and also so I could get close enough to you to get the message across. Everyone thinks I'm on the exorcists' side."

Morgarth's head bobbed up and down. "It sort of makes sense. Except, why pick on us?"

"Oh, well, I think you were just an easy target for the big green bloke. Everyone already hates you, he hates the Grim Reaper, and you're his most recent mistake."

"Oi," Yargvel said. "I thought you were on our side?"

"In the eyes of the public," Blunt said. "Let me finish my sentence. I think the toy people have manipulated the bloke in green."

"Toy people? There are others like us?" Morgarth asked.

"I mean the people who made you."

"Ah, the dark lords of Asgaroth have breached this afterlife from the demon pits, where we are born of spite. Those Beelzebub feeds with the souls of mortals to drag us out of the filth of sin—"

"Um, no. I mean the people who manufacture toys that are like the bodies you have."

"Ah. So this is all a manipulation?" Yargvel said. "This is excellent work."

"Yes," Morgarth said. "You must admire the craftwork that goes into an intricate plan like this."

Blunt shook his head, but as he was wearing a giant bunny head, nobody noticed.

The horde followed the three of them—and Sarah's trousers—ever closer to the towering Bleakest Day tree in front of the Office of the Dead.

Looking up, Blunt spied the cameras in the hands of some of the strange beings that dwelled on the outside of the Office of the Dead. Rumour had it they never descended from up there and that they ate the ravens, the only birds in the city. Yet Blunt could have sworn he'd seen them grabbing coffee first thing in the morning at the cafe next to the Office of the Dead.

It was then that he realised what the scene would look like from above. "Oh no," he said. "Oh, we are so fu—"

Stay Tuned

Lavender Holt and Crispin Neat were in conversation when Mortimer appeared in front of them again, looking flustered.

"Mister Mortimer?" Neat asked.

"His Lordship says he's going to stay outside."

Lavender nodded. "It's good for people to see him there. Makes it look like he cares."

"He does care," Mortimer said.

"Yes, and that's what it looks like," Neat said. "Now, we have another problem."

"Oh?"

"It seems we did not prepare the media for the change in arrangements. As people have entered the building, they've disrupted many of the live feeds and commentaries. This is very poor planning."

Ralph Mortimer looked around as people shoved each other towards the doors at the end of the reception area, where several Office of the Dead employees were attempting to corral everyone upstairs. They had trampled the media circus, and many members of the crowd had stopped to meet their favourite presenters or pull faces at the video cameras.

It is a universal given that should the opportunity to present yourself to a vast audience arise unexpectedly, then the correct course of action is to wave and pull the strangest face you can manage. And when it comes to strange faces, the dead have a distinct advantage over the living in higher pain thresholds, fewer consequences, and—for no apparent reason—much more elastic face tissue.

The crowd were now kicking cables and equipment out of the way, tripping over, and running rough-shod through the building's reception area amid a lot of angry, swearing talent and frustrated producers. Nervous support staff were debating attempting to blend in with the crowd to disappear.

"Mister Mortimer," Lavender said, placing a tentacle on his shoulder and pivoting the third assistant to the manager of the Office of the Dead towards the few screens still showing a picture. They all showed grotesque shots of Dead Square from above. Some of the more panoramic angles showed the horde approaching.

"Oh, that looks like everyone is running from… oh. Well, the commentary—"

"Sound is completely out. All that is being broadcast is coming from the cameras above us," Neat said.

"Maybe we should just cut the transmission."

Lavender smiled. It was not something Mortimer wished to see.

"First, there is no producer here who will accept cutting the transmission. The viewing figures for this are huge. Second, cutting the feed with no explanation will not calm the situation."

"Well, what are we going to do?" Mortimer

asked.

Neat pointed to a bulbous monitor. "We're going to watch and hope that the pair of trousers, the big bunny, the police, and His Lordship perform some kind of seasonal miracle."

"Pair of trousers?"

Ho, Ho, Ho

"I've got you by the baubles now," the man in green said as he stood in front of the stage. The great tree swayed in the wind, making creaking noises that grew in volume and something called ominosity.

Ominosity is not to be confused with ominousness, which cannot be empirically measured. Ominosity is measured on a scale from dripping tap, creaking floorboards, and strange scratching noises up to wolves howling at the moon and emails from bosses that read, 'See me in my office.' So ominous had the tree's sounds become they were in danger of becoming a measure of omnosity themselves.

Grim stood on the stage in his purple patchwork ceremonial robes. In one skeletal hand, he held a scythe. Holding a scythe was expected of Grim Reaper, but this was one he was particularly fond of because he had glued a festive star to the top of it.

"I see, so you stole my decorations?" Grim said. "Are you here to return them?"

"Ho, ho, ho," the man said, holding his belly like a bowl full of jelly. "Indeed I am." He reached into the hessian bag tied to his belt. "But the question is, have you been good?"

He pulled out several decorations tied together by a piece of string from the bag. The decorations were attached to a strange plastic and metal box that had wires popping out of the sides, which were held together by tape. On the top of the box were some brass buttons. The strings of the decorations were tied to a small aerial sticking out of the box.

Grim tilted his head to one side, increasing his own omnosity rating by a magnitude of ten. "Have I been good? On reflection, yes. Have you?"

The green-clad man grinned. In front of him, a small row of demons shuffled their feet, tails, pads, and ears without meeting the Grim Reaper's gaze with their own glowing red eyes.

"Uh, Your Lordship?" Chief Sowercat of the Gloomwood police said from behind the Grim Reaper. "The little green gnome things have all legged it. Do you want us to kick the green bloke's head in?"

"I don't think that would be wise," Grim said. "Go inside."

"Can't do that, I'm afraid, sir. Though it's kind of you to suggest it. There appears to be a demonic horde coming up the road, and it looks like that man might attempt to threaten you."

"Threaten me? Do you really think so?"

"Yes… sir."

"Hm. You there, beardy man, are you attempting to threaten me? And you, demons, why would you be threatening me?"

"They're here to destroy you," Sowercat said.

Grim lifted his arms, his robe sleeves falling down to his elbows, exposing his skeletal wrists.

"There seems to be some confusion," he said. The timbre of his voice changed, and the wind howled a little more. "Threatening Death is like threatening to splash water at the ocean."

The man wrapped a huge hand around one of the decorations on the remote control, a small globe with a snowman inside.

"Really?" he said. "I understand your decorations hold immense power. Inside each of these demons are another of these decorations and an explosive."

"What a strange thing to do," Grim said.

"Bloody Blunt and his bomb threat," Sowercat muttered under his breath.

"I'm going to unleash the power of these decorations unless you admit that this is Christmas."

Grim nodded. "I see. This is not Christmas. I can say that it is, if it makes you happy, but it won't change anything."

"These decorations contain power. I know they do."

"Yes, immense power," Grim said. "The power of sentimentality. Were they to break, I would be very upset. I'm quite attached to them. I have purchased a new one every Bleakest Day since it began."

"What?" the man and the demons in front of him all asked in unison.

"Every year, before Bleakest Eve, I go out and buy a new decoration for the tree. It's a tradition.

That snowman globe is from four years ago when the manager of the Office of the Dead and I had dinner at Mister Mortimer's house. It was delightful. We played charades. I wasn't very good at it, but we did laugh. The gingerbread house is from the year I spent Bleakest Day in Grimsby, which, it turns out, isn't named after me. Would you like me to go on?"

"But… the power? I was told there was immense power in these, just waiting to be released."

"Oh. I said that because people kept moving the box with them in. Every year, we have to go up into the attic and shift boxes. Tell people things are powerful, and they soon stop stacking other things on top of them. Now, is that it? All this so you could ask me to call it Christmas?"

Green Father Christmas, Faux-Santa, Papa not-Noel, deflated. His hand holding the remote dropped to his side, and, with his other hand, he pulled his hat from his head. The bell on it jingled once, then snapped off and bounced away across the cobbles.

"I just wanted to do the grotto."

Sowercat clambered down the front of the temporary stage. With his hands outstretched, he walked towards the man.

"Don't worry, fella. These things happen to all of us. I miss it too. When I was a lad, we'd get the whole family together and—"

"Don't move," the bearded man growled. He raised the remote in front of him, pointing it towards Grim. "If I can't have it, none of you will."

He paused as there came a sound like a high-pitched whistle. For a moment, the wind stopped, as if someone had silenced it.

Then, without a sound, neither cracking nor groaning, the tree fell. As it plummeted to the ground, the scream of the big man dressed in green broke the silence before the tree crushed him.

The remote flew from his hands into the air. As Sowercat launched himself at it, the demons did the same. Trem bounded from her place in front of the stage and, using Sowercat as a platform, threw herself in the air, catching the remote in her tiny rabbit paws. She whirled in the air until she landed on the shattered remains of the tree and the soft bed of dead pine needles.

Sowercat slowly got to his feet. He'd landed in a puddle and tried, unsuccessfully, to brush off some of the water.

"We're saved!" a demon said in the voice of a duck.

"I can't believe it," Sowercat said, a smile on his face as he shook his head and his nose swung from side to side. "What were the chances of the tree finally falling just then?"

"Yes," Grim said. "Very slim. If I recall correctly, though, it is after the jolly big man has been and gone that the celebrations truly begin."

The sound of a multitude of soft-footed toys and the gentle murmuring of voices trying very hard not to be too demonic began to fill the square.

Blunt, in his bunny suit, and the horde had arrived.

Media Snafu

"What just happened?" the Artificer asked.

She was standing with Neat and Mortimer in front of a monitor in the wreckage of the Office of the Dead's media centre.

"The tree crushed Santa," Mortimer said.

"Yes," Neat said. "That's an accurate description. However, it looks a little like…"

He reached forward and rewound the footage, pressing play once more and leaning closer to the screen. He hit pause and rewound it again, playing the footage back at quarter speed. Then he hit pause again.

"Wasn't there a star on top of His Lordship's scythe?"

"Yes," Lavender said. "It caused problems as it reflected lights at the camera. It was there, and then it… just vanishes."

"He's the Grim Reaper," Mortimer said. "Strange stuff happens around him."

Neat nodded. "Yes, like trees suddenly snapping along a perfect cut."

"The gnomes did that with their saw."

"Good point, Mister Mortimer," Lavender said, putting a tentacle around his shoulders. "Did you know you can beta-test advertising campaigns? A certain type of person can earn significant money doing that. It's all about really understanding the humdrum, face-value message companies want to spoon-feed you."

"What?"

Neat stood up, holding his hands together in a small pyramid shape as he considered the video. Still looking at the screen, he said, "He works for me, Miss Holt. Tentacles to yourself, please."

"Fine," she said, unwrapping Mortimer from her tentacles. "They should be reconnecting the other camera feeds and sound any second now."

Demons Arrive

"Happy Bleakest Eve," Grim said as the demons approached.

"We wish to make a statement," Morgarth said.

"That's what I said to Miss Holt, but apparently, leather chaps was a step too far."

The demons, Sowercat, and Blunt all held their breath while deciding whether or not the Grim Reaper was joking. He was not.

"Worry not, demons," Grim said. "The one who plotted to explode your friends is under that tree."

"Someone was going to do what to our who?" Yargvel snarled.

At Morgarth's side, Blunt knelt down in his bunny costume. To any observer, it looked as if he was kneeling in fealty to the Grim Reaper. Inside, though, Blunt was squeezing his eyes shut as he tried to stop himself from throwing up the ale, the only thing he could remember putting in his stomach, from the pub.

"Yargvel, your voice," Morgarth said.

Sowercat raised a quivering hand. "Are we all good now? Because, and I don't mean to be rude, I'm not standing here listening to demon voices for fun."

"Thank you for your bravery, Chief Sowercat."

Blunt stepped forward. "Send the crowd back

out, Sowercat. We need to stop the people from turning on the demons."

"Who the hell are you to tell me what to do?" Sowercat said, puffing out his chest. "Last I checked, the Chief of Police was me, not some demon bunny."

"You'd make a terrible demon bunny."

"That's not what I meant. I meant—"

"Yes, I got it. But you still need to send them out. The little green gnomes were dressing up as demons and making people hate them. While we're all here, we can clear this up."

"Of course a demon would say that. I mean, how convenient can you get?"

"It's true—"

"Really?"

"We didn't march all the way here just to say, 'Listen, Gloomwood, you better bow down to us, or we're going to control the Grim Reaper and turn the city into new Hell.'"

Bad Connection

"And we're live!" shouted a man in grey overalls, who, despite not working with anything that had oil involved in it, was covered in grease stains.

"Listen, Gloomwood, you better bow down to us, or we're going to control the Grim Reaper and turn the city into new Hell," declared the giant bunny standing before the demonic horde.

Silence descended in households, pubs 'definitely not still serving customers', on street corners, and at gatherings throughout the Grim Reaper's slice of the afterlife.

In the temporary media centre in the Office of the Dead reception area, there was a loud bang, and the smell of smoke filled the room.

"Sorry, that didn't work," a woman wearing overalls announced. "Feeds are down again, should be back up soon."

The name of the man wearing overalls was Hisham, and he was not a trained electrician or technician. His overalls were part of a fancy dress costume. He had come, ironically, as a ghost hunter, though he'd lost his neutron pack. He'd been following the crowd to the free alcohol offered when an irate television producer had berated him.

So furious had the onslaught of expletive-driven invective been from the producer, and the next producer, and the next, that he had pretended to be at work. Then came the talent, who were so filled with wrath towards him for issues that not only had nothing to do with him but also were beyond his comprehension that he'd given up and started trying to fix them. This, in the city of Gloomwood, is quite a common reason for sudden and seemingly illogical career changes.

Little did Hisham know that he would go down in the Gloomwood history books as 'some random guy who royally bollocksed it all up'.

All Together Now

The green and purple lights strewn across Gloomwood's streets swung as the howling gale grew stronger. Hail ricocheted off cobblestones made hazardous with black ice forming on already worn smooth stone. Despite all of this, the people marched.

The broadcast had caused a stir. The people had watched as Father of the festival that shall not be named arrived with his demon prisoners. Then, through some kind of demonic power, the tree had fallen on top of him. As if it had been called, the horde arrived when the Grim Reaper was most vulnerable.

Now the people would sort this mess out.

Wrapped in scarves, gloves and mittens, huddled together and fuelled by unique rage, the people of Gloomwood marched under one banner. 'How dare they?' people asked. 'Who do they think they are?' they cried. With ever-growing incredulity, their numbers swelled.

From the doorways of houses whose occupants would never dream of taking action stepped those who proclaimed, 'I've had enough'. Which was true, because many of them had certainly had 'one too many'.

Nobody had ever had the audacity to attempt a coup. 'Overthrow the Grim Reaper? Can't be done.' The biggest question on all their lips was the simplest one: 'Why?'

"We've always been good to the demons," Gillie Bailey said from somewhere deep within the confines of three scarves, two bobble hats, and a coat that was three sizes too big.

"I know. We let them come here from Hell. What have they got to complain about, anyway? Overthrow the Grim Reaper? Well, we'll show them."

"There's five hundred of them."

"Exactly, there's way more of us. What chance do they have?"

Onwards they marched. When one fell, dozens more swept in to ensure any valuables were swiftly removed and to help them up.

Shoulder to shoulder, gods walked with myths, nightmares held hands with hopes and dreams. Norms lifted pabies onto their shoulders. The braver, more violent types rushed to the fore, wielding anything and everything that might be a weapon.

Eric, level four thug and potential future stooge, had mustered his colleagues, and they were showing people how to palm cudgels in a menacing manner. He didn't openly say it, but there was a recruitment opportunity here.

An angry woman with an umbrella insisted on ensuring that everyone knew she 'had told them they were evil.'

Juanita regaled those walking with her of the giant rabbit demon she had seen in person. How it had the strength of ten men and hadn't even blinked when she had hit it with all her strength.

Miss Perkins, an odious woman at the best of times, found her encounter fascinated people. "One tried to steal my purse when I was shopping this morning, horrible creature,"

Tales of woe at the hands of demons crawled out of the recesses in people's memories. What were inconsequential moments now became nuanced, darkened with the realisation that the cuddly squirrel who had helped them carry their shopping was evil. That the squeaky turtle they had stepped on was a vile creature. That the friendly little elephant stacking shelves was secretly plotting to overthrow the city and torment them for all eternity… probably by putting everything you want the most on the highest shelves.

As they closed in on Dead Square, the demons were ready, in a tight square, a military formation. They were the soldiers of Hell.

Stand Firm

Blunt was ready.

There were more than he had expected, many more. He had imagined a celebratory crowd. Raucous, enthusiastic people who had decided to see in Bleakest Day in style.

Instead, he faced a mob. A large, angry, violent mob.

He clambered up onto the stage, but before he could speak, a police officer tackled him.

"Gerroff me, you bleedin' idiot!" Blunt wrestled with the police officer on the floor until the constable abruptly stopped struggling and let him go.

Standing over Blunt and the police officer was Chief Sowercat.

"Blunt, is that you in a bloody bunny costume?"

"It wasn't bloody before, guv. I think he broke my nose," the constable said, cupping his hands over his face.

"Finally worked it out?" Blunt said.

"Thought the voice was familiar, but when I saw you hit the floor like a sack of potatoes, it all made sense. Why the hell are you dressed up as a demon?"

Sowercat offered a hand and pulled Blunt to his feet.

"It's going to sound stupid now."

"Only now?"

"Fine. The idea was to bring the demons here, get up on stage, and reveal it's me."

Sowercat stared at Blunt, his nose growing as he tried to control his temper. "What would that achieve?"

"I'm using the fake news against itself. I can't explain everything that's gone on to people. They'll lose interest and turn off. The salient point is—"

"Good word that, salient."

"Thanks. As I was saying, the salient point is that the demons weren't the people who tried to burn down the stupid box," Blunt said, pointing to the rest of the cabin on the edge of the stage. "What is even the point of that thing?"

"It's more secure. People have been going in and out of the reception area all the time," Sowercat said. "In hindsight, it may have been a target."

"You think?"

"Oh yeah, have a go at the person who has been here doing his job all day while you dress up as a bunny rabbit. You think taking your costume off is going to make this mob back down?"

"Yes. They think I'm some kind of exorcist leader, a professional demon hunter. They have built me up as some kind of vengeful, demon-smiting warrior. I'm turning the tables on them. It's all about manipulation. I'm going to use what they've done against them."

Sowercat's nose popped. "That's the stupidest idea I've ever heard, and I work with this lot." He waved his hands at the few remaining police officers on the stage.

"Bit harsh, guv," one of them said.

"Shut it, Timmins, you brainless oaf," Sowercat roared. "You were hoping to stop civil war by going, 'Look at me'. You are one self-important gobshite."

"Well," Blunt said, "there's only one way to find out."

"Yes," said Grim, who, for a moment, had enjoyed being in the background of a conversation. It was quite a novelty. "Detective Blunt, you have the stage."

As he said this, the front of the mob rushed forward, but the demons, forged in the pits of Hell and with the benefit of years of combat training, held their ground—despite their diminutive furry bodies.

Dead Demons

She held the wound in her stomach closed and winced.

"Medic!" someone called from her side. The shouting and chanting of the surrounding crowd drowned out the voices of everyone but those nearest to her.

"I'm fine," Morgarth said. "Stitch me up. It'll take more than a pointed stick to keep this demon down."

"Morgarth, hold still," said the medic, a two-foot-tall green tiger by the name of Alejandro Cracked-screen. "It's... oh, Morgarth, it's through and through."

"Tell it to me straight, doc. How bad is it?"

"I can patch you up, but when this is over, you're going to need some new stuffing."

"Mortals and their obsession with stabbing. Perhaps we should show them what stabbing is all about?"

"Does it hurt?" Alejandro asked.

"Pain is our friend," she said. Her smile, terrifying even though it was made of felt and foam, grew broader. "Can you make the patch something different this time? The glitter one was nice, but I think people took me less seriously."

Around them, the crowd of others like her were waving placards as they roared. A chorus of demonic voices demanding to be heard.

"Demon rights are dead folks' rights! Demon rights are dead folks' rights!"

Alejandro stitched her up, and those standing around her helped Morgarth the destroyer, once part of the Devil's Elite Guard, to her feet. She glanced down at her stomach at her new patch. It was tartan. It didn't sit well with her purple belly or the light blue fur of the rest of her body, but it held the stuffing in.

Gone were the days when Morgarth stood eight feet tall with a body that screamed temptation and skin that could withstand temperatures that the mortal realm had never seen. These days, she was two feet tall—two and a half if she lifted herself on her tail—and inhabited the body of a blue furry dinosaur. She took some small comfort in the fact it was a tyrannosaurus rex, but it was a tiny comfort.

Her fellow demon outcasts surrounded her. All shapes and colours of the rainbow, if rainbows were painted in warm pastel colours with occasional neon splashes. Every demon in the city had gathered in front of the Dead Square to stand in the shadow of the huge dead tree as rain and sleet poured down upon them.

The feet of demons and the people of Gloomwood trampled and muddied festive decorations now strewn over the cobblestones. The Bleakest Day celebration was under siege as the demons faced off against a crowd of angry citizens calling for their furry heads.

"Morgarth, they said they're going to teapot

us!" Yargvel shouted at her. The white and pink unicorn was waving a sign that said, 'I didn't leave Hell for this!'

"They mean kettling," Morgarth said, "and they can try, but we're demons. Prepare for violence!"

The horde roared, a sound of promised terror and suffering that would have caused any post-mortal human to collapse quivering in a ball of terror.

Snow

The roar sent Blunt to his knees. Around him, police officers fell to the floor, covering their ears, and many were instantly brought to terrified tears.

Grim, though, was unaffected, and he stepped up to the microphone and tapped his finger against the device.

"One, two, one, two."

His voice carried across the crowd. The microphone was on, but it wouldn't have mattered, anyway. His voice went where he wanted it to go.

The roar of the demons subsided, and the crowd surged forward once more.

"And now," Grim said, causing the crowd to falter, "in a change from our scheduled programming, I invite a giant bunny rabbit to speak."

Things slowed on the skirmish's front lines until confusion took over as the people of Gloomwood watched a giant rabbit attempting to adjust the height of a microphone stand while muttering muffled expletives.

"People of Gloomwood. You have been tricked," Blunt said a moment later, gaining the attention of both demons and citizens alike, many still locked in positions of violence. "The demons you are attacking haven't been responsible for any of the things you've been told about. This whole thing has been an attempt to discredit them."

"Bollocks!" someone in the crowd shouted.

"You think that they've done all of this because of things you've been shown, because some idiot detective was looking for demons. You're right to think that. It's exactly what you're supposed to think, but it's easy to dress up like a demon."

The crowd murmured.

"Someone hired people to dress up as demons and do these things," Blunt continued.

"Why should we listen to you?" someone asked.

This was the moment Blunt had been waiting for. He reached up and pulled on the rabbit's head, but it didn't move. "Just a second," he said as he tugged, pulled, and twisted.

"Allow me," Grim said, stepping forward.

From behind Blunt, the Grim Reaper gripped the ears of his rabbit costume and pulled.

"Look, the Grim Reaper is fighting back! Get them!" a voice shouted.

"No!" Blunt raised his hands, and the head finally came off. "It's me, Detective Blunt! See? I just dressed up as a demon, just like the people who tried to set fire to the Grim Reaper. It's all been a lie."

The crowd seemed unconvinced, and Blunt looked down at the crowd, panic rearing its head like a creepy serpent winking at him from his subconscious.

Then he saw it. A small group of figures wheeling boxes along the front lines of the skirmish, handing out Talk like Tuck masks.

Chief Sowercat stepped forward with several of his constables. He grabbed the microphone stand and cleared his throat.

"Detective Blunt is correct. Thanks to the efforts of the Gloomwood police, we've captured the culprits. These people"—he lifted a green gnome up by its neck—"have been dressing up as toys. We found their costumes under the stage. We've all been duped, and the demons didn't do any of this."

Blunt yanked the microphone back and muttered to Sowercat under his breath, "Could've mentioned you'd caught them before I started this."

Then he gave a smile and turned to the crowd.

"Thank you, Chief Sowercat. The demons mean you no harm, and I'll prove it. While you all stand there ready to attack them… they're going to sing. You can join in, if you like, but if you keep attacking a bunch of toys singing Bleakest Day songs, who are the real bastards here, eh?"

He realised it wasn't the most eloquent speech.

Pressing on, Blunt cleared his throat and leaned towards the microphone. There are gambles, and then there are hopeless attempts to pull on the heartstrings of the dead. This was the moment where he would have to put all his hopes in a song, but the Grim Reaper put a hand on his shoulder.

"But first," Death said, "Happy Bleakest Day."

He snapped his fingers, and the rain stopped, the wind dropped, and snow fell.

"All together now," Grim said.

*Catch a snowflake on your tongue,
and it feels like life has just begun,
watch the showreel one more time,
and feel a taste of life sublime.
If life is not what you seek,
then maybe you can take a peek,
and visit places far away,
through Death's eyes,
just for one day.*

The crowd, and five hundred demons wearing duck masks, sang in unison. They didn't know the words, only Death did, but his voice went wherever he wanted. The demon voices, masked by Tuck the Duck's patented vocal modulator, sounded a little better, but they didn't have the same power over people as Grim.

Blunt stood open-mouthed as the words tumbled out, unbidden and involuntarily. He stuck out his tongue, catching a single snowdrop... and remembered.

He remembered dressing the tree, family dinners, curling up on the sofa, cold winters' walks and laughter. So many things forgotten, long summer days, shared in-jokes, the first of so many things that mattered so much. Everything that could lift a person's heart for just a moment flooded through him, and he understood. This was what it meant to have your life flash before your eyes... though only the good parts. The parts worth remembering.

THE MORNING AFTER

After the night's events, they had stumbled home arm in arm. Laughing at the absurdity of it all and the sudden change in the crowd's outlook when the snow had fallen.

"Why didn't anyone say that's what it was about?" Blunt asked.

"It's one of those awkward things. A bit like explaining sex to a perfect stranger."

Blunt's cheeks grew a little brighter, involuntarily and unnecessarily. He was glad he hadn't paid for extra blood.

"See, we're far from strangers, Augie, and you're still blushing. Now imagine walking up to someone in the street and saying, 'Excuse me, what exactly happens when people have sex?'"

Blunt coughed, choking on his coffee. They lay in bed, side by side. Outside the window, snow covered every surface. For just one day, Gloomwood would look like a winter wonderland. In return, they would spend the next week stomping through sludge in soaking-wet socks.

In the corner of Sarah's room was a Bleakest Day tree. She had covered it in coloured lights, and beneath it lay a box with 'Augie' written on it in black marker pen.

"Go get it then," Sarah said.

"No," Blunt said. "Your present is at the office."

"What? You got me this… lovely perfume and make-up gift collection… thing."

"Yeah, that was a backup. You don't like it, do you?"

"No, it's lovely, it's just…"

"What?"

"It's specifically designed for people with scales. Fish, lizards, that kind of thing."

"What? That's a pretty niche—"

"Seven percent of the population, apparently."

"Really? Well, good job I've got something better for you then. Give me half an hour, and I'll bring it right back. Save me a mince pie."

"You're not going out in this, are you?"

"Bah, a bit of snow never hurt anyone."

Sarah's eyebrows crept up. "I think that would be quite easy to disprove."

"Well, I'll nip to the office, and we can do it properly. Just like Chr… Bleakest Day."

She smiled. "You're a big softie, Blunt."

"Don't tell anyone," he said with a smirk as he rolled off the bed. It took him a moment to locate his pile of clothes on the floor. "Are you going to keep helping the demons?" he asked as he pulled his trousers up over his festive socks and began buttoning his shirt.

"Do you think it's all over, then?"

Blunt struggled to do up the top button on his shirt and gave up. "When Sowercat's men got to Leighton and her three little demon friends, they found forty industry leaders sitting on the floor, crying. It looks like a bunch of them had bought into some kind of deal to run small businesses into the ground. It was all about timing. Bleakest Eve, the biggest retail weekend in the entire year, and suddenly nobody is buying toys."

Sarah sighed. "I get all of that. I just... it doesn't quite make sense. That man we pulled out from under the tree. He hated the demons so much."

Blunt nodded. "No reasoning with some people. At a certain point, his entire personality became about hating demons and the Grim Reaper. I feel sorry for him, really. He just wanted to be Father Christmas."

"Hm, he turned up to a huge public gathering thinking he was going to blow everybody up. Including us and the Grim Reaper. So I don't feel too bad for him."

"Fair point. Right, back in thirty. Stick the kettle on, and don't forget the mince pies."

"Staying here today, are you?" Sarah asked with a smile.

Blunt smiled back, then slipped on his coat, grabbed his hat, and was out of the door.

The streets were pristine, as if Blunt's footsteps were the first to breach the freshly laid snow. For once, the frozen gloom of the city felt like magic rather than the physical manifestation of the bitterness of its population's hearts.

He lost his footing on unexpected ice and chuckled to himself. "Oopsie-daisies."

Someone opened their front door, and Blunt gave them a wave. "Merry Bleakest Day."

"Merry Bleakest… hang on, you're Detective Blunt."

"Oh, uh, yup."

"You were there last night."

"Well, I don't consider myself a hero—"

"Hero? The Grim Reaper saved us, and those Hopes who gave out the masks. Even the bloody police caught the gnomes. What did you do? Put on a bloody bunny costume. You should mind your own business."

"Right. Well, Merry Bleakest Day," Blunt said with a smile and a wave before walking on.

"Sod off," came the reply, just before he heard the slamming of a door.

Blunt wouldn't let it dent his mood. He walked briskly on and, ten minutes later, he was unlocking the door to his office on Pale Avenue. He kicked snow off his shoes before walking in and jogging up the stairs. As he walked towards his door, he saw it was open just a crack.

"Really should get that lock fixed," he said as he stepped inside.

The Boss

"Ursula?" Blunt said as he closed the door behind him. She was sitting behind his desk.

"What are you doing here?" she asked.

"It's my office."

"It's Bleakest Day, Blunt. You can have a day off. Especially after yesterday."

Blunt nodded. "Actually, as you're here, I got you a little something." He skipped to his desk and pulled open the top drawer. Inside were a handful of wrapped boxes. "Despite what people"—he gave her a pointed look—"may think, I do actually get presents for people."

On the desk, there was a handwritten note on headed paper. He ignored it for now and instead extracted a box from the drawer and held it out towards his business partner.

She looked down at it and, after hesitating a moment, took it from him and opened it. Inside the box was a scarf.

"This is…"

"Do you like it?"

"You're mocking me. You're not better than me, Blunt. You're a buffoon."

"Um, the more traditional response is 'thank you'. I wasn't expecting a gift myself, if that's why you're annoyed."

"This isn't over."

"Okay, it's only a scarf, Ursula. I was trying to

be nice. Look, I can see you're unhappy, but is this really the day for this kind of thing?"

"This is exactly the day for this kind of thing, you buffoon. As if having to spend eternity with these disgusting humans wasn't bad enough, now we have demons. It's all so... pathetic."

Blunt shifted his weight on his feet, then stepped backwards, his shoes squelching as he did. "Honestly, Ursula, until I saw your handwriting just now, I wouldn't even have realised."

"You were supposed to do your job, Blunt."

"I'm pretty sure this *is* my job, Ursula."

"Don't call me Ursula. I am not your friend."

Blunt took a deep breath. He held his hands out in front of him, fingers outstretched to be as unthreatening as possible. "Is this because of the sofa?"

In hindsight, he realised that was a mistake.

"You are the worst example of this place. You're not 'on the fence,' you're a nasty piece of work who should have gone to Hell, and I'll make damn sure it happens."

"Bit harsh," Blunt said. "I've done good things."

"Where's the line? Who decides?"

"Didn't the Grim Reaper decide?"

"And who made him the jury? A being who was never alive in the first place, who never even—"

"You were behind all of this, and you still tried to set me up," Blunt said, snatching the paper off the desk. "How flimsy is this? 'Dear Augustan, congratulations, the plot of land where the warehouse was is yours. I don't know how you knew it would burn down.' Bit of a desperate attempt, don't you think? Fortunately for me, I have another note." He reached into his pocket and unfolded a piece of paper. "This one was written for Charlie."

"Give that to me…"

The door creaked open behind Blunt, and Ursula Panderpenny's voice trailed off.

"Ahem." It wasn't a cough, but then, Death doesn't cough. He placed a skeletal hand on Blunt's shoulder. "Detective, thank you for your hard work in getting to the bottom of all of this. Miss Panderpenny, I am disappointed to find you were behind this. I thought you were happy."

"Happy?" she snarled, her face turning into something inhuman, the rage inside her doing something unnatural to her features. "I worked for years to become your receptionist, and then I was beheaded by a demon. While I spent my afterlife tolling away like some idiot, I watched people who deserved to be in Hell doing great things yet doing nothing to redeem themselves. Then, like some kind of twisted attack on me, you let demons in. Demons! Into my afterlife!"

"Ah," Grim said, stepping in front of Blunt. "So you're upset about the demons?"

"No. Yes. There's so much more. Why am I even speaking to you? This… this is the longest conversation we have ever had, and I worked for you."

"Ah yes. She did, you know," Grim said to Blunt. "She was excellent, though I recall myself and Crispin asking her not to take the job because it's very boring. Sends people loopy after a while as well, especially the clever ones. Good job you got out when you did, though, Miss Panderpenny. I mean, could you imagine?"

Blunt stared at the Grim Reaper. His mouth was moving, but nothing came out.

"Well. I'm glad we could have this chat, Miss Panderpenny. At least I got my decorations back."

"The decorations," Blunt said. "Of course. Who would know where the decorations were? Who would know how much it would bother, um…" Blunt looked at the towering skeleton beside him, "you?"

"You can call me Grim. I've told you that before."

"Yes, I know. Argh, and who has the contacts to manipulate that many people to be involved? Who is a master manipulator, over-qualified, arrogant, and worked with everyone? You hate demons because of the whole neck thing—"

"Neck thing?" she screeched. "That demon removed my head with thread from its tail. It sawed through my neck so I couldn't even scream. I was at work. You were both nearby and could have saved me."

"It's not like you died," Blunt said with a shrug.

She moved towards the window and opened

it. In her hand was a single bauble.

"That's not much of a threat. They're just sentimental," Blunt said.

She grinned, then started laughing. The laughter seized her shoulders first as it took control. "You're an idiot. An actual idiot. What happens at the stroke of midnight on Bleakest Eve?"

"It snows, and the snow—"

"Makes everyone sentimental?"

Blunt looked from his business partner to the Grim Reaper and back again.

"If it helps," Grim said, "my face would reflect grave concern about this situation."

"So they *are* powerful?" Blunt said. "You told everyone they only had sentimental power."

"That's right. Power. The phrase is sentimental 'value', but I said power."

"And if she drops that out the window?"

"It will probably break."

"And then?"

"It will be cold. Extremely cold. Everyone will freeze and be lost in their own memories, good or bad, for... a very long time. Like what happened when the snow fell, only far more concentrated."

"How long?"

"Is very long not bad enough? Try to remember who you're speaking to. If I think something takes a long time, then…"

"Fair point."

"Shut up," Ursula snapped. "This is where it ends."

"Oh. Seems a shame." Grim said. "You will, of course, suffer as well… possibly worse. You might end up reliving that moment with the tiny dinosaur. There are other options. How about we play a game instead?"

Ursula Panderpenny's eyes narrowed as she clutched the last remaining bauble. "What are you offering?"

"I believe the old tradition is that if you beat me at a game, you don't have to die."

"I've been dead for sixty years."

"Time"—Grim waved his right hand—"is everything and nothing. If you win, you can return. Perhaps you can do things differently, so there is no doubt about where you'll go? Of course, that will leave everything here as it is. Cursing these people to continue to live in this grey afterlife. I shouldn't have said anything. You have a noble cause, after all. Trapping some people in happy memories forever. I mean… that might be heaven."

Ursula glanced down at the bauble she clutched in her hand. Inside, shades of purple spiralled. She peered out of the window and back again towards the Grim Reaper.

"You have the power to send us back to life? Why didn't you just send us all back?"

"She's got a point," Blunt said in an indistinct murmur.

Grim shook his head. "It costs something. It costs a great deal, and I can't do it by choice. I must be compelled. Everything is a contract. If we have a contract where you agree to play a game and the price, if I lose, is life… then it can be allowed. You have the bauble, which I want, so we can make an arrangement. Neutrality is very important. Now, what shall we play? Cards? Chess? Checkers? Oh, we should play Monopoli! It's too appropriate to ignore it."

The Grim Reaper stepped around Blunt and picked up a wrapped box with 'Sarah' written on a tag on the side. He removed the wrapping paper with the delicate care of someone who believes the paper is as valuable as its contents.

Finally, he withdrew a Monopoli set, the Gloomwood limited edition. The game was almost exactly the same as a game from the mortal world, but the makers changed one letter, hoping it would prevent them from being sued across the mortal veil. It didn't work, but psychic court cases are very impractical and often take several lifetimes.

"That's a present for Sarah," Blunt said. "It's a clever half-joke thing because she knows I hate board games, but I said I'd play them for her, and… never mind."

Ursula Panderpenny and the Grim Reaper stared at Blunt until he trailed off. Then they turned away as if he didn't exist.

"It is your choice," Grim said to the woman standing by the window.

Ursula eyed the boxed board game. "If I win… do I keep the knowledge I have gained since I died? Do I remember?"

"Oh. I hadn't really thought about it. Would you like to?"

"Um," Blunt said.

"Really, detective. Fine, you can be the boot if you like," Grim said.

"What?"

"Would you like to play?"

Blunt stared at the seven-foot-tall robed skeleton as it unpacked the board game on Blunt's desk.

"I can play to escape Gloomwood? To go back to the living?"

"Yes. Everyone can, once. Whoever rolls highest starts."

Grim pushed the dice across the board towards Ursula Panderpenny, the mastermind behind everything that had happened in the last twenty-four hours.

She snatched them up and rolled a pair of sixes. With a smirk, she shrugged and put the decoration down on Blunt's desk.

"One question," Blunt said as he gingerly picked up the bauble. "Why did you knock down the warehouse?"

"So they had nowhere to go back to," Ursula said with a grin.

"That's it? Not some kind of real estate plan?"

She shrugged. "I didn't expect to get away with it all, and I wasn't scared of going to the library. I've had my head chopped off once already, Blunt. It's important to be single-minded in the pursuit of your goals. Now, are you playing?"

"No. I'm pretty sure that if you lose, you're going to Hell."

"Yes, that's right," Grim said.

Ursula shrugged. "Seems fair."

Hearing Demons

Morgarth woke up late. Finding somewhere to sleep had been difficult, but Mister Mortimer had found them a place, and she and the manager of the Office of the Dead had agreed it was a good idea. There were rooms. Not enough rooms for them to have individual space, but enough that there was some privacy, which was a luxury.

She rolled out of her makeshift bed, a desk drawer with a pillow inside, and walked down the corridor. There was a toilet further down the hall, and when she ducked in, she was surprised to find it not only empty but even moderately clean. After dragging a bin towards the sink, she leapt up and splashed water across her face.

From demons to soft toys with duck voices. She shook her head. It was hard to tell if they were falling or rising. Was this better than being a demon?

With one bound, she leapt to the floor. Tail swishing, she walked by several open doors. There were the sounds of laughter from some excited conversations. From one room came strange voices. She pushed open the door to find Yargvel, Trem, and Alejandro Cracked-screen, who had become known as their physician. The green tiger was exhausted after spending hours removing decorations from demons but hadn't been able to sleep.

"I thought I heard someone," Morgarth said as

she poked her head around the door.

"You did," said Yargvel in a voice that sounded like thick caramel over chocolate brownies. "What do you think?"

"You sound… you sound sexually attractive."

"I know," Yargvel said, wriggling his rainbow eyebrows.

"How?"

"Tuck the duck," Trem said. "It seems Father Christmas gave us something after all."

Morgarth nodded. "You can do this for all of us?"

"You and the six might be more complicated," Alejandro said.

"But we think so," Yargvel finished.

"I'm going to go look around," Morgarth said, too lost in thought to get excited.

She walked out of the room and headed back in the direction she had come from until she reached a staircase. She bounced down the stairs with small hops to the next floor.

"Morgarth?" Detective Blunt said from further down the corridor. "What are you doing here?"

"Mister Mortimer told us we could stay upstairs. There are entire floors empty."

"I know. The only business in the building is… was Panderpenny's. Hey, I've got a great idea," Blunt said. "Down the hall is my office. Why don't you pop your head in? There's someone in there who'd love to see you."

"Really?" Morgarth asked. "Me?"

Mind Games

As Blunt stepped out of the building on Pale Avenue, he jogged around to the alleyway his office looked out upon.

Narrow wasn't a reasonable description. As he clambered over bags of rubbish and discarded cardboard boxes, he could touch the walls on either side without stretching out his arms.

The snow covered the worst of the debris, but it also meant he couldn't see what he was standing on. His foot went through something that released a noxious odour into the air, and his sock added sticky to its existing epithets of wet and cold.

He looked up and could just make out his office's windowsill, and so he waited.

A little while later, a screeching voice howled, "—you!"

Blunt held his hands out expectantly.

The bauble fell from the window. It bounced off the opposite wall, and he winced as he watched it fall. He desperately tried to position himself beneath it until, satisfyingly, it fell into his numb fingers. He tumbled into the debris and snow, holding it close to his chest.

"Did you get it?" the Grim Reaper asked, poking his hooded head out of the window.

"Obviously," Blunt croaked. "We would all be frozen in memories otherwise."

"Hm," Grim said. "How would we know if we

weren't?"

Blunt gingerly got to his feet, being careful to hold the bauble in a tight grip. "I don't remember this," he said. Then he looked up. "How did you know that would happen?"

Grim put his hands on the window's edge and leaned a little further out. "Perhaps a better question is, how did you?"

"I... It just made sense."

"Hm. Merry Bleakest Day, detective," Grim said before vanishing back inside.

Blunt was left holding the bauble in one hand. He dropped it into his pocket and made awkward progress, crawling across the rubbish that filled the alleyway.

Once he reached the other end, he debated walking back up the stairs to give the bauble back, but the way the Grim Reaper had spoken... it could wait until another day.

He started walking home, head down, muttering a list of obscenities with every soggy step.

"Bloody Bleakest Day. Spent all day yesterday running around the city trying to save evil creatures from dead people who weren't decent enough to go to Heaven, stopping little green gnomes from cutting down trees and a fake Father Christmas from breaking decorations, then the whole thing turns out to have been a scam by a psychopath trying to destroy the demons, and ruin the Grim Reaper's afterlife, just because she got her head chopped off." He kicked a stone on the pavement, and it rebounded off a curb, a wall, and a fire hydrant before hitting him in the face.

"Argh!" He stopped in his tracks to rub at his forehead. "Bloody typical."

Laughter broke the silence, and he turned to see a man standing behind a shopping trolley full of blankets and pieces of cardboard.

"You laughing at me?"

"Yes," the man said. "It was hilarious."

"Well… you're bloody welcome."

"Merry Bleakest Day." The man rummaged in the shopping trolley until he pulled out a box. "This is for you."

"Yeah, I don't take things from, um, people's shopping trolleys."

"It's Bleakest Day. Trust me, you'll like this."

The man was skinny and had something that resembled a beard, but it was so matted and covered in filth it might have been mistaken for a dead rat. Except there weren't any rats in Gloomwood.

"Okay then." Blunt took the box. It was sealed and a little heavier than he'd expected.

"Merry Bleakest Day. Ho, ho—" The man's sentence was cut off by the kind of cough that sounds like it will never end.

"Yeah, you too," Blunt said as he walked away.

When he reached Sarah's apartment, which was on the second floor of a converted terrace house, he shook his head.

"Right, come on, Blunt. It's Bleakest Day and you can spend it with a beautiful woman. It's warm and cosy inside, with good food and good company. Put this whole mess behind you."

He pushed the intercom button.

"You said thirty minutes," Sarah's voice said over the distorted speaker.

"Alright, a little longer. I'm back, though."

She buzzed him in, and he jogged up the stairs.

When he walked into the apartment, she was sitting on the sofa in a dressing gown with her feet up.

"Well, what desperate attempt at a present did you come up with?"

Blunt sighed. "It's a long story—"

"Just give me the box," she said.

"Oh, this? No, it's—"

She was up and had taken it from his hand before he could finish the sentence.

"The thing is, I went to the office, and Ursula was there, then the Grim Reaper, and it turns out that all this time... oh, and Morgarth was there. Then on the way out—"

"Blunt? I thought you hated board games."

"I do... but I figured I could play one with you," he said, staring at a brand new, pristine Monopoli game. The Gloomwood limited edition.

"Oh, this card's for you," Sarah said. "Did you wrap it by accident?"

"Must've," Blunt said, taking it from Sarah. He opened it, facing away from her.

Inside, in elaborate calligraphy, were the words, "Merry Bleakest Day, detective. GR."

Blunt shook his head. "Not omniscient, my arse."

AFTERWORD

Things got weird.

They're only going to get weirder.

I'm not sorry.

ACKNOWLEDGEMENTS

Thank you!

ABOUT THE AUTHOR

Ross Young

Ross Young was born in Newcastle Upon Tyne in a hospital that has since been knocked down. He spent his childhood in a variety of international locales and uses this fact to affect an air of the windswept and interesting (badly). He enjoys diving and travelling and has lived and worked in a variety of exciting sounding places.

He writes novels set in the Grim Reaper's own slice of the afterlife: the city of Gloomwood. He does not write from experience as, despite his appearance and demeanour, he is not dead. You can find him @Rossyoungsulk on Twitter.

Visit rossyoung.ink for comics, games, and assorted fun times.

BOOKS BY THIS AUTHOR

Dead Heads

What happens when we die?

Why are dead people scared?

Who would take the Grim Reaper's head?

Welcome to Gloomwood, the city of the dead and the Grim Reaper's personal slice of the afterlife. In a city where the rules of the living don't apply, Detective Blunt's drowning in trouble, and he's never been much of a swimmer.

With the aid of a reality-challenged scientist, a bumbling bureaucrat, and a self-titled 'reporter extraordinaire', he's on a case where everyone's already kicked the bucket.

Dead gods, forgotten dreams, broken promises, lost hopes – they all end up in this city, and any of them could have a reason for exacting revenge.

Can Blunt uncover the villain decapitating the city's elite before the afterlife implodes?

Feel like laughing in the face of Death?
Better find his head…

Get Ted Dead

Teddington Rex is living his best life, star of the daily chat show and darling of the social elite. There's just one problem. His life is the only one there is. Everyone else in Gloomwood is dead.

Augustan Blunt has been fired and humiliated in front of the whole city, but a mysterious stranger has a job for him. All Blunt has to do is find someone living in the afterlife. It's an impossible task, but he's got nothing better to do, and it isn't as if anyone else is going to employ him.

The Grim Reaper isn't feeling himself. He isn't feeling anyone else either, but he's never been accused of being 'handsy'. Something is wrong in the city of Gloomwood.

The dead are coming to life, toys are causing problems, and an old friend has turned up in town.

Whatever happens, everyone seems to have the

same goal.

Get Ted Dead.

Printed in Great Britain
by Amazon